THE CRYSTAL GAME

THE CRYSTAL GAME
A Western Trio

MAX BRAND®

SAGEBRUSH
Large Print Westerns

First published in Great Britain by ISIS Publishing Ltd
First published in the United States by Five Star

Published in Large Print 2007 by ISIS Publishing Ltd.,
7 Centremead, Osney Mead, Oxford OX2 0ES
United Kingdom
by arrangement with
Golden West Literary Agency

British Library Cataloguing in Publication Data
Brand, Max, 1892–1944
    The crystal game: a western trio. – Large print ed. –
    (Sagebrush western series)
    1. Western stories
    2. Large type books
    I. Title II. Brand, Max, 1892–1944. Fugitive
    III. Brand, Max, 1892–1944. Uncle Chris turns north
    813.5'2 [F]

ISBN 978–0–7531–7768–6 (hb)

Printed and bound in Great Britain by
T. J. International Ltd., Padstow, Cornwall

Table of Contents

The Fugitive

In 1926 Frederick Faust published twelve short novels and twelve serials, all but two appearing in Street & Smith's *Western Story Magazine*. "The Fugitive" appeared in the issue dated July 24, 1926, under the Max Brand byline. In it Faust made use of one of his favorite themes, the good badman. And like many of Faust's protagonists, Stephen Macdona falls outside the law, not because of anything evil in him, but rather because he had been "equipped with a resolution to do everything too much", and because "temperance was not in him". He is as wild in nature as his beloved horse, Christy, who is stolen from him, as is his heart, by Constancia Alvarez.

CHAPTER
ONE

Like the true prodigal, Mother Nature gives freely of the things that she has by her. When they are exhausted, the next guest may have to go supperless to bed, as it were. It was in exactly this manner that she fashioned Stephen Macdona. Somewhere in the not distant past there had been a "gh" on the end of that name, but Stephen's father had dropped it after he made a fortune in cattle. He felt that there was a distinction in the abbreviated word. Perhaps there was. Certainly there was distinction in his son and sole heir. What young Stephen Macdona was like in his childhood must be omitted for the sake of space, and also because it would break the heart of any young mother to think of what Stephen was, and then look at her own offspring.

Let us look, rather, at Stephen as he was when he entered his early twenties. He stood exactly at the romantic height of six feet, not a scruple more or less. Very adroitly distributed in perfect proportions were 180 pounds, sleek, smooth, and supple — not the sort of muscle that gymnastic performers wear, like rolls of padding, not the kind that heaves vast weights slowly but surely from their rooted beds, but that kind of

3

sinewy strength that wings the runner down the track, that whips the jumper over the bar, that entangles the wrestler in a thousand lightning grips, and that strikes down the boxers with a blow as swift as the tongue of a lightning flash and as resistless as a thunderbolt.

This same Mother Nature, knowing that Stephen was destined to grow up under the torrid suns of the Southwest, furnished him with an olive skin calculated to resist the blast of the fire. She gave him features that might have been struck in marble as a flawless model. She set a quantity of rather curling, brown-black hair above his brow. Beneath it, she furnished him with brown eyes that could cast forth sparks or melt the hearts of the ladies.

Nor was that all. Having poured forth her plenty upon the matchless head and body of this favorite child, she went on with the inward equipment of his being. Surely it seemed that the evil fairy was absent when this spendthrift mother was at work. First, she turned over the shining treasures of her armory and said: "What gift is first and peerless, for that he must have." She found that gift, the brightest of all. And she gave him courage.

Then, turning from this stern and kingly virtue, she gave him the opposite quality of kindness, which surely should go with courage always, to keep it from tyranny. Still she had not done spending. She found for him ceaseless good nature, the sunny talent of loving his fellow men; she gave him equanimity in the face of misfortune, nerves of truest steel, a heart of the most dauntless fortitude. More, she furnished him with wits

4

as quick as the lightning that lived in his own fingertips. Generosity she gave him, mercy and tenderness. She heaped richly upon him the sense of the rightness of this world in which we find ourselves condemned to live our lives.

All of this was done by Mother Nature, and, when she ended, it was as though she rejoiced in the things that she had done and said to herself: "What is there that I can give to his soul that will make it better? What better than a soul like mine own?"

So the last gift of all was the nature of a spendthrift like herself.

Alas, poor Stephen Macdona. From the very first day of his life, it seemed as though he were equipped with a resolution to do everything too much. Temperance was not in him. As he grew older, that quality that could be laughed at in his infancy could no longer be laughed at in the boy. If it were a matter of setting forth with other mischiefs to break a window or two, there were those contented with a pane or two in a distant barn, but Stephen selected the stained glass of the western portal of the church.

If it were the baiting of the peddler that diverted the boys of the village while they stole a bunch of carrots for their pet rabbits, Stephen Macdona overturned cart and all and frightened the horse, who scampered down the street — wrecked everything.

When it came to a bit of a fist fight, such as is supposed to be good for the soul of all who wear short trousers, Stephen must elevate it to the dignity of a war. If he were entangled with a hopelessly older and bigger boy, he fought like a tiger until they bore his senseless body home. When he grew a little older and stronger in the arms, the time of defeats ended, and that of victories began. They were not little victories in little frays. Single combat no longer contented him, for he soon reached the period when no boy in town dared stand before him for an instant. Then he organized the youngsters of the west end of the village and led them against the youth of the opposite sections. How many a bruised cheek bone and cracked ear were carried homeward!

Deputations of fathers called upon the elder Mr. Macdona. He did what he could. But Nature had made him a mild man, and he was dazzled by the brilliancy of his boy. There was not always a father to foot the bill for the indiscretions of young Macdona, however. The cattleman died within a year of the death of his wife. The estate was confided to the guardianship of a partner who decided that he would make his protégé a millionaire before the year was out. It was a grand year of visions and great attempts. But when it ended, the money was mysteriously gone, and Stephen was left without an income.

However, there was always a shift and a new expedient in the wits of Stephen. He took as a foster parent the goddess of chance, worshipping her as devoutly as his nature was capable. He would not become her intimate, however; he would never learn the devices of a crooked gambler. When he played among honest fellows, he reaped a rich harvest, but, just as his capital had mounted to a comfortable sum, some clever sharp was sure to appear and scoop in all of his winnings in a single high hour of play.

It might have been said very honestly that he had done nothing a whit worse than a hundred other youths of his day and age were doing, but it was different in the case of young Macdona. When men looked upon that magnificent brow and upon that glorious body, they told themselves that it was a bitter crime that such a grand engine should be put to such base uses. Moreover, there was an innate dignity about the person and the manner of this youngster, even in his gayest moods, so that people could not help taking him very seriously.

For instance, every boy in the county had fallen wildly in love with pretty little Elena Ramirez in that romantic Mexican house by the river. Her father, like a sensible man, had told himself that one cannot rear roses without making the world stop to stare. But when Stephen Macdona appeared on the scene, it was different. He took the youngster aside and asked him about his intentions. And why was it, pray, that Stephen came so regularly, three and four times a week, to see Elena?

"I am learning Spanish, you know," said Stephen instantly, and he kept his smile out of his brown, serious eyes.

Señor Ramirez grew worried. He let as much be known by two or three of Elena's Mexican wooers, and so they waited for Stephen in the cool of the evening by the riverbank. It was a memorable occasion for several reasons, three of which were the bodies of the assailants. The coroner, of course, pronounced it self-defense, but he could not help indulging in the request that Stephen might defend himself just a little less vigorously on the next occasion, if there ever should be one.

Alas, there were many more. For one of the important results of this evening's amusement was that Stephen made a grand new discovery, which was to the effect that cards had their place in the scheme of this joyful world, and so did the riding of wild horses, and so did trick target shooting, and so did the hunting of grizzlies, and the following of the puma into its dark lair — but all of these were as merest nothings compared to the supreme joy of finding oneself standing before mature men armed to the teeth, and resolute to fight.

A grand appetite is bound to be fed. You would say that, after that first affair by the river, other men in that country would be somewhat wary of the manner in which they crossed the path of Stephen. To be sure, they were. But this cleverly devised world is so arranged that he who wants trouble can usually find it. Through the town in which Stephen lived, strangers from other parts of the cattle country were constantly passing — men with keen, quick eyes and lightning hands, inured to their work by long practice. Among so many, all perfectly sure of themselves, there were some who were bound to fall foul of Stephen.

The end would have come much earlier than it actually did were it not for the fact that Stephen's shooting improved. He did not have to aim for head or heart. A shoulder or a leg would do nearly as well. And if there were a doctor's bill, it was less than the cost of a burial.

However, even these matters mounted and mounted. Add little to little and finally you will hit your million. So it was with young Macdona. One day a grave deputation called upon Stephen. They addressed him with respect, but with firmness also. They understood, of course, that he had been unlucky, that much trouble had come his way, that he would willingly have avoided it. But after all, the nerves of the people in that community were beginning to be a bit fine drawn. They suggested firmly that he should take a vacation. They suggested that a change of air would probably be wonderfully beneficial.

Stephen agreed with them, sympathized with them — but did not leave. A week later a rough fellow from Denver lay wounded and cursing in the street — cursing his gun that had hung in the draw. It was always that way with the men who stood up to Stephen. Something happened to their guns before they got out of the holsters; something always slipped.

Another deputation called on Stephen, but he was not at home. He had gone whirling off up the country and he came back in a month with a perfect beauty of a wild young mare, which he named Christy. She was a black chestnut, darker than polished mahogany, with a dappling, like leopard spots, showing plainly when the light struck her from the right angle. Stephen loved her with a passionate devotion, as he loved all things that were fair to look upon. For many a day after that he was too busy grooming his new treasure and teaching her tricks to pay much attention to the rest of the world.

One bright, clear morning, as he rode Christy down the street, he encountered three men, riding sternly abreast, three silent, gloomy men who carried rifles. They were not Indians or Mexicans or half-breeds. They were purest white, except for the tan that the desert sun had given to them. No one knew exactly how the trouble began — Stephen least of all — but it was some ridiculous thing about the right of way. Suddenly a gun flashed in the early sun, and the wild, sweet madness of battle was flaming across the brain of Stephen Macdona.

When it cleared a little, two figures were writhing in the street, staining the dust with an ugly crimson. But the third man lay upon his back, with his arms thrown wide, and his blank eyes looking mildly up to the sun of heaven, seeing nothing at all.

Stephen took note of this. He took note, also, that most unfortunately there were no living witnesses to this affair except himself and the three. And what they would have to say might be the hanging of him.

Discretion had never been a promising virtue in Stephen, but on this morning it suddenly took possession of him. He gave mute thanks to God that he happened to have the sleek and supple speed of Christy beneath him, and he rode straight out toward the mountain desert, not even pausing to take his new rifle as he passed his house.

CHAPTER
TWO

Seeing Stephen riding across the desert in this fashion, with nothing but a brace of revolvers in his holsters and a very few dollars in his purse, what had Mother Nature to say for herself, she who had searched among her best gifts, to squander them all upon this rapscallion? Certainly she must have hid her head with shame. Yet there was no shame in Stephen. It must be recorded that he was whistling as he galloped down the trail, only stopping his music to shoot a mountain partridge as it rose on heavy, humming wings out of the thicket before him.

He built himself a little fire and roasted his meal, and no man ever enjoyed food more, as he sat there upon his heels, watching the honest sheriff and his dusty posse toiling across the flat beneath him on his trail. After picking the last bone of that big, fat bird — with the others a half rifle shot away, and spurring wildly to get at him — he mounted Christy and slid away into the wilderness.

They headed him off at Caxton Pass. He turned back and tried the western trails. They stopped him again with numbers at the edge of Lake Tucker, and it was said that surely at least two bullets had been shot into him at that encounter. But here rumor lied, for he went unscathed.

He made a pause, helped himself to a prosperous rancher's wallet and best rifle, and continued toward the south. They nearly snagged him not two miles from the Río, then hunted grandly north and west again, while the newspapers published bulletins every day, morning and evening, to tell how the war against the desperado was continuing. And every young boy, north and south and east and west, prayed daily that the hero might be spared.

Stephen Macdona was having the very best time that he had ever had. Yet, when two posses nearly caught him on successive days, and when Christy began to grow thin and lost the sharper edge of her speed, he saw that something radical would have to be done.

He went up into the mountains and lived for eight months like a hermit. He grew in that time a luxurious young beard and a mustache. His good clothes turned ragged, and the mare became a glossy thing of beauty again, ready to flirt her heels in the face of the world.

Then he caught a stray mule, made up a pretended pack, and tramped across 1,200 miles of desert and mountain and farm land, with the mare led at the side of the mule. When they asked him questions, Christy was a wild horse that he had caught and that he would sell, when he found a man to ride her. Would you like to try? They tried, but he had taught her to buck like a young fiend, and no one ever managed to stick in the saddle.

Stephen Macdona passed across the country and drifted south and south and east and east, until he found himself at his goal — a seaport, with a dumpy steamer lying in the harbor bound for Central America.

He bought new clothes, trimmed his beard and mustache to a fashionable semblance, shipped Christy, and walked on board himself with the air of a young duke traveling incognito.

What had Mother Nature done to him now, driving him away from his native land, which he watched that evening, as it turned blue and soft in the distance? She had done this much — she had made him laugh softly and sweetly to himself, and let him think of sundry industrious and ant-like toilers who were still floundering here and there among the mountains, laboring at broken trails, following false clues, and forever trailing a man **about twenty-four years old, six feet tall, 180 pounds in weight, looks a little younger than his age, of a gay nature and very prone to laughter, smooth shaven, handsome, dark hair and eyes.**

But that was no longer a description of the fugitive. Now, under the name of Valentin Guadalvo, there appeared a gentleman who looked some twenty-eight or thirty years, with a neatly cut imperial and a well-shaped mustache, with lips that smiled but rarely laughed, a gentleman speaking the most fluent Spanish, a man of ease and quiet deportment.

Who could have looked in him for the fire-eating young Macdona? Certainly no one aboard the steamer, *Santa Lucia*, regarded him with any suspicion. Most wonderful of all, even that exquisitely beautiful mare, Christy, was not eyed with any undue curiosity. She had a Negro from New Orleans to look after her — a rascal who was a fugitive, also, due to certain eccentricities connected with betting at the races. He knew horseflesh.

"Give this Christy girl another inch of legs," said George, the Negro, "and she'd be winning frequent on the track. There ain't any doubt about that."

They steamed south and west, with the old boat rebuffing the waves at the rate of nine knots an hour, and her wake sweltering slowly in the rear while the skies grew hotter and closer. The warm gulf winds brought a sense of drowsy comfort to all on board the ship.

Stephen Macdona, alias Valentin Guadalvo, lounged in cool flannels and smoked rich Havanas on the deck, turning his brown, sparkling eyes on everyone who passed by him. He liked them all, simply because they were human creatures like himself. He liked the ship and felt grateful to her for the steady way in which she bucked through the waves and put precious leagues between the hungry sheriff and him. He liked the sun, because of its strength, and the sea, because of its delightful blueness, and its foaming waves that crisped about the bow. For the wind that was ever playing about the head of the ship he felt almost a personal affection and affinity. She was a wild thing, yonder wind, and a wanderer without a home, a gay and reckless wanderer, like this same Valentin Guadalvo. But of all the things living and dead that lay under the eye of Stephen, that which he approved of most highly was Constancia Alvarez.

He would not give himself many glances at her; indeed, there were not so very many chances. When she walked the deck, it was always at the side of a billowy old lady, dressed in black, who often obscured the view. Her deck chair was in a quiet and most removed part of the deck where, to see her, one would have to stand directly in front of her place and stare. And Stephen never stared — except when he was about to draw a gun.

But he saw her now and then, and every glance added something to the picture of her that was lodged in his brain. Other young men on the boat, without exception, had attempted to make themselves agreeable to her, but she had avoided them with perfect ease. She could make her glance as dead as the eye of an Egyptian mummy and as cold as ice. After a time, she was left alone to take her turns on the deck, to lounge in her chair, and to remain in her cabin, the best on the old ship. The other gentlemen aboard hid their chagrin under a mask of surliness and swore that she was a stupid face of frost and not worth the knowing. But for Stephen, she remained like a touch of salt that makes food edible. No one could have known that he was watching her, when she went past. His glance always seemed fixed at something far away, but all the time he was adding some new feature.

And then something happened which gave him a chance to know her better. It began with Jamaica rum, old and beautifully aromatic. The second mate could not resist this excellent drink. In addition, there was a strong headwind, cutting a bit across the starboard quarter and making the ship pitch like a sparrow in choppy flight, up and down. Too, there was a sharp-crested sea running, throwing points and ridges of foam up against the blue ocean, whirling keen volleys of spray over the rail. Finally there was a low place in the rail.

All these elements combined. The rum had just made the second mate's head swim; he had just reached the low place in the rail; at the very moment the ship rolled with a heavy pitch into a quartering sea.

The mate staggered against the low rail, his legs flew out from beneath him, and his screech was stifled with amazing suddenness in the waters beneath.

CHAPTER
THREE

In that crowd the majority did what the majority usually does in time of emergency. Some of them clutched the edges of their chairs and stared with bulging eyes; some halted in mid-step and gaped; many screamed; some gasped; some started up; a mother caught her child into her arms; but two people acted.

The old duenna and Constancia Alvarez were passing along that side of the ship, at the instant, taking their usual exercise. The chaperone clasped her hands with a shriek, but Constancia snatched a life buoy that hung at the rail and flung it accurately at the spot where the mate had disappeared. The buoy had not yet landed in the blue water when Stephen Macdona went over the rail and headed for the water in a graceful arc.

The ocean heaved before him, but he went through it. Something flashed with a white twinkle beneath him — the sun gleaming on the flannels of the wretched mate, filmed over with the shadows of the brine. Stephen closed a hand in the hair of the man and started upward; clinging arms and blind, desperate legs were flung around him, so Stephen, feeling himself sink, turned and considered what to do. Striking through water, one's fist is a powerless tool. But there

17

was still might in a sharp elbow. He drove it home against the side of the mate's head, and then swam to the surface, bearing a leaden burden.

By the time he had gasped out the dead air from his lungs and breathed in a fresh supply, he saw the life buoy, not a dozen strokes away. To it he clung, keeping the head of his man above the tossing of the waves while a boat was lowered to fetch them in.

The wits of the frightened mate returned, sobriety, also, before they climbed up the side of the vessel. He was stammering out some sort of thanks to Stephen, but the latter laughed him away.

On the deck of the steamer a pinch-faced missionary reached for his hand. "What a noble thing, *Señor* Guadalvo!"

"Piffle," said the hero, and went to his cabin to change.

He waited in his room until the excitement should have died down a little. Then he came up and found Constancia Alvarez. "I have come to thank you for that life buoy," he said.

Even the duenna considered that this was introduction enough.

They sat on the deck, that evening, watching the rail dip down to the steel-gray waters and then pitch up and cross the face of the moon with bars. The duenna was discreetly asleep in her chair.

"I bless the mate," said Constancia.

"And why?" asked Stephen.

"Because I was dying of weariness."

"There was no need to. I watched twenty men try to comfort you."

"How could I talk to them, and be reported to my father by the *señora*?"

"Is he a dragon?"

"He is *two* dragons."

"I thank the rum," said Stephen, "and the roll of the ship that knocked him against the rail, and the lowness of the rail there, and the pitching of the waves, because they give me a chance to tell you what I have been thinking about."

She settled back in her chair. The shadow of her hat did not shelter her face quite as completely as she thought, and he could see her smile. Even the white moonshine could not make that smile cold.

"The first thing that I discovered after I came on board the ship . . . shall I start at the beginning?"

"Of course," she said.

"The first thing was the fragrance of jasmine."

"Oh, that was what you were studying, when you looked at the sky with such far-away eyes?"

"Of course you are surprised," said Stephen.

"Tremendously," said Constancia.

They turned their heads at the same instant and, of one accord, they smiled. Her glance flickered toward the duenna, but all was well. That good lady slept, or seemed to sleep, and there was such a good understanding between Constancia and her, that either of the two amounted to the same thing.

"The next thing that I noticed was the way the hair curls at the nape of your neck."

"I am old-fashioned and do my hair high."

"I saw nothing else for a considerable time, until one day you stopped and I saw your hand against the rail. However, I saw at a glance that was a subject I could never learn at a distance."

Her hand appeared from beneath the steamer rug.

"You are a scientist, then?" said the girl.

"I read the future by the hand," he said, "which is a common art, isn't it?"

"I suppose so," she said.

"And would you like to know what will happen to you?"

"I feel rather foolish. But I suppose that I would." And she gave him her hand.

He held it where the moonshine turned it to a transparent whiteness; he held it with the lightest and most gentle of reverent touches. All the while her curious, thoughtful eyes were studying his face.

"Begin, then," she said. "But I never heard of a person who could read the *back* of a hand."

"The palm," said Stephen, "is only important in a soft, gentle, and yielding person."

"And I am none of those?"

"We'll see what the hand says for itself about the future. At the very first glance, I see trouble."

"Of what sort?"

"Oh, many kinds. Young trouble and old trouble. Tall trouble and short. Trouble with black and gray heads."

"But what will come of it?"

"Much talk."

"That is always a terrible bore," she admitted.

"Exactly. Most of this talk will be about love. All of these troubles will tell you that they love you and ask you to marry them." He leaned his head a little closer to the hand. "In fact, I see that there has been a great deal of this sort of thing already."

"Oh, nothing at all worth mentioning. But what is to come of the future?"

"The worst of it all is," he explained, "that none of these troubles, not even the old, gray-headed ones, will really know what they are talking about."

"What in the world do you mean by that?"

"Why, they will think that you are like the palm of this hand, soft and yielding and gentle. As a matter of fact, you are not."

She sat up a little straighter. "You are an odd person," she observed, "and I think that . . . well, go on. Tell me what I am."

"Here are knuckles all even, firm, strong, and straight. They tell me that your strength is even, regular, and steady, and that it will never leave you. These thin, strong fingers tell me that, when you make up your mind, you generally can take what you want. The roundness of this wrist says that there is much endurance in you. Then, there is no trembling in the fingers. But they are quick and sure and restless. See, they are always moving just a little. And they mean that you are restless, impatient, stern, cruel, gay and . . ."

She took back her hand and stared at him.

He continued: "And fierce, determined, cunning, and apt to be desperate if you are crossed."

"*Señor* Guadalvo!"

"Yes, *señorita*."

"Perhaps I should be insulted, by such talk."

"No. Other girls would be. But you are only interested because I am telling you the truth."

"You are a very self-satisfied fellow. But it is the truth, and yet . . . how in the world could you ever know me? Who is our mutual friend? And . . ."

"I'll tell you how it is. I know a lady who is exactly like you."

"Ah. Do you really?" There was a cold, little rising inflection in her voice.

"Exactly like you," he said. "She is beautiful, as you are. Yes, even when I look at you now, when a bit of anger makes your eyes larger than usual . . . even as you are now, I think that she is more beautiful."

"I don't think that we have been talking about beauty," said the girl sternly.

"I don't think that we have, but this is a good time to begin, if you don't mind. I should like to talk about it a long time. The lady of mine has a head as proud and as highly poised as yours. She has a great, bright, wild eye, like yours. Her feet can step as light as the wind. And her body is one of exquisite perfection."

"I think that we have talked enough about beauty," said the girl in haste.

"At the first glance," said Stephen, "I fell in love with her."

"Ah."

"Yes. Hopelessly in love."

"Just because she was pretty, then?"

"It was not only because of her enchanting beauty, but because she had, like you, wonderful virtues mixed with her faults."

"Indeed?"

"Oh, yes. With her stubbornness there was mixed a fine patience, like yours. She was rash and headlong, like you, but, like you, she has a magnificent courage. There is no fear in her. And when I saw that brave, bright eye of hers, I loved her, and I knew that I should have to have her or die."

"You are still alive, however."

"But I have her, *señorita*."

"You have her, really?"

"Yes, indeed. Shall I tell you how I won her?"

"Yes, if you care to," said Constancia a little more coldly than before.

CHAPTER
FOUR

He sat forward, where he could look more fairly at her. "This is in the manner of a confession," he said. "Does it bore you?"

"I am wonderfully interested, of course, if you care to talk about this thing."

"I would not ordinarily," he admitted. "But she is so perfectly like you that you will understand why I can confide in you. Besides, you are to learn a great lesson out of this."

"Of what sort, if you please?"

"You will know that until some man woos you exactly as I wooed my own dear, you will not have met the right person to marry. I tell you as a prophet."

"I hear you . . . as a prophet." The girl chuckled.

"Very well. In the first place, I went on her trail."

"She was not a stationary beauty, then?"

"No, she was a great lover. I followed on her trail for a long time, and, when I caught up with her, I took her suddenly in such a way that she could not resist me. She had to place herself in my hands."

"Good heavens!" exclaimed the girl.

"She was desperate. She struggled against me with all her might. But I subdued her with a stern hand. I even went so far as to give her scarcely any food, and no water, until her spirit left her and she was so weak . . ."

"Can you sit here, in this century, and tell me such a thing?"

"Of course. Take notice of every point. It will be useful for you, later on. First, I knew that I had gained a point when her hatred of me turned into fear and when she cringed at my coming . . ."

"Oh, dreadful."

"When she cringed at my coming, I knew that I was on the way to victory. I was more stern than ever. Suddenly, one day, she submitted out of weakness and pain. Her fierceness and wildness had left her. She gave herself into my hands. The battle was ended. And after she had submitted, I had only to give her a little liberty, and she began to love me."

"I won't believe it."

"Oh, yes, but she did. She loved me tremendously. So much so, that when you see her, you will find the love shining in her eyes. She does not care one bit if the whole world should know."

"I am to see her, then?"

"Yes, indeed. She is on this boat, you know."

"On this boat?"

"Yes."

"But . . . where is she?"

"She is confined to her cabin."

"Is she ill, poor thing . . . and in these dark little cabins in such weather?"

"As a matter of fact, I don't care to have her mix with the people on the deck. And when men see her, you must understand that they lose their minds completely. They would lay down their souls to have her. So I have to watch her with the greatest of care."

"But does your wife . . . ?"

"Oh, she is not my wife. No. We decided that we loved each other so perfectly that marriage was an unnecessary ceremony. I knew, when she began to come at the mere crooking of my finger, that it was unnecessary for me to go through the formality of a marriage. So we have been living together as happily as two lovers in the Garden of Eden."

"Thank you for the . . . confession," said Constancia.

"You must take it carefully to heart," he said, "because, unless some man comes to you with a high hand, you'll never find a husband worthy of you, Señorita Alvarez."

"I am a little sleepy," she said. And at that instant, the duenna wakened.

Stephen rose. "I shall introduce you to her as you leave the ship," he said. "When we land tomorrow, you shall see her. Then you will confess that she is the most lovely thing in the world."

There was no answer from Constancia, and therefore he bowed to her and went down the deck singing softly to himself. He was very pleased, because he knew that she would never forget. He also did not intend to let this thing slip from his mind.

But he did not dare to come near her during the rest of that evening, or the next morning, as the shore came toward them, blue, and then turning to green, and then glossy and glistening under the hot sun. Back beyond these too rich, feverish lowlands, where the rain fell every day, and the steam was drawn up by the sun, stood the mountains, beyond which were the fine, high tablelands that were the wealth of Venduras — where the city of Venduras stood, surrounded by its ring of dependent towns, in which rebellion was constantly raising its head. In the mountains themselves were the mines, and any one of the wealthy owners could turn the political world of that little country topsy-turvy at a moment's notice. For all was ever at a fine balance, ready to waver at the first hostile breath.

Not for the mines or the rich farmlands, or the cattle ranges where cowpunchers could find work — not for any of these things had Stephen Macdona come to Venduras, but because of those same political upheavals, those wars that commenced at a card game in the evening and continued in street fighting and massacres the next day. In such a world there was sure to be a place for him, as soon as he could make himself known to the powers that were. He thought of these things as he watched the ship being brought to dock and the cover taken from the main hatch, and the derrick with its long sling lowered into the depths.

He hurried down to take charge. For, of course, Christy would treat them as a tiger treats dogs if they started to fit the sling around her without her master's presence. He arrived at the critical moment. They had her placed on a little platform, and Stephen lashed her

27

to the sides. Then, standing beside her, he was swung ashore.

It was the old story. The instant the mare was freed from the ropes of the sling, men began to gather. Ragged fellows in tattered clothes, that had once been white, came peering and grinning and nodding their heads until the great brims of their straw hats were flopping up and down. In the meantime, Stephen groomed her, gave her a mouthful of oats, and fitted the saddle on her back. Then he let her walk about in a narrow circle, getting her land legs under her once more, and breathing the land air, with her eye brightening each instant.

His luggage was brought. A porter was shouldering it. But where should he go?

A little avenue opened through the gaping throng. It was Constancia Alvarez and her duenna at her side. Constancia Alvarez with glistening eyes.

"*Señor* Guadalvo! That is the lady . . . that is the beautiful lady."

"See," said Stephen. "She is not ashamed to show the world how she loves me."

For the mare had come up from behind and rubbed her muzzle at his shoulder.

"She is a lamb," said Constancia. "Tush, are you afraid of me? Look, *señor*, we are friends already. Oh, what a lovely thing."

"*Señorita*," said the warning voice of the duenna.

Yonder, surrounded by men carrying heaps of luggage, appeared a dignified gentleman, with the crowd giving way before him. Constancia Alvarez hurried to rejoin him. She had time for only one bright smile to Stephen Macdona, and, as he swept off his hat and bowed after her, he heard her voice saying *adieu*. Then the crowd closed around her again.

Even the beauty of Christy could not keep all eyes in her direction now, for the father of Constancia was a great man in Venduras, and every face was turned to watch the progress of *Don* Rudolfo across the square, toward the one respectable building that fronted on the plaza.

When her duenna and she were alone in their room, Constancia hurried to the window and looked out. Still she could see the flashing body of the mare.

"Tita, Tita," she moaned.

Tita was, in the presence of others, the most circumspect of elderly ladies, but with young Constancia she was the opposite. And she said now: "Is it really the horse or the man, my dear?"

"He is the most impertinent rascal in the world," said the girl, frowning. Then she laughed. "And the bravest, Tita."

"All brave men are dangerous," said Tita with the gravity of one reading from a book.

"No, I don't mean that he means as much as that," corrected the girl. "Only . . . I wish to see more of him."

"Shall I tell your father what you wish?"

"Oh, Tita, that would never do in the wide world. Never. He would begin by asking questions . . . who is this *Señor* Guadalvo and all the rest. But . . . if this

Don Valentin . . . if he were to follow us to the city . . . do you understand? How can it be done?"

"A word from me, my dear?" said the old woman with a faint smile.

"Oh, a word might never do," said the girl. "He is all fire and words, this Guadalvo. On the ship he had nothing to do . . . except to pull drunken sailors out of the water and talk to a girl, one evening. Talk nonsense . . . but you heard, of course."

"Of course . . . every word. And it was not such very foolish talk, *señorita*. However, if you wish to have him follow you, suppose that you take his horse away from him."

"His horse? His horse . . . He would go mad, Tita. He would kill a hundred men for her sake."

"What are a hundred men?" Tita smiled again.

"But how could the horse be taken?"

"Is there anything that your father cannot do in this country of ours? And suppose that you point out that horse and say that you want her . . . why, my dear, the thing is done."

Constancia stood with her eyes closed, her smile going and coming. "It is tremendously wicked . . . such a thought," she said. "And tremendously delightful."

CHAPTER
FIVE

There were two things of which Rudolfo Alvarez was prouder than of all else in the world. The first was his title of general, which he had obtained on a certain occasion in the city of Venduras. A too-ambitious president had overtaxed the mine owners, and the result was an invasion of hardy fellows from the mountains, well armed, with European and American leaders, their ranks bolstered up with more than a little of the same sort of fighting blood. They took the city of Venduras and put the president to flight. As one American in the fray put it: "There was nothing to it but come and take while the taking was good."

Alvarez had not been among the enemies of that president. Indeed, he had been so enriched by the land grants of the chief official of the republic of Venduras that he had been included in a little impromptu proscription list that had been published by the mine owners. So, along with a crowd of others, he had been driven helter-skelter out of the town. That evening they had camped upon the hills overlooking beautiful Venduras, saw the sparkle of its lakes beneath the moon, and trembled in the naked, chilly air.

Then Alvarez breathed inspiration from the air, sweetened with the scent of the pure pines. He gathered the downcast throng together and pointed out that they were a scant ten miles from the town. The victors were now engaged in celebrating their victory. What more simple than to sweep down from the heights, rush across the city, rout their drunken enemies, and reclaim all that they had lost, plus glory.

The idea was a catching one. By mutual assent, *Don* Rudolfo was placed at the head of the expedition. It was too perilous a task for other heroes and important men to envy him his place at the head of the silent column. It was not over-silent, at that. But in the city of Venduras all was hilarious noise. For the men from the mountains were making up for the heat and the dust of their long, hard march across the plains. They had found wine by the hogshead; all was dancing and singing and joy, as long as head and feet could hold out.

In the midst of this there came a sudden, sullen rumble out of the south, and then the crackling of firearms. It only meant that some of their friends, of course, were celebrating the battle with powder and lead. So they remained at their jollities until the streets were black with an onrushing throng. There were guns, indeed, and guns that were pointed to kill.

In half an hour after the attack reached the vitals of the city, all was over.

After that, Alvarez was seen rushing about the city on a conspicuous white charger, carrying the word everywhere that there were to be no reprisals. For he had had a second inspiration. He had determined that, by this *coup d'état*, he should make nothing but friends. The next morning he could count the heads of a dozen important mine owners in the city prison, and other people of much note, here and there. He gathered the miners together in a single chamber.

"If the last taxes were oppressive, what can you afford to pay?" he had asked.

And they had told him, meeting frankness with frankness.

The late unhappy president was straightway boosted from his place by Dictator-General Alvarez. He himself was too wise to wish to stay in power long. All that he collected were a few modest square leagues of good timberland in the hills, farm land in the river bottoms, and cattle range on the plains. He put in another figurehead at the helm of the republic, and, for his part, he was contented to go back to his ranch and let time roll again beneath his feet.

It was the one great action in his life. Before that, the most distinguished thing that he had done was to inherit a large property. But upon that one turbulent night and the deeds of the days after, his fame was based as upon a rock. Thereafter, he was looked upon as sort of a deity behind a cloud. He could do no wrong. He could not ask too much.

The foreign capitalists whose whims and fancies so often upset the political situation of the republic always made one exception in the list of the proscribed, and that exception was sure to be Alvarez. He had been their friend in the hour of need, and they blessed him for it ever after.

As for the politicians themselves, they looked upon him with even a greater reverence, for he was the only citizen of Venduras who, being at the head of the state with resistless power — for the nonce — had had the modesty and the strength of will to step out from the chair of state and give the scepter to another.

These affairs were now many years in the past, but General Alvarez had never lost his overnight title, and he had never lost his prestige. In fact, he had never allowed his reputation to become tarnished by being used. This, then, was the most memorable thing in the life of the general, and rather than lose that title, he would have given up both legs and ten years of his life.

However, there was another possession of his of which he was proud to a degree only less than his fame. That was his daughter. He considered her from a thousand angles, and, from every new viewpoint, he found that she was perfect. And when it came time to send her away to a far country to be "finished", the general had been buried in grief. Every evening he wrote a letter to her — no mere note, but something that told her everything that had happened in the course of the last twenty-four hours. He was certain that all that happened to General Alvarez was of real importance to the world, therefore, how trebly important to his daughter.

She wrote him in return a scrap of news twice a month, perhaps, and disregarded volleys of frantic cables in between. It was not that she did not love him, but because she was a continual procrastinator.

Now, as the general sat and twisted his long, gray mustaches and worshipped her with his eyes, wondering how God could ever have made a creature so beautiful, so delightful, so perfect — as he thought of these things, he heard her ask if he would do one thing to make her the very happiest girl in the world?

One thing? He would do a million things. Ah, let her see.

She led him to the window. "That black chestnut mare. Father, she is the most exquisite thing that ever walked on four feet. I have seen her. My heart is breaking to have her. Can you . . . ?"

"My dear child, my dear, silly child, if he were a Derby winner, he should be yours. Instantly." He said to the servant who came in answer to his summons: "There is a horse yonder in the square. A pretty, dark chestnut. She belongs to young Valentin Guadalvo. Buy her and bring her instantly to the hotel."

"And the price?"

"Buy her," said the general, and frowned.

"But a thousand . . ."

"A thousand or a hundred thousand *pesos*. Be off."

The man was off, gaping. He went to young Stephen Macdona and found that gentleman in the act of getting into the saddle, while Christy turned her head to watch her master with loving eyes.

Their conversation was not as brief as Stephen Macdona would have had it. He listened for five minutes, while the offers constantly climbed. Finally he leaned from the saddle and placed his strong hand on the shoulder of the other.

"Have you a wife and children, *amigo mío?*"

"I have, God be praised."

"Would you sell them for gold or diamonds?"

The man fell back, amazed, and he carried this strange story to the general.

"It is as it should be," said General Alvarez. "I look about me and wonder what there is to show my girl that I love her. Now fortune brings this way into my hand. Very good." He changed his coat, took his polished stick, wore his heaviest gold chain, with the Swiss watch at one end of it, and a certain rich medal at the other. Then he went to see *Señor* Oñate.

Oñate was not an official. He was more. He was the power that pulled all the strings at the seaport town. He listened to the general with respectful attention. It was not for him to ask questions. It was sufficient that the general had a desire for yonder horse.

"It is done," he said, smiling most agreeably.

"May I ask how?"

"The horse is sick," said Oñate. "The horse is sick, and the veterinary . . . the lazy scoundrel . . . who pronounces upon every animal that enters the country . . . will see that it would be fatal to permit this mare to live for five hours on this land. Very well. The mare is taken . . . she disappears. If another horse very like her should come into the hands of General Alvarez, it would be an odd coincidence. And there is nothing more to it." He waved his hands and bowed above the gesture.

Alvarez said: "You are a thousand times kind, Oñate. I wish you to take this to remember me by . . ." He put a thin sheaf of bills on the table. There were 3,000 *pesos* in that stack.

Oñate looked at that money, and his heart ached for it. However, he knew policy too well to accept. This was the first time that he had been lucky enough to have Alvarez ask a favor of him. He only wished that such favors were asked every day of the year.

He actually turned pale as he caught up the money in both hands and carried it to Alvarez.

"General Alvarez, you crush me," said Oñate. "How could I take this money? It would haunt me. My first opportunity of serving the great benefactor of his country . . . *señor* . . ."

"It has left my hands, Oñate," said the general. "I cannot take it back again." And he left the room.

CHAPTER
SIX

The worthy who stopped Stephen Macdona was splendid above the waist and negligible below. He had a uniform coat of brilliant blue, surmounted with staring epaulettes of gold at either shoulder; enormous brass buttons flamed down its front. He had crossed belts, each set off with cheap gold-and-silver threadwork. The cap on his head was set off with a towering plume of crimson, and his belt supported two revolvers, to say nothing of a magnificent sword. But below the waist he had on a pair of white cotton trousers, frayed to rags halfway down the calves of his legs, and his bare toes wriggled in *huaraches* that had withstood much battering, in the service of his country.

It was very unlikely that Stephen Macdona would have paid much attention to him, in spite of guns and sword and stout and useful knife. But behind this dignitary strolled half a dozen others, all loaded with weapons, looking exceedingly familiar with the use of them. They had been accustomed to terrifying the peaceful populace of that town for years, and therefore they knew that they were invincible. So Stephen stood by and listened, while they informed him that he was guilty of a great crime in having introduced his horse into their country before the veterinary inspection. Already, the seeds of dreadful disease might be speeding abroad to depopulate the myriads of cattle on the wide uplands.

Stephen listened with patience and accompanied them to the veterinary inspector. It was a purely honorary post. No one in Venduras had ever dreamed that such a thing as disease might be brought into the country by foreign cattle until the last president wished to find another easy post with which to reward one of his minor followers. So the necessity of a veterinary inspector was discovered at once.

The school in which this doctor had been trained consisted in a degree as banker's clerk; this was followed by a year of service in the police; he left the force to follow the fortunes of various candidates for political honors, all of whom failed lamentably with the exception of the very last. So, tired from a dozen years of poverty, rags, starvation, and fighting, he sank with a sigh into this comfortable post.

He was to be seen ordinarily with his feet displayed on the window sill, a cigar of unspeakable badness fuming between his teeth. But when a ship came in, he put on his uniform coat and put away the bottle of mescal, which was otherwise beside him. He had never done anything about the arrival of the ships and the cattle aboard them, but, when he put on his uniform coat, he felt vaguely comforted and important. Sometimes he took a turn up and down before his office, with his hands clasped behind his back, and was seen to chew his cigar with a savage insight and determination.

The inspector received Stephen Macdona in a Napoléonic attitude, with one hand twirling his mustache and the other resting upon the hilt of his sword. They all had swords in Venduras. To be without one was a sign that one was a nobody — at least, in a governmental sense.

The patience of Stephen was a little thinner than one of those spider webs that are invisible except when they are drenched with the morning dew. He said: "You are to examine my horse, *señor*, or are you to examine me?"

Stephen spoke an excellent brand of Spanish, for pretty Elena Ramirez had been well schooled. The veterinary inspector stared. But after all, his orders were precise. And the great Oñate himself waited beyond to receive the mare. He turned his attention to the mare and again he blinked. Although he was prepared to do his duty, he had not expected to see such a beauty as this. For this horse he could understand how anything might happen, including a revolution in Venduras. However, he walked around her and laid a hand on her shoulder, frowning at the ground in critical thought while he fingered the supple steel of her muscles.

On such a horse, I am an eagle, ran the thoughts of the inspector. *I range through the country. I dash here and there. I take what I wish. No man may follow me. But after all*, he concluded, *my office is comfortable, and winter nights in the mountains are very cold.*

"This is a critical case," he said out loud. "I shall have to continue the examination." And he had the mare led away.

Stephen Macdona would have followed, but seven bright, tawdry uniforms barred his path, so he retreated and sat down to wait, anticipating the thing that was to come.

The veterinary came back, shaking his head. "Do you know, señor, that you have brought a dreadful blight into the country?"

"My horse is sick, is she not?" Stephen hissed through his teeth.

"She is mortally sick," said the veterinary.

"I had an idea that I was about to lose her."

"She will be destroyed and the body burned at once."

"Very well," said Stephen. "I shall be present to watch."

"That," said the veterinary, "is not ordered." And he turned on his heel.

Again Stephen would have followed, but again seven tawdry uniforms barred his path.

Stephen retired to a corner of the plaza and smoked a cigarette. After all, he was not well furnished with money, but he saw that a time had come to use what he had. He stood up at the end of a half hour, and found the veterinary in his office.

The latter was in the act of producing a bottle of mescal which he hastily put away again as he scowled at his visitor.

Stephen said: "I was grieved, *Señor* Colonel, to learn that my mare is sick."

"That was unfortunate," said the other.

"But the air of Venduras is so wonderfully healthy," Stephen continued, wiping away three or four mosquitoes that had clustered on his hot forehead, "so wonderfully healthy that perhaps she has already entirely recovered and may now be just as healthy as ever."

"You speak of miracles," said the veterinary.

"However," Stephen said, "I believe that this is the very land of miracles. Will you not go and see if one has not been accomplished?" And he placed fifty dollars in the hands of the doctor.

The eye of the latter burned. The currency of Venduras went up and down like a bird in flight, but chiefly it went down. A *peso* today was apt to be half a *peso* tomorrow. And although the veterinary inspector had very little use for the *Estados Unidos*, he was sure that the fields of heaven grew American greenbacks. He stared at this money and he counted the figures in the corners of each leaf. The very heart of this citizen was stirred, but then he remembered Oñate and all that Oñate represented. He balled the money into a knot and hurled it through the doorway. "Dog!" shouted the veterinary inspector. "Do you offer me a bribe?"

The patience of Stephen had already been rubbed thinner than thin. Now the last thread of it snapped. He saw only one thing, and that was the protruding midriff of the inspector, bulging against the buttons of his uniform coat so tightly that Stephen could not help wondering if this balloon might be burst, and if his was the hand appointed for the pricking of the bubble. With 180 pounds of concentrated might and fury, he smote the inspector just upon the sixth button, counting from the top.

The inspector had had time to reach for his gun, but by the time his hand closed on the butt of it, his whole body was benumbed in every nerve, and he himself was hurled upward and backward. He catapulted over a chair, crashing against the adobe wall, and half a dozen rain-rotted bricks of it crumbled under the impact.

By the time he had gathered enough breath to shriek — "Treason! Murder!" — the villain was away. Still he was too helpless to rise. He could only lie on his back and writhe and gasp and fire bullets through the roof of his office, praying that the slugs, descending, might find human targets.

The seven gentlemen in bright uniforms caught a fleeting glimpse of the form of Stephen disappearing past the farther corner of the plaza. When they learned what was wrong, they started on horseback to find him, for this was work exactly to their taste. However, the streets of the seaport town were exceedingly twisting and winding, and, before they were well under way, Stephen was in the jungle that pressed just against the back of the little city.

He had taken his little traveling pack with him. Now he squatted on his heels by the edge of a marshy stream and shaved off his beard and mustaches, shaved them with a sigh, feeling that he was denuding himself of a very precious dignity. However, Christy was in the balance.

Not half an hour later, a muleteer, driving his pack animals up the narrow road from the town, was seized from behind. Before he could turn his head, a coat was clapped over eyes and mouth. Presently he lay on his face in the dust, with the major portion of his clothes stripped from him. And half an hour after that, a ragged young man — tall, strong, light of stride, with a face sun-browned above but strangely pale below, entered the town again with a pack at his back, a whistle trilling from his lips. Stephen was on the trail of Christy.

He passed straight across the plaza and under the eyes of the inspector. The latter gave him not a glance, and Stephen felt that he had equipped himself with a bulletproof disguise. He went on toward the corrals that stretched behind the warehouses, to learn what he could learn. As he walked, he felt more and more that this was a country of many possibilities — if only one could learn the right ropes to follow and the correct strings to pull. Perhaps, in the end, he would be very much at home here.

But in the meantime — Christy.

CHAPTER
SEVEN

There was no trace of beautiful Christy in the corrals. She seemed to have vanished like a vision. So he went to a little cheap café and ate stale bread and tamales of a wonderful and fiery pungency and drank *pulque* not too fresh. He learned something there.

There was no rich citizen in this town. There was really not a single person of the first rank in the place. As for the rich and the distinguished, of course they dwelt in the interior, in the great and beautiful city of Venduras, with the snow-topped mountains standing in a cool circle around it. But who would choose to swelter here by the sea, if he could avoid it?

Stephen Macdona, drawing breaths of that humid air with difficulty, could not help agreeing.

There was only one great highway that led from the town toward the uplands and the great city beyond the blue mountains. Along that highway Christy must pass, because certainly she had been stolen from him by the veterinary inspector, not for his own use but to be sold to some other dignitary of real importance. Therefore, she would leave the seaport, and therefore she would travel by that highway, and, accordingly, beside that road he determined to wait — for a month, if need be.

In the dawn he was at his post. It was now livably cool, although the moisture in the air surrounded him as with a wet blanket. But the billions of insects had not yet begun to fly and to sting; their dreadful humming did not fill the air, and in the silence of the wind he was surrounded palpably.

He looked behind him to the dim blueness of the great mountains of the interior, and before him to the sparkling blue of the sea, with the whitewashed town between. For some reason, a sense of confidence filled the heart of Stephen.

In this land where the railroad, as yet, was a mere experimental affair, the rails had not been brought farther down than the farther edge of the marshes. There had been no available funds for bridging the great acreage of soft, drenched land that lay to the landward from the seaport. For that reason, the poor and the proud would all have to cross by this causeway. Only a desperate man or a strong wild beast would venture to leave the road and go by the miasmic jungles. He watched the day brighten and the sun rise. The instant it was above the horizon, it threw warmth as from a campfire into his face. But he pulled his cheap, tall-crowned hat of straw lower over his eyes and watched the road.

A caravan of mules wound up the way, with shrill oaths coming from the lips of the muleteers. Yonder, the last of the lot, was his friend of the day before, a little more ragged than the rest. However, he was taking payment for his loss out of the hide of his mule. A group of wagons followed. Then, after a considerable time, a party of horsemen, wild fellows bound for the cattle ranges. They rode little ponies as shaggy as dogs, but the brightness of their eyes and the fineness of their legs told Stephen their quality. Still he crouched behind his rocks and watched the procession grow thicker and thicker.

Presently a group of three stalwarts, well mounted, heavily armed, passed at a moderate pace up the road. It was easy to see, from the glances that they cast behind them, that they were the outposts of persons of importance who followed in the rear. Those persons came now into his view, but, before he knew a human face, he saw the bright body of Christy.

He crouched lower, like a beast about to spring, and a savage impulse set all his nerves on edge. How beautiful she was, and how true to him. For now, as the procession drew nearer, he saw her pulling back on the rope that led her along. Her neigh rang again and again to him. She was calling for her master, and he knew it as though the call had been phrased in human words. But who were these who had secured her? Perhaps they were persons who were innocent enough and had simply bought her from that trebly dyed villain, the veterinary inspector.

He saw a tall, gravely dressed gentleman, with the well-groomed mustaches of a Venduran of importance. At his side was a girl, the carriage of whose head was oddly familiar. She came closer — closer — Constancia Alvarez. A thousand plagues light on her lovely head. Innocent? No, she knew the mare as well as she knew him. Now she was turning back and murmuring baby talk to Christy. But the wild mare would have none of her, and it made the heart of Stephen swell with a savage satisfaction.

Stephen began to calculate chances. If he aimed his leap well, he would be at her side before anyone could mark him. A slash of his knife would sever the rope that tied her, and a bound would place him in the saddle. After that, both his hands would be free for his weapons, for he could guide her by the touch of his knee or the sound of his voice. Once on her back, he was seated on a strong wind that obeyed him like his own thoughts.

But it would not be easy; it would be far from simple. Behind them came four more men of the rear guard, and two in addition were close beside the mare. All, including the tall father of Constancia, were armed heavily.

As the fury grew in his mind, he thought of taking careful aim from behind his rock. At this point-blank range, he could tumble them over like the iron ducks that circle around in the shooting gallery — and with a dozen bullets in his two revolvers, how many would be left living from that party at the end of two or three seconds? Constancia and her duenna — and no others.

However, he checked that furious impulse. He had never fired from ambush before, and he would go to the end of his days without committing such a sin against manhood. Besides, it might not be necessary. One second to reach the mare; another to gain the saddle and cut the rope; another to run her down the road, hurtling through the four men of the rear guard, while his revolvers scattered death and destruction among their ranks.

He crouched there in his covert and laid his plans with cold fire in his eyes, and a cruel smile curving his lips. Ten yards away, the mare came to a sudden halt. Her hoofs braced and thrust firmly into the deep dust of the road. Her head went up. Her neigh was a call of agony and hope.

He had forgotten the wind — the cursed land breeze bringing the scent of him squarely down the road. But now she had it and presently she would go mad to get to him. Yes, now she reared — she pitched. She hurled herself backward against the rope like a frantic tigress. All was confusion. *Don* Rudolfo was turning back. The duenna screamed and clasped her hands. The two who had been assigned to handle the precious mare danced here and there helplessly — and the rear guard came hurrying up while the vanguard turned back.

Stephen groaned and set his teeth. If only she had been three strides nearer — but, if he acted at all, he must act now. For the eight men from front and rear were hurrying up, and he would be helpless against such numbers. He sprang silently from behind his rocks. He would have come unmarked, but the quick eye of Constancia caught him, and her warning shout made the nearest of the men turn.

The man snatched at a gun as he glimpsed Stephen, but he snatched too late. A hand of iron was in his face, and he went down, with a spurt of crimson from nose and mouth. The heavy hilt of the hunting knife crunched along the head of the second man, and he rolled in the velvet dust without a sound.

One spring again, and Stephen was in the saddle, slashing at the rope. Alas, had it been the stoutest hemp in the world, it would have been shorn through at the first cut, but it was rawhide, almost as tough as steel, flexible as a serpent, now that it hung slack. Twice and again he slashed at it, and the lariat yielded and swung away from the edge of the knife.

Then the four from the rear were around him. Half a dozen bullets had whistled around his ears, but now that they were close, they dared not fire again, for the bullets might strike *Don* Rudolfo or his daughter. They clubbed their rifles to smite him to the ground.

He had one backward glimpse of them and knew that the battle was lost. So he came out of the saddle as a lynx comes from the branch of a tree. Instead of teeth and claws, he had a Colt in either hand, and they were speaking while he was still in the air.

One man spun around with a scream and clasped his body in his agonized arms. A second dropped into the roadway and clutched at his wounded thigh. And Stephen Macdona, springing through them, headed for his one chance of escape — the marsh beside the road.

He saw its black waters, filmed with green scum. To touch it would be like touching leprosy. But yonder was the half-exposed curve of a fallen trunk. He leaped for that, felt the rotten wood crunch and sag beneath his weight, and sprang instantly again. A little ridge of mud received him, and he floundered out of sight among the trees.

50

Bullets followed him, but they were fired from shaking hands. All these who rode with *Don* Rudolfo were followers worthy of their famous master. They had been proved in the wars. But after all, they were not prepared to fight a lion, hand to hand. As for the marsh, they dreaded it hardly less than a pointed gun. Few had been known to enter it and come forth alive. If they escaped the engulfing mud, the fever poisoned them, and they died afterward. So they looked upon this sudden madman as one already dead. Why should they pursue him? They turned to the work of helping the wounded. There was plenty in that task to employ all hands.

CHAPTER
EIGHT

Out of the marsh, in the dusk of that day, a mud-incrusted monster crawled. He staggered with weariness for even the panther-like strength in his body had been exhausted by the brief mile he had toiled through the marshes. When he came to a stretch of clean grass, he flung himself down on his back and lay gasping, his misted eyes fixed on the stars, his chest heaving convulsively.

Half an hour, and he was up again. He found a clear rill from the mountains flowing into a clean, gravel-bedded pond, and into it he dipped, clothes and all. He swam out on the farther side, refreshed and purified, and strode on up the trail toward the lights beyond.

Walking and the warm wind that blew through the night dried him. When he reached the town, he stopped at a little lunch wagon, where tortillas and tamales were for sale. Keeping to the shadows, he ate and ate to repletion, and listened to the talk.

There was only the one theme — the wild man who had attacked the great *Don* Rudolfo. However, this man was now dead, or as good as dead, since he had spent the day in the marshes. Strict watch had been kept. He could not have escaped. There he would perish, or else crawl out, a fever-stricken refugee, and surrender himself to the hands of the law.

Stephen Macdona listened and smiled. He bought a flagon of dreadful *pulque*, downed it at a draft, and then he continued his quest.

Christy was not in the railroad village. She had been shipped on toward the mountains, and the rumor went that she had been heavily guarded. So, that night, when the freight pulled pantingly out of the yard and up the first severe grade, Macdona lay upon the beams and closed his eyes to keep out the flying cinders. They had not yet shaken him from the trail.

He made half the distance to the mountains, on that first stage. When the freight stopped in the cool of the morning, he went out to forage for food. It was a very rash thing to attempt, and he paid the penalty of his rashness. For a fat policeman saw him and, without asking questions, emptied a revolver at him as Macdona zigzagged down the street and around the corner. He heard the route of the pursuit behind him, and therefore he simply dived through the back window of a hovel and into the midst of a humble family circle, sitting around the breakfast pot.

So Macdona squatted in a corner of the room with a gun resting on his knee.

"Eat," said Stephen.

And they ate, while he helped himself to a remnant of roast kid that remained from a feast of the night before. When the pursuit poured past that door, a voice shouted a query.

"You have seen nothing except your breakfast," Stephen whispered.

"We have seen nothing except our breakfast," said the man of the house in a trembling but loud voice.

And the crowd rushed on.

An hour later — "Here is one *peso* for my breakfast and four for this lodging," said Macdona. "I am the man who attacked the party of *Señor* Alvarez, and, if you help to catch me, you will have some thousands more to reward you for your work over me." And he left by the window through which he had entered. It would be pleasant to state that his frankness disarmed the host. But truth is that he had not gone fifty yards, before the wild clamor was raised.

He found a saddled horse in the next street with a stalwart youth climbing into the stirrups. Macdona plucked him out again and tossed him over his shoulders. Then he rode for the hills.

They hunted him, hot and close, all that day, and just as he was safely distancing them, on the third horse he had borrowed for the day's riding, a random party of *vaqueros* came down and blocked his way. They had not placed themselves across that trail on purpose. But they smelled mischief while it was still a long distance off, and their guns were out. Most willingly would Stephen have given them the road, but the rocks climbed upward on either hand into the heart of the sky. Even a mountain goat would have turned dizzy with one glance along their polished sides.

He bent over the pommel of the saddle and spurred straight ahead, his guns flashing from either hand.

Three went down, and one, perhaps, would never rise again. But they had had enough. There were five of them left, but it seemed to them that the light was very dim — and yonder stranger must have the eyes of a cat to shoot so straight at such an hour. They paused to recruit their forces with the posse that followed after.

In the meantime, Macdona was deep in the heart of the mountains. He came out through a narrow gorge the next day and looked down on the loveliest valley of creation. In a mighty ring against the sky stood white-headed mountains, and beneath them lordly forests marched down over the hills to the plains beneath. All those plains were green as emerald and streaked with the winding silver of many a stream, that paused here and again in flashing lakes, and passed in their leisurely journeyings villages and towns that were white blurs upon the landscape. There stood the central ring of cities. In the midst of all was Venduras with its clustered lakes around.

The heart of Macdona swelled as he looked on all this beauty. But he could give it only a casual glance, for yonder was Christy. Somewhere among those green plains or in those white cities, men were wondering at the beauty of the mare, and that was more to him than all the rest of the world beside.

Down the valley, he met a girl, pacing up the road with a jar of water poised on her head, climbing patiently toward her father's little whitewashed hovel on the hillside. Perhaps Venduras was backward in many respects, but at least the country possessed telegraphs enough to spread such news far and wide.

She knew him the instant that her eyes fell on him, and turned with a scream. The jar fell to the roadway and cracked in a hundred pieces on a rock.

Stephen, with a shout, spurred his horse ahead. He jumped the hedge and caught the girl beyond it. The strong sweep of his arm lifted her onto the horse before him, and, still laughing, he placed his hand over her mouth and watched her terrified eyes widening at him as she strove to scream again.

"Yes," he said, "I am Valentin Guadalvo, but I shall not cut your throat, sweetheart. See, here is a *peso* to mend the jar. And here is another to make you happy, and here is another for the news which you are going to give me."

Now, when Mother Nature made Stephen Macdona with such loving care, she placed her master touches in the creation of his eyes, making them just that shade of brown that no woman, north or south or east or west, can look into without a leaping of the heart.

This maiden of the mountains was standing presently close to Stephen by the roadside and telling him all that was locked in her little head. Afterward she waited until the dust he raked had wound out of sight down the trail, and she was left again to the lonely brightness of the morning sun, and cold, shaggy mountains, and the empty sky.

But Stephen had found out where the ranch of *Don Rudolfo* was situated, and he made toward it as straight as the needle of the compass points. They sighted him by chance near San Gabriel and hounded him down the valley until he twisted out of their traces among the lowest hills. Another night march carried him toward his goal by a long distance. Then a keen-eyed goatherd saw him in the distance and sent in the warning. They picked up his trail with hunting hounds and pressed him so hard that he had to turn back toward the hills again. And only the skilful use of his rifle kept them at a safe distance.

He lurked in the foothills and tried again, three days later. And again he was marked and ridden until his horse staggered. That might well have been his last day on earth, but he saw the white walls of a little town and rode straight for it. He found there what he expected — more than one gun blazing at him as he passed. But he also found what he had hoped — a fresh, strong horse standing at a tethering post in the plaza.

He made the change in an instant and rode safely out into the plains beyond, with only a bullet hole through the crown of his hat to tell of the encounter. But although he shook off the pursuit on this day, also, he felt that he had already more than half failed in his quest. For by this time the whole of Venduras knew that he was desperately bent on regaining the black chestnut mare, and, of course, *Don* Rudolfo knew a little better than the rest. So, even if he could gain the ranch, would he not find the mare guarded heavily, day and night, with chosen men close to her?

Now, resting in the hills, and drifting restlessly here and there while he strove to make new plans, on a day, he saw a solitary horseman on a nearby hill, stationary, with something held glittering before his face. Some look-out had evidently spotted him with field glasses, and Macdona with a groan resigned himself to another hunt.

He got down first and looked to his cinches, which were somewhat loose. When he climbed into the saddle again, he saw a strange thing — the single rider was coming toward him with both hands raised above his head. Macdona paused with his rifle at the ready and let the other come into close half pistol shot — and then nearer. He began to see that he had nothing to fear from the stranger, who was an unshaven rascal with two pistols in the saddle holsters and two more at his belt, to say nothing of a rifle thrust into the long gun bag beneath his knee. The clothes of this man would have shamed a beggar, but his horse was fit for a prince to bestride. It seemed to Macdona that there was only one sort of man in the world who would be thus accoutred.

The other stopped ten paces away, with both his hands still shoulder high. "Consider, *Señor* Guadalvo," he said, "that two are stronger than one, and that three are stronger than two."

"You speak" — Macdona smiled — "like a schoolbook. But where is the third?"

The other pursed his lips and raised a whistle that blew screaming down the wind. At once a dozen riders started to the crest of the nearest hill.

"*Señor*," said Stephen, "I see that there is more to you than meets the eye. Are we to be friends?"

"Ah," said the brigand, "it is for that purpose that God made us."

CHAPTER
NINE

To be a bandit, in other countries, was to be a cut-throat, a thief, a vagabond, and a general scoundrel. But to be a bandit in Venduras was something else. Guido de los Pazos, that same roughly dressed and splendidly mounted thief who had encountered Stephen Macdona, was decidedly something else. He had been, at one time, a rich landholder, a man of education, and a senator who sat in the tobacco-flavored senatorial chamber in the capital city. The cross currents of two or three revolutions had altered his manner of living and his ambitions. He had risen, you might say, from the comparative obscurity of a politician and ranch owner to the bright fame of a bandit. From the western to the eastern sea he was known and well considered.

Now he sat in his village, and, reclining in his favorite chair, he comforted himself with cool drafts of scented smoke, drawn from a water pipe. He looked through the window upon the rough rocks of the mountainside, pleasantly crossed with a cedar bracken, here and there, up to the point where the goatherd drowsed on a stump and watched his flock that was scattered higher up, beyond the view of *Don* Guido's window. He smoked with the calm content of a philosopher, and like a philosopher he received the news that was presently brought to him.

There had been a rattling of horses' hoofs outside, and a stir of voices. Now his daughter Lila came running in to him.

"Andres Castellar is dead!" was the first word that she wailed to him.

Then she shrank away and waited, for Andres Castellar was one of the bravest and most trusted men of her father's band. That morning, he and a few others had gone up into the mountains for a day's hunting, taking with them the new man, that richly famous Valentin Guadalvo, who had recently filled the country with his deeds, flashing here and there across Venduras.

Don Guido removed the mouthpiece from his lips and emitted fragrant smoke. "Valentin Guadalvo killed him, then?"

His daughter looked at him in utter wonder. "Is it true, *señor*?" she said. "Do you know things when they happen? Do you see everything?"

He waved a magisterial hand without answering, for *Don* Guido made it a rule never to commit himself as to his own weaknesses and limitations. "Why did not the others bring me word of it?"

"They were afraid. And now Gualterio has rushed into the mountains with more men to revenge Andres. Ah, is it not dreadful?"

She turned up her face in a pious horror, and her father watched the sun turn her hair to flaming gold.

"This is very well," he said.

She stared at him again. She had never been able to understand this father of hers. Even in his talkative humors, he was strange enough. In his silences, he was more mysterious to her than an oracle.

"When *Don* Valentin returns . . . " he began.

"Alas, *señor*, will his ghost come to haunt us?"

"Who spoke of ghosts?"

"But even though he has been able to kill Andres, how can he stand against that terrible Gualterio? Oh, no, he must be dead even now."

"When *Don* Valentin returns," he went on, not regarding her, "you may see him before I do. And then you must be sure to smile at him. Because, my child, that will be a sign that I am not angry, and I do not wish him to doubt me."

She left him and stole back to the grave circle of waiting men. "Even Gualterio will not be able to kill *Don* Valentin," she whispered to them. "My father has said so."

Perhaps other men in other countries would have smiled, hearing such powers of prophecy attributed to anyone. But these fellows did not smile. They knew their leader far too well to question his wisdom. But an air of tense expectancy settled over the village, and all eyes scanned the hillsides anxiously.

Presently they saw the return of the hunters. First came the mules, driven along with shrill-voiced, brown-footed boys, and carrying the quartered bodies of five deer, the fruit of the hunt. Behind these came a group of three: Andres Castellar in the middle, and upon one side his brother Gualterio, on the other Valentin Guadalvo himself.

Who could say, after this, that Guido de los Pazos did not possess the gift of second sight?

It was no dead Andres, then, who came back to the village. But there was a bandage around his shoulder and the first swift rumor, as the riders came in, was that there had been a fight, indeed. When Gualterio reached the hunters, there had been another battle, but bloodless, this time. In both *Don* Valentin had conquered. But who could think that there had ever been strife among them to see Andres smiling faintly, and Gualterio laughing. No, they came in like the three best comrades in the world.

Someone ventured to question the fierce and battle-scarred Gualterio. He merely shrugged his shoulders. "Is it any shame," he said, "to be beaten by a mountain lion? Besides, I have now two brothers, instead of one."

Stephen Macdona had gone into the house of the chieftain, and at the door he met the blue eyes and the golden hair of Lila.

"My father knew that you would come back safely," she said. "I, also, am glad, *señor*." This she said, obeying the very letter of her father's command, for she smiled up into the brown eyes of Stephen.

He went in to de los Pazos, leaving the girl behind him with a slender hand still pressed against her lips.

"And it was a pleasant hunt?" *Don* Guido asked, when he had placed a box of long, brown-coated, oily

Havanas before his guest. "A hot day, but a happy one, señor?"

"We found some deer and brought them back with us," said Stephen. "It was a fine day and . . . you have a glorious lot of fighting men, *Don* Guido!"

"I selected them with care," admitted de los Pazos.

"However, I am curious about one thing."

"Ask whatever you choose."

"You are known in this country, *Don* Guido. You have done enough to fill the lives of half a dozen men. And yet you can settle down here peacefully in the mountains . . . for how long? How is that managed? Why have they not sent men up here to take you?"

"In part," said the bandit, "you have answered yourself. I am known in this country." He made a slight pause as he drew on the water pipe and crossed his legs. Then he continued: "Besides, they have sent men for me, once or twice. The men found me, but only part of them went back to tell what they had seen."

He waved toward the white-headed mountains. "Consider, my friend, that in the throat of one of those passes, half a dozen men could make hot work for a hundred. They would need a little army to take me. And a little army is an expensive thing. And while the little army was away catching me, might not some clever politician make a revolution? You see how this thing is."

"I begin to see." Stephen smiled. "So you might go on here forever?"

"One never can tell," answered the leader. "I live each day for its own sake."

"If President Smith sends an army out to catch you, Senator Jones takes the lucky chance to raise a revolution and the good work of bandit-catching will have been done by Smith for Jones. That is very neat."

"Venduras is Venduras," said *Don* Guido. "We have our own little ways in the world. Besides, I am moderate. I take what I need and not what I want. My own goatherds on the mountains, you see, furnish milk and cheese and flesh enough for my men, and for me. If we need more, why, you have seen the deer that run in our valleys. The streams are crowded with trout. Watercress grows in the pools. We have our patches of maize here and there, enough to make our tortillas. What more do we want? A little money, to be sure. I must have enough of that to satisfy my brave men. But that is soon done. When the silver is brought down on the backs of the mules from the higher mountains, if I stop a train here and there and take a few loads, is that a great crime? No, because what I take in moderation, others might take in gross. And no other bandit dares to show his head in these mountains except my men. Some call me a thief, to be sure, but then there are others who call me a chief of police. Or again, if some owner of a ranch grows too fat and proud and like a tyrant in the lowlands, I slip down on him in the night, and, when I come back, he finds that he has become thin between dark and dawn."

He settled back in his chair and smiled at the young man, who watched him with smiling lips and fiery eyes.

"*Don* Guido," he said, "I begin to understand you very well."

"Now the first thing," said the leader, "is that mare of yours. We will start at once to —"

"De los Pazos," broke in Stephen, "it seems to me that everything is for me, in this arrangement. Suppose, then, that I take the mare and ride away?"

"We are gamblers," answered *Don* Guido. "And this is a risk which I must take."

"This is very fine, frank, generous talk. I have to answer it in the same tone. This is a jolly life that you lead up here . . . a free and cheerful life, *Don* Guido, but I shall not stay with you long. Enough to make some return for Christy . . . and then we say goodbye."

"Tomorrow" — the brigand smiled — "takes care of itself."

CHAPTER
TEN

In the cool of the evening *Señor Don* Rudolfo Alvarez always sat on his balcony. He retired there shortly after the last meal of the day and remained there to think in peace. For he could look from this balcony across the flower-starred gloom of the patio gardens beneath, and beyond the walls of the patio to the level thousands of his acres, patched with lights here and there, where his villages stood. Beyond these nearer beauties arose the hills where the great forests that he owned were slumbering, and beyond these still stood the mighty mountains, unseen, except where their outlines blotted out the stars.

It was an old habit with General Alvarez. He felt that it surrounded him with dignity and calm. In a way, he aspired to be considered a sort of George Washington of Venduras. So he maintained these evening vigils, and, after dark, the fragrance of his Havanas crept down and mingled with the perfumes in the patio, and sometimes, a little later, the soft murmur of his snoring descended, also. However, the general never dreamed that the servants dared to smile, even behind his back. He was a rare soul, who saw so few faults in himself that he could not guess where others might criticize him.

On this evening, he had finished his first cigar and had wrapped the goatskin rug closer about his knees as the night breeze grew a little chillier. He looked drowsily forth across the dark until he was not at all sure where the lights of his outermost villages ended, and the stars of heaven began. Just at this moment he was drawn rudely back to the earth by the sharp tapping of heels that crossed the floor of his library, behind. There was only one person with authority to break in upon him in this fashion.

She came out onto the balcony with the swishing of her skirts about her like the noise of a wind through ferns. "Father, it is not true," she said. "You haven't sent Christy away."

Some of his sense of greatness departed suddenly from *Don* Rudolfo. His aura, as one might say, grew dim, and he bundled the silken softness of the goatskin tighter around him. "Sit down beside me, child." She did not budge from before him, looking down at him with blazing eyes. He was glad of the dimness of the night, which screened his face, although some of the lamplight from within shone upon her. In these moods she was very like her mother — a little too splendid — a little too like. "There is one's duty to be considered as well as one's pleasure," said *Don* Rudolfo.

"Duty? Duty?"

"To one like your father, who must think of his country as well as himself."

"I'm not talking about the country. I'm talking about Christy . . . just when I'd taught her to take sugar from

67

my hand . . . and . . . and I would have ridden her in another week."

She fairly stammered in her passion, and her father looked at her with a vague uneasiness.

"If it were only this Guadalvo, he would have been nothing to your father. But when de los Pazos comes in . . . ah, that is another matter."

"Guido de los Pazos," echoed the girl.

Her father sighed. He had not been sure that even this name would impress her. "That same Guido," he said.

"But de los Pazos, the bandit . . . what has he to do with *Don* Valentin?"

"This much . . . that they ride together, my dear. I heard it this morning. And the instant I heard it, I knew what I should have to do."

"Guido de los Pazos," said Constancia again, breathless.

"The party was sighted near San Lorenzo. Troops rode out."

"And caught the wind!" cried his daughter. "Oh, that is all that they ever catch when they try to net that terrible man. Oh, go on."

"They did catch the wind, and it proved to be a hurricane," said her father. "They laid an ambush to surprise de los Pazos twenty miles north of San Lorenzo . . . twenty miles nearer to me and to you, my dear, if you know the map of your country."

"Yes, yes."

"When they had arranged their troop, there were enough of them to swallow de los Pazos and all his crew, they thought. And then they saw *Don* Guido coming across the plain with a little handful . . . hardly enough to be worth talking about . . . and they prepared themselves to capture the old lion at last."

"Ah, but they never could do it!" exclaimed Constancia. "Tell me what he did?"

"Nothing but ride straight forward toward the government men. It seemed plain that he suspected nothing."

"Ah, how splendid!" cried Constancia.

"Child, child, do you love nothing but bloodshed?"

"Quick . . . tell me everything. When he came closer . . . he slipped away?"

"He came too close to them to slip away. He came right on into the range of their rifles."

"Dreadful."

"Is this de los Pazos your brother that you love him so well?"

"Every brave man is my brother. Go on."

"The troops saw that they had him in their grip. They held their fire, ready to blast *Don* Guido to bits. They only wondered that there were so few of the bandits with him. Forty had been reported in sight at San Lorenzo. And here were a scant dozen with him. And of the government, nearly two hundred, say the reports."

"Two hundred, and poor *Don* Guido had only a dozen. But that would mean a miracle, Father."

"Do you think so? Well, it was a miracle that came from a different direction. Just as they were ready to open fire and blow de los Pazos to bits, there was a rattle of hoofs from behind the rocks of a tall hill that lay at the side of the troops. And down came a little crowd of horsemen at full speed, each man with a pair of revolvers spouting fire and lead. As they galloped, they shouted . . . What do you think they shouted?"

"They shouted for de los Pazos. Did they not?"

"That was only part of their yell," said *Don* Rudolfo. "They shouted for de los Pazos and for Guadalvo. De los Pazos and Guadalvo. They made the hills ring with their cheers. And in front of them rode a tall young man whose guns killed from either hand."

"It was Valentin Guadalvo. And he crushed them."

"He tore the troopers to shreds. They rode away as fast as they could, and that left the field to nothing but the bandits and the wounded. There were plenty of the latter, and plenty of dead, also."

She threw up her face and laughed softly. "Did I not tell you that he was such a man?" she said. "Oh, I saw it in him. Soft as silk, but a tiger's claws under the velvet. A dreadful man, Father. A glorious man. And now that he and *Don* Guido are together . . . will they not burn through the country like a great flame?"

"My dear," said her father, "I'm glad to see that you agree with me. Now, if a man has a bear's cub in his tent, and he sees the mother bruin come raging down the path, does he not put the little one outside where it may be seen? And in exactly the same fashion, would I not have been a fool to retain that mare with me when I knew that Guadalvo and *Don* Guido were riding together?"

"Oh," said the girl, "to surrender without striking a blow."

"Consider, my dear, that I have something beyond myself to think of. There is my country, as I said before. Who can tell when this poor, bewildered, harassed Venduras of ours may need me again? Am I to throw myself away fighting brigands? Will you tell me that, Constancia?"

Constancia looked down at him for a long moment. Then she leaned forward and kissed him on the forehead. There was something almost like pity in that kiss, and it disturbed the equanimity of Alvarez more than anything that had ever happened in his entire life.

"Dear Father," she said, "of course, you have done exactly the right thing."

And she went from the balcony, although *Don* Rudolfo could not settle again toward drowsiness. He was filled with a coldly disturbed thought. It was as though his daughter's eyes had been looking through him, and finding in his inmost nature something of which he himself was not aware. What could it be?

She found Tita enjoying a covert cigarette in her own room. That worthy old woman hastily put out the cigarette, and Constancia pretended not to see.

"Do you know what it is?" she cried.

"And what, then? I thought that you would be down there much longer than this, complaining."

"It is de los Pazos."

Tita clasped a little pendant ruby that glowed at her throat, and she looked about her in terror.

"De los Pazos and Guadalvo have joined hands. And Father, like a wise . . . politician . . . has sent Christy away, where they can find her more easily, you know . . . sent her away without a guard. Oh, how could a man's pride let him do such a thing?"

"Yet you do not seem unhappy, child?"

"When he has Christy will that be the end, Tita?"

"Will that be the end? Will that be the end? Of what are you talking, Constancia? What should be the end?"

Constancia sat by the window and watched the stars and clasped her hands across her throat and laughed and shuddered. "Will he stop when he has Christy . . . merely?"

"Oh, Constancia, are you mad? Do you mean . . . do you guess . . . would he dare?"

"I have never seen the stars so bright," crooned Constancia contentedly. "And what is that bird singing out yonder in the darkness, Tita?"

"Is a screech owl a singing bird, Constancia?" asked the other, still breathless.

"I never knew," said Constancia, "that the world could be so beautiful before."

CHAPTER
ELEVEN

It was the manifest intent of *Don* Rudolfo to avoid trouble with the bandit if he could, but it was also most necessary that he should maintain a bold and politic front. Because, worse than death itself, he feared the compromising of his dignity as a national figure. Therefore, he made the most careful preparations to impress the public eye.

He called in from the hills some scores of his hardy herdsmen on their shaggy, wild-eyed little ponies, all looking as formidable as tigers. He brought down from the forests and the rougher upper mountains a number of woodsmen and goatherds, more stolid than the riders and therefore, it was felt, suitable for use as a sort of infantry to be thrown about the house of *Don* Rudolfo and protect that house from the onset of the enemy.

But a mere defensive campaign was not what *Don* Rudolfo pretended. He would have people believe him capable of still more than this. Accordingly he sent out a few scouts, riding in the direction of the supposed line of the bandit's march. The people of the countryside were given to understand that *Don*

Rudolfo was merely concentrating his forces before launching an irresistible attack against de los Pazos.

However, it was never the intention of the politician to do more than strike a few attitudes for the sake of impressing his fellow countrymen. He posed as a great upholder of law and order. All the while he earnestly prayed that *Don* Guido would exercise discretion and good sense and forbear the battle. If the terrible de los Pazos had made an ally of Valentin Guadalvo, there could really be nothing that the pair wanted from him, Alvarez, except that same unlucky mare, Christy. So he had sent Christy out to pasture on the verge of his dominions, in an unguarded range. Let the bandits pick her up as they would. So ran the thoughts of *Don* Rudolfo.

The very next day they had news of a kind that convinced him he had nothing more to fear. Word came over the wire that the government, while de los Pazos was ranging across the lowlands, had dispatched a flying column that had penetrated softly through the mountains and had reached the valley where the bandits kept their headquarters. There the men who remained in the place had fled to the fastnesses of the higher ravines. But they had captured several children and women — a small booty, to be sure, except that one of the girls was none other than the daughter of de los Pazos himself.

Don Rudolfo, rubbing his hands together, communicated these tidings to his family at the noon meal. What would be the result? Why, that grim bandit would whirl about and scour across the plains, breathing death and destruction and headed for the misguided spirits who had dared to violate his valley in the mountains. This was clear to Alvarez, and he wondered when his daughter dropped her head and frowned.

But of the actual movements of de los Pazos, there were no tidings. He was lost in the vast sea of the plains and there was no word of him, until late that afternoon a flying rider rushed to the Casa Alvarez with the word that de los Pazos and his men had been seen — many miles away. There was word that they had paused to capture a certain black chestnut mare.

Alvarez was in a quandary until he had had a chance to think the matter over. "It is all clear," he said. "De los Pazos has not yet heard about his daughter. But now he knows the truth and he will turn back."

Constancia had ideas of her own, and Tita heard them before the day was ten minutes older. "If *Don* Valentin has taken Christy again, tell me, Tita, will he turn back until he has come to see me, also? Or has he made all of those desperate rides across the plains only for the sake of a horse?"

"All the saints have mercy," whispered Tita. "Do you think that he would try to steal you out of your own house?"

"Steal me? Oh, no, he would not dare to do that. How could they face all my father's men? No, but before tomorrow morning . . . you will see if I lie . . . he will attempt to slip into the house and see me. He will come on with Christy. He will try to see me if it is only to berate me for having stolen his horse."

"Child, child, is he a madman, then?"

But Constancia merely laughed, and all the rest of that day she was as happy as a child. In the evening, she watched from her window as a broad moon lifted its golden face above the eastern trees and covered the plains with soft shadows and unearthly light. She could not sleep; she could not read. But she sat for a long time listening to the voices from her father's little army that was housed in the outer sheds, living happily, and waiting for the word of command that was to send them out against the bandits.

They would never receive that command. Constancia knew her father far too well to expect that. But it gave her a pleasant sense of strength to hear those distant, murmuring sounds. They began to die out; they passed into a few faint laughs; the men of Alvarez were going to bed. And what of Valentin Guadalvo?

When Tita came to say good night, she stood at the window, saying: "You see, you have been only dreaming, child. Even a madman would not dare to come here . . . but why do the men of your father keep up such a noise?"

For a sudden tumult had broken out again from the sheds. Then it seemed to Constancia that she could hear a single voice, far away through the night, shrieking a distant, dim warning. After that, the clear, small ringing reports of guns half covered up by the thundering of hoofs that swept rapidly toward the house.

Tita clutched her. "What is it, Constancia? Oh, my guardian angels, what can it be?"

Constancia put her suddenly away and sprang to the window. The noise from the sleepers had turned into a deafening babble of sounds. Men were shouting commands, questions. She could see them pouring out, half dressed. Some carried rifles. Others went about half asleep, half bewildered with fear, their hands empty.

From a window farther down the house, the voice of *Don* Rudolfo shouted orders. There were no obedient ears to hear. Half a dozen riders came swirling into the confusion of men. They were gesticulating wildly and pointing behind them.

"Constancia!" gasped Tita. "Tell me before I die . . . what is it? What can it mean?"

The door of the room was dashed open. *Don* Rudolfo ran in, girding a cartridge belt about his hips.

"Constancia!" he cried. "Come quickly! There may be little time. They are coming. That devil . . ."

The uproar outside drowned his voice, and Constancia, clinging fascinated to the window, heard the roar of the charge rush louder and closer. She strained her eyes and saw a long line of shadowy horsemen pouring out of the night. A wild voice went up from them: "Pazos! Pazos! Guadalvo! De los Pazos!"

Guadalvo. Her mind flashed back to the deck of the old *Santa Lucia* as it weltered through the warm gulf seas, tossing its rail against the rising moon. Guadalvo had held her hand gently, and spoken as no other man had ever dared to speak to her.

"Constancia!" shouted her father at her ear. "Do you hear? Are you mad?"

She did not turn her head. She would not lose one iota of the magic scene outside. "We are as safe here as anywhere!" she exclaimed. "Ah, what men."

"I am coming again. I shall have the horses placed at the rear of the house. Do you hear me?"

"Yes."

"Come there instantly."

He was gone, racing from the room, and there was only Tita, sobbing convulsively on the floor beside her. But yonder came that line of galloping shadows. They gleamed clearer in the moonshine, and the yelling cut like knives against her ear:

"De los Pazos! Guadalvo! Guadalvo!"

Words of magic, it seemed, so far as those heroes who had been drawn together by her father were concerned. They had heaped themselves together, forming in some semblance of solid ranks, like infantry about to receive a cavalry charge, but, under the thunder of those approaching cheers, they began to melt away at the flanks where the men skulked away into the shelter of the house and the sheds.

As soon as they were a little distance away, fear seemed to leap upon their backs. She saw them throwing down guns and racing off at full speed. The body of horsemen that had been forming staggered as though struck by a tidal wave of terror. Then they, too, wheeled away wailing:

"All is lost! All is lost!"

There was a grim attraction between them and the remaining body of foot fighters. One or two discharged their guns into the air, unaimed, and then, as though

78

their own daring had paralyzed them with fear, the whole mass turned and fled in a screeching body that turned into a churning mass, leaping and scrambling, and falling down, tearing one another to the earth in a wild effort to get first to safety.

But they would have paid dearly for their stand had it not been that, in front of the wild band of riders out of the night, there rode one taller than the rest and on a taller horse, a creature as beautiful as a glistening black panther beneath the moon. He rode in the lead, a revolver in one hand, his horse perfectly guided by the pressure of his knees apparently. His other hand was raised high above his head as he shouted in a voice that sounded with a wonderful clearness through the uproar:

"No bullets! No bullets, *amigos míos!* All is over!"

At his command guns that had been leveled were lowered, and the horsemen drew rein hard to keep from driving their frantic horses into the tangle of fugitives.

And that was Valentin Guadalvo.

CHAPTER
TWELVE

That fascination left Constancia now, and its place was taken by a grand terror. She raised Tita with a vigorous hand. "Tita, Tita, there is no time for crying and fainting. Run!"

Tita ran with all her might, her mistress behind her. They found that the halls of the house were already deserted. Truly, they were very late. Only, as they passed the dining room, they saw the old butler, who had always been so deeply trusted, raking the silver into a sack. She did not have time even for indignation.

They rushed breathlessly to the little rear door of the house where her father had said that horses would be waiting. She stumbled out against the figure of a man in the night. A hand of iron caught her by the throat and shoulder and hurled her back. She struck against Tita. Both went to the floor inside, with Tita shrieking. But a grim, careless voice followed them:

"If you try to come out again, I'll use the quirt. Keep inside."

The door was flung shut, and in the ears of the girl, as she raised herself to her feet, were echoing such words as she had never heard before. Even Tita had time to understand that this was no occasion when screams would be of any service.

They stole back toward the room of Constancia, and, as they went down the hall, they heard the bolt of the great front door being shot back, and then the door itself grating open while the familiar voice of the butler was raised cheerfully.

"Enter, *Señor* Guadalvo. I have prepared the silver in some sacks for you. It is waiting in the dining room."

In her own chamber, Constancia sank into a chair and said to Tita: "Now, Tita, don't make a sound. I want ten seconds of perfect silence, while I think."

Tita sat like a mouse and watched the face of her mistress grow stern while her blank eyes turned their glance inward. Whatever the thoughts of Constancia, they made her start up and shoot home the bolt of her door. She had barely done it when there was a voice in the hall — was it not that same Teresa, that young maid for whom she, Constancia, had done so much? Yes, it was her voice crying out cheerfully:

"This is her room, *señor!* I watched every moment. She did not get away. She is in there now, I swear."

A hand rapped gently at the door.

Constancia leaped up and cried: "*Señor*, I am standing within here, armed. If you force that door, I shall shoot, and I shall not miss!"

A man's voice laughed softly in the hallway, and a thrill of ice went to her heart. That was the voice of Guadalvo. She had heard that same laughter on the old steamer, but she had never dreamed that it could have so many meanings.

"Be warned, however, *señor*, in the name of heaven," broke in Teresa wildly. "If you touch that door to break it down, she will fire . . . and she shoots straight. I have seen her."

"We shall see," said Stephen Macdona from the hall, and instantly the heavy door groaned inward. The stout bolt bent under the terrible pressure of his strength. It was a thing to wonder at and hardly to believe.

Constancia caught up the revolver that she had already laid upon the table. From outdoors, there was a great sound of battering. Someone, some place, was smashing down doors. She had to raise her voice almost to a scream to top the racket. "*Señor*, I have warned you . . . I am not a fool or a child. If you . . ."

At that instant, the bolt was ripped from its screws, and the door swung open, while with a great, lurching step Stephen Macdona entered the room.

Savage pride and white fury made the girl raise the revolver and fire straight at the mark. Then, as an instant's darkness swam across her eyes, thinking of the thing that she might have done, her wrist was seized by a grip by no means gentlemanly, and the revolver was plucked out of her hand.

"Is he dead?" gasped Constancia, her eyes closed.

"He is not harmed," said the voice of Stephen Macdona.

She opened her eyes. There was the tall fellow standing above her and his brown eyes cold and stern as he looked down to her. "Are you not a horse thief only, but a murderess, also?" He turned and called out. Half a dozen wild-looking men crowded instantly through the doorway. "Leave the old woman," he said, "but take this one." And he strode from the room.

To Constancia it was very much like the difference between dreaming of battle and battle itself. Battle dreams may be glorious, but battle itself is apt to be a dusty, dirty affair. These stained hands gripped her on either side.

There crouched Tita, swaying back and forth, her face raised, her eyes blind and closed, her hands clasped together as she prayed. It was not a prayer for herself, but for her young mistress. The heart of Constancia swelled. Trying to stop, she called gently: "Do not be afraid, Tita. They will not dare to hurt the daughter of Alvarez."

"You she-wolf," snarled one of the men who led her along. "If I had my way, I would cut your throat and hang you up by the heels. Take her along."

She was jerked violently ahead. They brought her rapidly through her father's house and into the open night. It was a scene of grand turmoil. Men were running here and there. And not all of them were the bandits. More than one face of her father's servitors she recognized, and wrote them down in her heart for a future reference.

Yonder sat a rough-looking fellow on a tall gray horse. She recognized that horse. It was her father's favorite thoroughbred on which he was accustomed to ride at the head of parades now and again, or on which he pranced along when he was showing some distinguished guest over his estate. But if this were her father's horse, where was *Don* Rudolfo himself?

She was brought forward through the swirling crowd to a little inner and open circle, and there she saw her father in person, with his hat thrown off, his long hair disarranged so that he looked more like a cartoon of a musician than a great patriot. His hands were tied behind his back. She stared from him to the man on the gray horse. That was de los Pazos.

The bandit pointed a gloved hand at the girl. "She is there," he said.

Alvarez turned his head, and his wild, despairing eye lighted as it fell upon his daughter.

"Now, Alvarez," said the chieftain, "I could take you along with your daughter and sell the lives of the pair of you for a good fat sum, but there is something that I prize more than money. You are free. You have lost nothing, but a little spilled wine, a few horses and cattle, and perhaps a pound or two of silver . . . besides your daughter. I could have gutted your house and set fire to it afterward. But I have spared everything except the girl. If she behaves herself, she will be treated well enough. She is in the hands of a gentleman. You are free, Alvarez. The instant that you arrange to set *my* daughter free, you will receive yours back."

"Then stop now, in heaven's name, de los Pazos," said the politician. "That is a thing which can be done instantly and I —"

"And one little thing more. I have with me a young gentleman who may grow tired of this cheerful life that we lead together in the mountains. His name is Valentin Guadalvo. I shall wish to have a pardon for him, also."

Alvarez raised his voice again, but de los Pazos cut him short by placing a whistle at his lips and blowing a rapidly thrilling note.

Instantly the place was crowded with men, mounting and riding toward their leader. Alvarez himself was lost in the swirl. She saw one fleeting glimpse of him as he shouted to one of his captors. She could see the movement of his lips, but she could not hear a murmur of his voice. Then the whole body of men was thrown into rapid forward movement. She herself was put into the saddle on a fiery little mustang, with a lead rope running to the pommel of the bandit beside her. And suddenly they were away through the night. As they gathered headway in the moonshine, beyond the trees that surrounded the Casa Alvarez, she could see the whole of them with a glance forward and a glance behind. And behold, of the little army that had scattered the forces of Alvarez in such a shameful rout, there were hardly more than twenty couples cantering across the plain — not more than forty men. Yet they had done such things.

It reminded her suddenly of other tales that she had heard out of the past, of how a score of buccaneers, English, Portuguese, French, and renegade Spaniards, mixed with Indian half-breeds, or Negroes from the West African coast, had been able to scale the sides of the tall Spanish galleons that sailed the Spanish Main — twenty against 200, sometimes those odds had been. With the fury of mad dogs they had ripped up and down the decks until the crew fled below.

Now she could believe those old stories and understand them. These fellows were of the same breed. Each man, careless, wild-eyed, stern of jaw, was ready to risk his sacred life and soul for the sake of a half penny of gold or pleasure. The result was that ordinary human beings could not stand before them.

The canter increased to a grand gallop. A cloud of dust rose from the hoofs of the horses that ran before her. Then a voice rang through the night. She heard someone come flashing up from the rear on a beautiful horse, cursing in Spanish most magnificently, and demanding to know if the leaders wished to run their horses to rags before they had well begun the return march?

The order was instantly obeyed, although Constancia trembled with expectation as she saw the scowls that passed over the faces of those moonlight riders. Still, not a voice dared to be raised in answer, and the rider of the beautiful horse fell back again to his position of captain of the rear.

That was Valentin Guadalvo.

CHAPTER
THIRTEEN

Afterward, of course, Guadalvo would come and ride at her side. Then she would tell him firmly enough what she thought of his way of life, and these new associates of his — and the raiding of a peaceful house in the middle of the night, and the taking away of a helpless girl. But Guadalvo did not come.

They halted toward the gray of the dawn, when she was very tired, and that instant Guadalvo came. "You are not to be watched," he said, "or troubled so long as you do not leave the sight of the column. There is your blanket." He threw it across the pommel of her saddle, and rode on.

Constancia dismounted slowly. This was not the way matters went in books. This was not the way of heroes to heroines. A girl's voice came past her, laughing gaily. It was Teresa, walking beside a swaggering giant of a bandit.

"Teresa!" she called. "Unsaddle this horse and put the —"

Teresa stepped before her and snapped her fingers in her face. "What are you," said Teresa, "to give me commands?" And she whirled about and went off with her cavalier, who was nodding and chuckling approval.

The head of Constancia was spinning with bewilderment. This was not the habit of her life. The whole world had turned topsy-turvy. But could it be that in a world of men, the beauty of a woman, of a wronged and helpless woman, had no power? She stood as one stunned.

A blaze went up. They were tearing up small brush and piling it to make a fire to break the chill of the night wind. And then a harsh voice beside her: "Go fetch in wood, lazy one. Be quick." That was that double-dyed scoundrel, the butler. She looked at him, helpless with fury. He caught her shoulder and thrust her away. "Be off!" he commanded.

She stumbled away, her teeth set. She passed a tall man seated on a fallen log, making a cigarette and whistling softly to himself while others made a bed for him out of the tips of evergreen branches from the woods and spread his blankets over the top. That was Guadalvo.

Once in the brush, she leaned automatically and laid her hands on a small shrub. As she leaned, a thought came to her. Suppose that she scurried softly away; no eye seemed to be upon her. Once among the shadows of the rocks, they could hunt far and far before they would see her. With a little luck . . .

A quirt cracked not an inch from her ear. "Are you dreaming, little fool?"

She looked up to a swarthy monster that swung the whip in his hand, only anxious, it seemed, for a fair excuse to lay the lash on her shoulders with his next gesture. Constancia tugged at the shrub. Her grip failed. A thorn tore her palm.

"Quickly," commanded the brute behind her, and she wrenched the brush from the soil and carried it back toward the fire.

The flames were mounting. The bandits were scattered about it, laying down their blankets, making a comfortable place for de los Pazos. Yonder came Teresa, fairly staggering under a great load of wood, but laughing with her burden. Willing hands lifted it. It was flung onto the fire.

"Brave girl!" they called to her.

One of them leaned and kissed her cheek.

So Constancia threw her own burden on the fire and heard a harsh roar behind her: "Is that all at one journey? Go back and fetch an armful."

It was the tyrant of the whip, and she turned bitterly away, and heard the soft, easy voice of Guadalvo saying: "Come here, Gualterio, my brother."

She glanced sharply back and saw the form of the giant with the whip striding toward Guadalvo. Was it possible, then, that he could call such a monster "brother"?

She was staggering with weariness and her very vitals were pinched with hunger when, at last, she was allowed to stop her work. Packs of provisions had been opened. Food was being passed around.

"And this is for you," called a voice. Two or three cold tortillas were flung toward her. She stepped aside in haste, and they fell in the dirt.

"Very well, she will go hungry, then. She is too good to take food from my hand?"

Constancia crept to her blanket and wrapped it around her. She was bitterly tired. But hunger was worse than weariness. It was a wolf in her. With all her heart she regretted that she had not snatched those tortillas from the air.

It seemed to her that she had barely closed her eyes when a whistle sounded. She opened her eyes wearily, wondering what alarm this could be. All about her, men were saddling their horses. She saw, yonder, Guadalvo riding up and down on the panther-like beauty of the mare. What a queen was Christy with her master on her back. She disdained the earth that she trod upon.

Constancia stood up to saddle her own down-headed mustang. While she tugged at the cinches miserably, a voice cried:

"What, is the whole march to be held up for one stupid woman?"

She threw over her shoulder a frightened glance at that same monster of the quirt — at him who had been called "Gualterio, my brother". Then she drew the cinches taut with a wrench, tied the slipknot, and climbed into the saddle. Yonder was Teresa, laughing at her and scorning her — Teresa, looking as fresh as a lark.

She was the only other woman from the ranch. But there were half a dozen men, the very choicest spirits from her father's house, men trusted for courage and faithfulness. Such as these, apparently, were wanted by the bandits, and perhaps for the same qualities. She could understand now, why the strength of de los Pazos did not wane. He knew how to recruit his forces through the very actions that wasted away his flying columns. He would return to the mountains stronger than he had been when he set forth.

It was nearly noon when, looking up from the sun-whitened ground, dizzy with weakness and with hunger, she saw Guadalvo passing. It was the sliding shadow of the mare that had roused her.

"*!Señor!*" she called.

Christy was turned instantly to her side.

"*Señor* Guadalvo," she said, "I do not wish to keep you long. I only have to say that I understand everything. You have set on these men to bait me and torment me and bully me. You hope to break my spirit and my heart. But I understand and I despise you, do you hear me?"

"Are you finished?" said Guadalvo.

"Yes. I shall never open my lips to speak to you again."

Christy carried him swiftly up the line of the marching column, and she heard the shrill cadence of his whistle come back to her. Another shadow crossed her. She looked up to the giant, Gualterio, with his quirt hanging from his wrist.

"Insolent devil," said Gualterio. "My brother Valentin may let you speak as if he were your slave, but I shall not permit it. Do we not all know that you stole a horse and drove him into outlawry to take back what was his own? Do we not know that you would have sent a bullet through his heart, if a kind God had not turned it aside, last night? What wrong had he done you, then? And if it were not for the daughter of de los Pazos for whom you must be a ransom, I would tie you to the tail of that horse, and whip it through the cactus. Do you remember this thing . . . and watch your tongue."

He glared at her for an instant, and then fell back, but Constancia rode on in a weary trance. Surely, in her life, she had done a thousand worse things to other men, and they had thanked her for it. They had come a thousand miles when she beckoned. And when she was tired of them, she had dismissed them with a wave of her hand. Yet they had willingly forgiven her. And she could call them back a second and a third time. But it seemed that there were differences between them. Some were lead, and some were steel that had passed through fire and cold water. Valentin Guadalvo was steel, indeed.

They made a late noon halt. Once more she and Teresa moiled and toiled to carry wood for the fire. Once more the crisp voice of a man called — "This is for you!" — and threw a few tortillas at her.

She snatched them out of the air. Nothing had tasted half so divine as this food. She saw yonder man grinning and nodding.

"Hunger teaches us better things than Latin," he said.

She stared at him. What did he know of Latin? What was he beneath his shaggy whiskers? But what were all these others? Perhaps not altogether the scum of the earth, but free men, valuing themselves and their freedom.

★ ★ ★

All the eastern faces of the hills were painted crimson with the low-hanging sun. Long purple shadows crept from the western mountains, and every ravine was pooled with blue-like water.

"There will be something more than talk in a day or so. See those two heads together."

So said someone in the procession of riders near to her. Constancia looked ahead, seeing de los Pazos and Guadalvo sitting their horses, side-by-side, in close conference. She looked back in her mind to other things — to the dreamy brown eyes that had seemed to look through her and have no knowledge of her as she walked past on the deck of the *Santa Lucia* — to the flashing arc of a man's body diving over the rail and then cleaving through the deep waters of the ocean — to the wild man who had leaped from behind the rocks and charged down upon them for the sake of Christy, like a tiger upon a dog pack — to the form that had thrust open her door and strode toward her, making her eyes dim as she pulled the trigger of her revolver.

She stared at him again as he sat beside de los Pazos. He was not far away, and yet he was as distant and unknown as the farthest star in the heavens. A thing to be guessed at rather than known.

CHAPTER
FOURTEEN

Twice they shifted the angling course of their march. Once, looking down from the lofty shoulder of a mountain, they saw a long cloudy streak of white across the face of the sandy plain below them. The soldiers of the president, marching in pursuit of the bandits. And those hardy rascals looked and laughed. How sublime was their faith in their leaders.

Then, in a gray morning, they came out of a mountain defile and swept down toward a little valley, round as a basin, and green as an emerald, with a dozen watercourses streaking it with silver. The line of riders opened out, ten yards between each man. They looked, as they rode, like a long, supple, curving whip. Like a whip, they curled around that little valley and drove all that lived into a central pool. Horses, cattle, sheep, goats, and *vaqueros*, goatherds, villagers all were assembled on the bank of the river beneath the great sabina trees.

"You may be the judge, Valentin, my son," said de los Pazos. "You should have training in these affairs. Suppose that a bullet should snuff me out, one of these days? My men must not be left without light."

Guadalvo sat on a rock on the edge of the river. The captives went before him, one by one. Besides Guadalvo he had selected three poor men, two goatherds, and a ragged beggar.

"What is this man?" he would say.

"That is Domingo, the money-lender."

"But a kind money-lender, is he not? He lets the day go by and waits for his money?"

"Alas, *señor*, business is business with Domingo."

"Gualterio, take our friend Domingo. Talk to him and learn where he keeps his money. Perhaps you will have to persuade him. When you find what he has, take what you think is a fair share. Now who is this man?" He would point to another.

"That is Agustin Almadares, the rich owner of sheep. It was he who loaned me enough to make a beginning of my flock."

"That is enough. For that kind act to a poor man, Almadares, you are free. Let the next man step out."

So ran the judgments. Constancia listened and wondered. It was all very swift. When it was ended, they left the little valley with fat spoil in cattle and fleet-footed goats, to say nothing of hard cash. Yet she felt that there was little bitterness left behind the plunderers. There had been a certain justice in all that was done. She herself wondered at it. However, perhaps *Don* Valentin was a little more lenient than the chief would have had him.

"Justice, my son," said de los Pazos, "is sometimes a luxury. You must remember that."

Now they wound away through the steep mountains, driving their spoil before them. They had taken enough. All hearts were happy. Their valley homes were not far away. They came down into the long gorge, and Constancia, staring at the twisting line of adobe houses, wondered why it was that the government troops had failed to destroy the nest of these wasps, once they had mastered the place.

"I'll tell you about that," said one of the brigands of whom she asked that question. "Too many of those fellows did not know when they would be wanting to find a home in one of those same cottages."

That, perhaps, was the answer.

A rider came spurring to meet them. Other riders came in his wake, shouting and waving their hats. People began to gather in front of the houses, like little spots of moving color in the distance.

That first messenger carried news that had a meaning for Constancia. Word had come into the mountains that the president of the republic had considered the matters proposed to him by *Señor* Alvarez. He would gladly liberate Lila de los Pazos in exchange for Constancia. But as for Guadalvo — he was something too much beside the mark.

Constancia, fixing her eyes on the face of Guadalvo, saw that his expression had not changed. He bore this news with the faintest of smiles. A sort of helpless rage swelled the heart of the girl. If she could once startle him from his self-control — if she could see him again, as he had been on the never-forgotten day when he fought for Christy against such great odds.

96

She was given a place in a hovel halfway down the scattering street of the village. In a cracked half of a mirror she saw herself for the first time in long, long days. She was a new creature. Her clothes were tatters. Her black hair was sun-faded a trifle here and there. Her face was a deep, deep walnut brown, with a big gray streak across the cheek where a chaparral thorn had scraped a day before. The palms of her hands were bruised with work. She looked, indeed, like one who has really faced a long and mighty storm.

From this same storm and stress, Guadalvo emerged cheerful. But it was a false smoothness, she felt. Once she could strike beneath the surface, she was certain that the tiger would show its head as she had seen it before.

At least, physical hardships had ended. The old woman who kept the house cooked and cleaned. There was nothing for the girl to do except to fill up the long, idle hours as best she might.

Evening came. A great bonfire was lighted in the rude little plaza that composed the center of the village, where the goats cropped the grass short in the day and the gossips gathered in the evening. In honor of the return of *Don* Guido, there was rejoicing on this day of days.

Guitars were thrumming, castanets clattered musically, and around the light of the fire the girls whirled through their dances. They danced alone, until, at a given signal, which was a shrill screech uttered by one of the men, the cavaliers also sprang into the circle.

97

Each chose the lady of his pleasure, and they whirled through a breathless measure or two.

Constancia watched. She watched with a smile, and then with her head nodding to the rhythm.

Don Valentin himself stood among the onlookers. The signal came, and he stepped forward leisurely, while the other men sprang like panthers. He stepped forward at ease, sure of himself. Constancia saw that same pretty vixen, Teresa, dodge past the outstretched fingers of two other admirers and come laughingly home to the arms of this Guadalvo. How enchanted was Teresa to dance with so great a man. How her eyes shone, and her face flushed, until she outshone the other girls as the moon outshines the brightest stars.

The dance ended, and there stood Guadalvo, his arms folded, mildly amused, smiling on the merriment. It angered Constancia, and it something more than angered her. She felt that she hated this Teresa, and yet she had no reason for hatred. It was simply a burning thing in her breast, without a reason.

Now see Constancia hastily at work. She thrusts from the garden of the little house a great red rose in her hair, and she pins a cluster of slender buds at her breast. Her ancient hostess looks on with a toothless grin of understanding and of excitement. And she brings suddenly a net of opalescent spangles that she throws over the shoulders of the girl.

Before the cracked fragment of a mirror, Constancia turns herself about and about. There are plenty of tatters still to be seen, but the spangles are a brilliant veil. The rose in her hair is a blur of color — and she hurries out into the night.

Through the outer circle of the watchers she passes, unnoticed. But as the dance began again, and as the girls whirled through their steps with the yellow tides of firelight washing about them, Constancia danced in turn. She knew those steps of her native country. She knew, also, certain refinements of grace that dancing masters in older and politer lands had schooled her in. When she began her dancing, she did not need the rattle of a castanet to call attention to her steps.

She saw the face of Teresa, with the dancer's smile frozen on her lips and her eyes big with anger and envy. But the others were not even close enough to rival her. They could wonder and applaud with smiles and nods, like so many men.

And the men? She saw them sit up and then come to their feet. She saw their eyes glistening, and the white flash of their teeth as they smiled in appreciation. But that was not all. Yonder, Guadalvo, the proud and the complacent — what of him? She saw that his smile had gone out, and that was her first triumph. She saw that his face had grown stern, and that was the second step.

But here was the tall, grim figure of Gualterio. Before him she danced — for him she danced — for him she smiled, but, ever from the corner of her eyes, she watched closely the face of Guadalvo. It was not a hard look to read and the print was not exceedingly small. In another man, she would have called this jealousy, plain and simple. Why not in Guadalvo himself, for he was mortal.

The screeching signal sounded. Gualterio, his face aflame, started toward her, but she spun away. She whirled toward Guadalvo through the crowd and saw him suddenly leap forward to meet her. There was no calm complacency in him, now. He came with a set face and a stern eye. Almost in his touch, she floated back like a feather before the wind — Gualterio and Guadalvo met at the same instant.

The tremendous bass of Gualterio was crying: "She is mine, Valentin! I touched her first!"

"Gualterio," said the other, "you are wrong."

"Do you tell me that I lie, Valentin?" The music had fallen into an uncertain melody. The dancers were ceasing on every side. She heard the voice of de los Pazos shouting in the distance and coming rapidly closer, sternly commanding them not to touch one another.

But they had gone much too far to stop. She herself stood between them. The great hard-fingered hand of Gualterio gripped one of her arms. That of Guadalvo held the other. Their chests were rising and falling rapidly. Their eyes flashed at each other. These were the men who had been in the habit of calling one another brother. She remembered that, and laughed softly in her heart of hearts.

"This is not a place to be taking advantage of your place as lieutenant, Valentin."

"You use me, Gualterio, because I have been kind to you."

"Do you accuse me of that?"

"I do."

"Then you lie."

"Have a care."

"Bah. Guadalvo, I despise you. This is for your heart."

High words and even a blow, perhaps, she had expected. But this was something more. She saw the knife leave its sheath at the belt of Gualterio. It flashed in the firelight like a streak of crimson, straight at the throat of Stephen Macdona. But the latter was a shade faster. He had not waited to draw either gun or knife. A set of hard knuckles thudded against the jaw bone of Gualterio and turned his eyes to glass. He fell on his face, with the knife rattling on a stone, far away.

Over him Macdona leaned for an instant, his whole body tense, until it seemed to the girl that he would throw himself on the stunned form of Castellar.

He recalled himself instantly, however, threw a wild glance at her, and walked hastily through the circle and away into the black of the night.

CHAPTER
FIFTEEN

Out of the midnight, Stephen Macdona came to the door of the hovel where Constancia was a prisoner, and she herself heard him parley with the old woman.

"Is *Señorita* Alvarez here?"

"Yes, *Don* Valentin. But she . . ."

"No more talk. Tell her that I wish to speak with her. Quickly. Then go off and study this by the light of the moon. Quickly."

"De los Pazos has told me."

"Here is something more. Forget de los Pazos. These are new orders, so far as you are concerned."

The hand of the crone touched the shoulder of Constancia. "Waken and dress quickly. It is *Don* Valentin himself."

The old woman was gone; Constancia, as she dressed, heard the harsh, dry coughing of her guardian outside the house, hurrying away.

She came from the inner room and saw the black silhouette of a man in the outer doorway.

When he saw her, he said in a shaken voice: "Will you come out of this darkness under the open sky, Constancia?"

She went silently past him and stood beside the hedge, with the narrow cypress behind her pointing like a dark finger at the white stars above. Yonder, in the black square of the plaza, the dying fire had sunk to a sullen red eye that watched them.

"I have tried to keep away from you," he said, standing at a little distance. "I went out and rode up and down through the valley. I have even tried to leave the valley, Constancia, but I could not. I have lost my pride. I am beaten. I have come back here to surrender."

"You say it fiercely," said the girl.

"Because I despise myself. But I cannot help it. I love you to a madness, Constancia. When I saw you in the circle about the fire, willing to dance with those ruffians, I felt that I had dragged you down and degraded you to that. And it snatched away the last bit of my sense and self-control. I began to pity you. Then I was helpless."

"What shall I say?"

"Tell me whatever you please. Tell me that I am a fool for confessing these things to you."

"I only remind you that, when we sat together on the deck of the *Santa Lucia*, you told me then that the sort of man who won me would treat me . . . as you treated your horse, *Don* Valentin."

"I believe it still. Only a man strong enough to do that can conquer you. But I am not strong enough. I tell you, Constancia, when I saw you in the tattered dress and with the tawdry spangles thrown over you, it stabbed me to the heart. And when I saw the red rose

103

in your hair, and the red of your lips, parted and panting, I lost myself. I have not come in hope. But only to confess. I am surely beaten. You may use me as you wish to use me."

She thought of the shadowy rush of horsemen out of the night and the splendid form of Guadalvo at their head. He had been like a king; now he was like a slave. She was dizzy and weak with the shock of the contrast.

"Then tell me first what you are."

"I am a penniless adventurer and wanderer. I have no home, no family, no friends. I was driven away from my country because I would have no law but my own pleasure, and I killed men like mountain grouse. My name is Stephen Macdona. Everything else that I have seemed to be is a pretense and a lie."

She was very glad that she had the cypress behind her. She put back a hand now, gripped a slender branch, and steadied herself. "Then tell me this . . . it was you who suggested to de los Pazos that he come to my father's ranch and steal me away in the place of his daughter. De los Pazos would never have dared to think of such a thing by himself. It was you?"

"It was I," he admitted.

"And then you determined that you would break my spirit as you had broken the spirit of Christy, before me?"

"Yes, I thought that that was the only way in which you could ever come to love any man. To be mastered, Constancia."

"And when I was proud and surrounded with servants and with wealth . . . why, then you could treat me coldly enough. But when I went and danced by the firelight, like any beggar might have . . .”

“Yes. I could not stand it. There was one thing that unnerved me. A scratch along your cheek. I know that I am a fool. But you see, I am telling you the whole truth. I want you to know what I am . . . a very weak man, but loving you enormously, Constancia.”

She raised her hand, and he bowed his head a little. “You took me from my father’s house, and it is only right that you should take me back again. Will you do that, Stephen Macdona?”

He struck a hand across his face. “Listen to me,” he said. “Guido de los Pazos has been like an older brother to me. There is no kindness that he has not offered to me. Now, if I steal you away from him, I am stealing his own daughter, also.”

“And your own hope of a pardon?”

“Ah, do you think that would trouble me?”

“Look, Stephen Macdona. The night is running away. Will you take me off with you?”

“You tear up my honor like a piece of paper covered with scribbling. Is there no other thing that will make you forgive me?”

“Nothing.”

“Constancia, if I do this thing, you will despise me afterward. Tell me if that is not true? Oh, I shall talk no more. Be ready in two minutes . . . the horses will be there . . . behind that clump of poplars.”

He was gone, hurrying through the night.

Constancia, watching under the shadow of the cypress, presently saw two glimmering shapes of horses drawn toward the poplars that had been pointed out beforehand. Then she went, hurrying. She found Christy waiting, and a tall and powerfully made gray horse — that same magnificent creature that had been stolen from her father's ranch. Once in the saddles upon the backs of this pair, there was no question of them being overtaken in their flight.

She was helped in silence to her place on the back of the gray. Stephen Macdona mounted Christy, and it seemed that the horses turned of their own accord up the long side trail that wove across the wall of the valley. There was not a word between them. They worked their way steadily up to a high shoulder of the mountain above. Looking back, they could see the valley, half in shadow and half in the moon, with thin white ribbons of waterfalls leaving the opposite cliff. The murmur of the cascades came up to them like the faintest of voices. Below, pointing east, there was the downward ravine that would lead to the great plains and to safety, for her. She looked to Macdona, as he rode with her out of the shadow and into the moonshine, and she had never seen such torture as was on his face.

She checked the gray. Christy stopped, also.

"Are we free to go on?" she asked him.

"Yes, and quickly in the name of heaven. I want to turn my back on that valley and my conscience."

She loosed the reins, but drew them tightly again before the gray could take a step. A strange pain was wringing her heart. "Stephen," she said, "if you go on with me, you have left your honor behind you forever."

"Yes."

"But what if your honor should become my honor, also?"

Christy seemed to whirl back of her own accord, and here was Stephen Macdona sitting his saddle, facing her.

"Tell me quickly, Constancia. My brain whirls. I cannot think my way through this thing. What do you mean?"

"I mean that I am a foolish, weak girl. I thought that I wanted to match strength with you and conquer you, Stephen. But now . . . I see that I am breaking my own heart."

"Constancia, Constancia, by all that's wonderful and beautiful and dear in the world . . . you are crying."

"I am a great fool, Stephen. But I cannot . . . help it."

"Does it mean that you care for me, then?"

She made an impulsive gesture with both hands. "If you had half an eye, Stephen, you would have seen from the very first instant that I loved you. Take me back to the valley. I would rather die than have you break your faith with *Don* Guido."

They went slowly, slowly down the slope again, with many pauses. Just as they reached the valley floor a swirl of horsemen came rushing toward them. There was a chorus of shouts. To left and right the wild riders sheered away and left them facing Guido de los Pazos.

"It was too fine a night, Guido," said Stephen Macdona. "We went out to watch the valley in the moon."

CHAPTER
SIXTEEN

On the balcony before his library sat *Señor Don* Rudolfo Alvarez. His guest, who was none other than that same Diego Catalon who had recently resigned from the presidency because his mines were more important to him than political glory, smoked one of *Don* Rudolfo's best Havanas and looked with him across the softness of the night. It was not complete darkness. There was just a stain of color in the west, and only the brightest stars and planets were visible.

"When I look back upon your life, *Don* Rudolfo," said the politic guest, "I see one clever stroke after another. Until, at last, you have completed the picture of a successful man. That much is entirely clear. But let us go a little further. There is often a flaw in the finest diamond. And it seems to me that there is one weakness in your career."

Don Rudolfo lifted his brows in the dimness of the evening. "So?" he said.

"May I speak outright, like an old friend?"

"By all means."

"Very well. Since ancient days, wise men have always realized that one of the surest ways of founding their fortunes was in making wise marriages for their children. Is not that really quite true?"

"Most undoubtedly true, my friend. Continue."

"Very well. You could look about you in Venduras and select whatever family you chose and then make the marriage proposal for an alliance between your daughter and the heir of the other house. Is not that true?"

"I hope that it is true. Continue. I shall have something to say when you have ended."

"Very well. You might have selected the son of some great owner of a ranch like your own, and, uniting your interests, you could have dominated the plains. Or you could have allied yourself with some of the mine owners . . . I do not mention myself. But others, still richer and stronger, perhaps. Or again, you could have selected the son of a powerful political family, such as the Vegas. Could you not?"

"All of those things were possibilities, of course."

"But, instead of all that, you select this man from a foreign nation . . . a wild American . . . a daredevil and a hero, I grant you, but a fellow who came to you without anything much greater by way of reputation than the number of times that he had flirted with death. Now, *Don* Rudolfo, tell me in what way you have strengthened your position by this alliance?"

Don Rudolfo considered for a moment, eying the dark of the night. "All of these things, to be sure, I have thought of," he said. "But I had to consider other things, also. I had to have in mind that, if I married my daughter to the son of some other rich man, people might begin to be envious, because this is an envious country of ours, Diego."

"That is true."

"And it might have looked as though I were trying to fasten too strong a grip on the wealth of the country. However, there is something lost in one way and gained in another. Consider this, *Don* Diego, that in the past year there have been waves of revolution passing here and there. *Haciendas* are burned to the ground, and men are murdered in their houses. All around me there have been calamities, but my lands remain unharmed. There has not been a single sheep driven away. Every cow remains to me. My horses have not been stolen, and what is the explanation, then?"

"It is true." *Don* Diego sighed. "We suffer from these bandits. I cannot tell what sort of a lightning conductor you use. But it is notorious over the entire country that you are no longer harmed by them . . . not since your daughter was carried away . . . and returned to you."

"Very true. Now I shall tell you the reason, *amigo*. I keep with me a young tiger, and the robbers fear him more than the devil. Because if they dare to offend him, he follows them not like an ordinary man but like one of their own kind. He runs them to the ground and slaughters them without mercy. Besides, the greatest robber of them all . . . that great de los Pazos . . . is like a father to Stephen Macdona. And I have nothing to fear. By this marriage of my daughter to the adventurer, I have made my property safe. It is better to keep a little in safety than to build a great house that may one day be burned to the ground."

110

"But when this property comes into the hands of Macdona . . . will he not be a waster?"

"A conqueror is not a waster, my friend. Besides, he follows a master."

"Is his wife his controller, then?"

"His wife? There is no such thing between them. They are like one. No, but they are the two proudest people in the world and they have both given up their pride to another thing."

"Very well. But tell me what that thing may be."

"Listen, and you will hear the voice of the master of them both . . . there, it begins again."

Don Diego canted his head. And out of the distance he heard the thin, far, high-pitched crying of a child.

Uncle Chris Turns North

The year 1923 saw sixteen short novels and ten serials published by Faust under various pseudonyms, mostly in Street & Smith's *Western Story Magazine*, his primary market between 1922 and 1934. This story, "Uncle Chris Turns North", appeared under the Max Brand pseudonym in the December 8, 1923 issue of *Western Story*. It is an unusual story about power and tyranny, in which Chris Martin, the czar of the local village, tests the extent of his reach when he takes on Willie Merchant, the hard-working young man who has fallen in love with his niece, Jennie.

CHAPTER
ONE

What Willie Merchant decided, when he had finished dressing and looked at himself in the glass, was that his face was not so bad — it was his name that damned him. There was nothing spectacular even in his appearance, to be sure. That is to say, he was of about average height; his hair was between sandy and brown; his eyes were between gray and blue and looked a little green in some lights; his features were simply as average as the rest of him, except that his mouth was a little wider. He stretched that mouth with a grin, and the effect startled him.

"But, after all," he decided, "old Chris Martin won't give a hang about my looks. It's my bank account that he'll inquire after."

He stepped to the door, and the hot wind rolled heavily against him. It burned up his perspiration in an instant; it scorched his body even through his clothes. But it was better than the stifling closeness of the atmosphere inside. He scowled, so that a steep shadow fell across his eyes, and, thus sheltered, he was able to look forth upon the landscape.

"Mostly flat," he said to himself.

In truth, it was not a very attractive picture. There was just enough roll to the ground to spoil the grand effect of an absolute plain level standing away to the horizon, but there was not roll enough to give the comforting variety of hills. The surface was simply thrown into little waves 100 yards apart — that was all. It looked to Willie Merchant as though that landscape had been turned out with a gigantic rolling pin. The only bit of mountain sculpture was the Diablo range to the south and west. They were a huge distance for riding, but the eye went to them so easily through the dry air that no tint of the horizon blue was on them in the midday.

They were simply big, brown, naked ugly masses, a poor monument to the Creator of this wretched country. Yet Willie Merchant surveyed the scene with much complacence — if in some respects it were ugly, in others it was delightful. For instance, that sunburned bunch grass, withering still more in this hot wind, had the most astonishing nutritious properties. It fattened certain scores of wide-horned, red-eyed cattle that roamed the desert, branded with a peculiar scrawl and cross. A most delightful hieroglyphic, in the eyes of Willie, because it meant that they were his property.

No wonder, then, that he looked fondly at that brown grass, and then away to a single form of a cow that strolled into the skyline across the top of a knoll and then disappeared. Only a fleeting glimpse. But he knew the creature. It was the four-year-old brindled mongrel among the half dozen he had bought for a song from Peterson last winter, when they were half

116

starved. He had nursed them through the bad season almost by hand. Today five of the six were living and prospering. They were money in his pocket. By such shifts as these he had built up his little herd in the amazingly short time of two years. After all, he had not received the weight of a single hand to help him. It was all his own work. The only previous preparation had been the year he spent accumulating his pay. That saved cash, and then infinite labor to eke out his capital, had given him these returns.

So great were the returns that Willie Merchant lifted his brown face and smiled toward the white-hot sky; his ideas concerning a divinity were very vague, very less real than the wisps of cloud forms here and there that the sun had not yet been able to burn up. But to whatever God there were, he rendered up his thanks.

The house in which he lived was small, but it was his own. His own money had bought the remnants of old Sam Chandler's shack in the draw. How few dollars had been needed to persuade the whiskey-loving old scamp. His own labor had brought that lumber across the hills; his own uninstructed hands had, somehow, contrived to erect the shack. For two years he had struggled on, propping it, refitting it, making it finally ugly enough, but sound and strong. He rejoiced in the possession of three rooms. There was a kitchen-dining room. There was a bedroom. And there was another room more splendid than the others. He himself hardly knew what to call it. Surely it would be presumption to name it a parlor.

117

At the thought, he turned from the door and went to the front of the house and gingerly pulled open the door of the sealed chamber. The window was kept tightly shut lest sand and dust blow in. Accordingly the room was furnace hot, and the stinging smell of new varnish, half melted, came to the nostrils of Willie Merchant. But that he did not mind. What he looked at was the grass rug on the floor, embroidered with a brilliant Indian design, and two pictures on the wall that had been cut from magazines, but which looked well enough in neat frames, and, most of all, he regarded three great bundles wrapped in coarse cord and paper. The biggest was the rocking chair. The other two were straight. Willie regarded them with a leaping heart. *Her* hand was to cut the strings, remove the paper, and bring those chairs to use and the light of day.

She was pretty Jennie Martin, so gay and so happy that the only blot on her life was the freckles across the bridge of her nose. But Willie was blind to such small defects; to him she had seemed an angel, on a day, three years before. The sight of Jennie had made him begin his savings. The sight of her had made him toil and slave for two more years. Now, at the last, he was ready to marry her.

There was a single last hurdle to be jumped. Jennie herself was willing; she had told him so two months before. She had ridden to the ranch. She had inspected everything with cries of delight. She had nodded with a flushed, uncomprehending face of joy as he explained with magnificent gesture, how his little ranch would expand west and west toward the Diablo range, and how the cows would multiply. She had been escorted through two of the rooms of the house and had declared it was more than good enough to start housekeeping in. And to think that he himself had planned and executed this dwelling. How big and wise and strong he was. The heart of Willie ached to think of her words. And how she had teased and pleaded to be allowed to peek — one single glance, no more — into the sealed chamber. But he had been adamant. He had wondered at his own strength. In the end, when he took her home, she had cried for pure happiness into the hollow of his shoulder, and all the stars in heaven had seemed to look down upon Willie Merchant to bless their union.

Yet still there was one hurdle to cross, and that was to gain the consent of Chris Martin, her uncle. He had raised her. Therefore he had a right to speak as to her destiny in her years to come. What answer he would give was the great question now, and, although Willie Merchant could not imagine why he might be refused, yet no one could be sure of what old Chris would do. All the old-timers declared that his mind was as unreadable and whimsical as the mind of the Sphinx. Yet to Willie himself he had always seemed a kind and simple man, singular only from the fewness of his words.

There was no time to ponder now, however. So Willie picked rope and saddle from the wall and went out to the corral. The four horses began to swirl about when they saw him coming. It did not confuse Willie. He opened the gate, stepped inside, dropped the saddle upon the top rail of the fence, and with a single wrist movement shook out the noose of his rope. Then he advanced. It was the roan he wanted, the fiery, ugly-headed roan. He wanted to feel the strength of that indomitable little mustang under him on the way to town for the momentous interview. It would give his very mind greater power. So he sifted through the others, and let the three fly to the far corners of the corral. But the roan he cornered and advanced on tiptoe toward him, prepared to spring to either side. For the roan was rope-wise to a degree. And it could dodge like a house cat. In one hand Willie held the rope end, noosed. In the other hand he carried the real noose. When the roan plunged to one side, he feinted with the nearest hand, and the horse finally was backed into the corner, watching him with glittering little eyes of hate.

At length, desperate, the roan made a blind charge for freedom, neither to the right nor the left, but straight at Willie. Willie dodged like a bullfighter, just before those gaping teeth were in reach of him. The rope slithered out of his hand. The noose floated out, formed in a perfect circle above the roan, and then dropped around his neck. The roan stood still. He had been rope burned too many times not to surrender the instant that prickling coil had hold on him. He stood like a lamb while the master saddled him, and like the most well-trained saddle horse he cantered off when Willie Merchant had mounted him. Only his ears were flattened along his neck, and his little bloodshot eyes watched the rider from their corners. Someday that horse would make him trouble, but Willie never worried about the future.

He was in the presence of Martin before he even saw the old Tartar, for, when he entered the town, he was upon Martin's land. All the town and all the houses upon it belonged to the little czar of the district. There were twenty houses or shacks. They were all Martin's. There was a combination hotel and general merchandise store. It was Martin's. There was a blacksmith shop. It was Martin's. So were broad stretches of land outside the town and the cattle that grazed on them. All belonged to Martin. Perhaps he was not worth, actually, many hundreds of thousands of dollars. But he seemed to be richer than a millionaire, for, what he owned, he owned with an absolute right. The families that were his tenants were almost his slaves. They owed him money, and they were powerless in his grasp. But he never pressed his tenant debtors for the money they owed him. He gave them freely his keen, practical wisdom. There was not a man in his village who did not live in comfort. Yet they feared him, rather than loved him, for they knew that to differ with him was to be ruined. Rebellion he would not tolerate. In short, he was a tyrant. He was a kindly tyrant usually, but, when his fur was rubbed the wrong way, his claws were instantly out.

Willie Merchant could not help thinking of these things as he entered the town, and for every step his horse advanced his heart sank lower. If the czar refused him, what would he do? What could he do?

CHAPTER
TWO

His courage returned when he actually faced the great man. Old Chris kept a room in a corner of the hotel as his office. It was a most unpretentious place. It was up two flights of stairs, in the little corner room that was all that the third story consisted of. The stairs were unpainted, rickety, with the center of the boards hollowed out by the treading of many rough boots. The door of the office sagged upon one hinge. For three years old Chris had let it hang like that, lifting it carefully open, and shutting it again with equal caution. He used to say that he could read the character of a man by the fashion in which he opened and shut that door. The office itself was a heap of scraps and a little of odds and ends. Whatever old Chris found, he picked up; whatever he picked up, he saved.

Martin was dressed, when Willie Merchant found him, in a soft white shirt with a double stripe of blue and red lines running through the cloth. It had shrunk so that the collar and the sleeves were much too small for him. But he made short work of those hindrances. He cut off the sleeves at his fat elbows, and he left the collar unfastened. Such was the shirt of the great man; the rest of his costume consisted of a pair of old brown

122

trousers, faded to a tan across the knees and the seat, and bagging beyond conception at the knees. They were held up by a single suspender, which was used out of preference and not carelessness. It crossed the left shoulder, and Chris used to say that this gave him a little more freedom in his right shoulder and arm. What he needed that slightly greater freedom for, need not be said. His boots, to complete his costume, were heavy, unpolished, shapeless things, and, most of all offensive to the eye of a cowpuncher like Willie Merchant, who would not have donned other than shop-made boots had he starved to buy them.

Martin was short and heavy without being wide of shoulder. He was simply very thick through. He had, in fact, a round build. His strength was enormous, but it was disguised even on his ponderous forearms by a thin layer of fat that was spread over the surface of his body. His muscles, indeed, showed at only one place, and this was at the base of the jaws, where a great permanent knob pushed out on either side, and, when he set his jaw, as he was continually doing, either in meditation or in anger, those knobs turned into corrugated knots. He had a rather pale face, for, much as he talked about the value of labor, he no longer touched any sort of work. His face showed fat and soft. The flesh under the chin was flabby. His nose was short and flattened a bit, like the nose of a pugilist. He had great, flapping ears, which thrust out on either side of his face, and which were even exaggerated in size by his habit of keeping his hair closely cropped. All of him, as might be seen at a glance, was extraordinarily commonplace, with one

123

exception, and this was that he possessed a pair of those bright blue eyes that never falter, and which denote, without exception, a bull terrier courage, an indomitable will, and a cool, steady brain in all trials.

He sat with his chair tilted back and his cowhide boots resting on the face of his desk. That desk was piled with papers blackened with house dust and yellowed at the edges. They had lain there for years, with a bit of iron lying on the top of each pile. Those piles of paper were never touched. Perhaps they stood there to give the office an appearance of a lively industry. But the singular inertia of old Chris kept him from maintaining the bluff or removing it. The only vestige of recent industry consisted of certain handfuls of iron junk, red with rust, which he had recently picked up. His hands were red with the same rust; where he had rubbed the side of his face there now appeared what seemed to be a broad marking of dried blood.

All the drawers of his desk were stuck fast. They could not have been opened without a hammer and chisel and many wedges. That is, all were fast sealed by the warping of dry summers, with the exception of a single one. This was that in which old Chris kept his cigars. He had one expensive habit only. That was his choice of tobacco. Some said that on a time after prosperity came to him, he made a long trip to the West Indies, studied tobacco on the spot, and selected for himself a certain type of leaf of a certain type of tobacco; he even selected the maker who was to prepare the tobacco, and instructed him in the exact shape of the cigar he desired. It was a long fat cigar. Its color was a pale, yellow-brown. It was rolled very compactly, and, although it drew clearly, it made a slow smoke at the best, even for old Chris. It produced a long, black ash. That is to say, it was really a mottling of gray, but so much darker than an ordinary cigar that it seemed black. It was commonly supposed that old Chris spent his time in his office smoking steadily at these cigars and thinking of little other than the length to which he might draw out the ash of that particular smoke.

Certain it was that he handled his cigars with the greatest delicacy, that he kept his eyes constantly on the length and condition of the ash, and that he never knocked them away. He waited until the ash fell of its own weight, or was pried away by a draft of the wind.

Into the presence of this soiled, ash-streaked figure, then, walked Willie Merchant. And, oh, thought he, for another name than this name Willie. Cursed be the day when that name was applied to him. But for that matter, it was not the fault of the world in general. It was the fault of his dear mother, who had insisted upon calling him Willie long after all the rest seemed united that it was time to call him Bill. Bill was a good name, a good, manly derivative from William. But Willie? The soul of the young fellow shrank within him. He talked like a frightened pupil reciting a lesson when old Chris, in his quiet voice, asked him what brought him there.

It was Jennie who brought him there, he explained. They'd agreed that it would be a good idea to marry.

"You've both agreed that?" asked old Chris.

"Yes," said Willie. He would have added a "sir", but his breath was too short to admit of that.

"Go back home and think it all over for a week," said old Chris. "Then come back a week from today and talk it over with me again."

Willie Merchant went out, and the rich odor of the Havana followed him down the stairs and to the street. He found himself in the open air at last, and he made a fierce resolution never to smoke another cigar so long as he should live. That decision, for some reason, made him feel more at ease. He started, but not for his home. Instead, he drove out to the Martin ranch house, and there he found Jennie under the mulberry tree and told her what had happened.

"It don't mean anything," Jennie assured him. "He's just taking his time about it. That's his way. It'll all turn out all right in the end. Besides, Will dear, how can he stop us from marrying if we really want to?"

It was an angel voice to Willie. He went back to his place, and, because he could not sleep at night nor remain quiet during the day on account of the tumult and the hope in his brain, he worked like a madman during that next week. So that it was a weak and haggard fellow who stood before Martin at the end of the week. Old Chris was smoking with a concentrated frown of attention, for he had actually succeeded in smoking two-thirds of a cigar without having the long ash drop off. This miracle of skill and good luck seemed to mean far more to him than the interview with the young man who had come to talk to him about marrying his niece. He kept watching the ash.

"Well, son," he said as kindly as ever, "you been thinking all week?"

"All week, sir."

"Well?"

"I've made up my mind. I'd rather die than not to marry Jennie."

"You would, hey?"

"Yes, sir."

"I've talked with Jennie," said old Chris. "She says that she'd die rather than not to marry you."

He considered his own statement for a time while the heart of Willie Merchant beat with triumph. Then, from the street beneath the window, there arose a nasal, droning, drawling voice — a cracked and ruined tenor of an old man that began to sing the old ballad, so appropriate to this very moment:

> **Of all the girls that are so smart**
> **There's none like pretty Sally;**
> **She is the darling of my heart,**
> **And she lives in our alley.**
> **There is no lady in the land**
> **Is half so sweet as Sally;**
> **She is the darling of my heart,**
> **And she lives in our alley.**

Here old Chris started from his chair so violently that the long ash tumbled from the cigar and struck his knee and, still remaining solid with a wonderful firmness, rolled off and struck the floor before it cracked apart. Old Chris looked down on that small ruin with a black face. Then he strode to the window and peered down into the street.

"It's that darned old fool, Ballon . . . old Hank Ballon, I see," said Chris. He jerked the window up wider and leaned out. "Hey, Hank!"

"Aye?" called the nasal voice of Hank.

"Stop that damned noise!" He slammed down the window and turned on Willie Merchant. "Look here, Willie, what have you got to marry on?"

"I got a bit of land . . . I got some cows that are doing fine . . . I got a house that Jennie says is good enough to live in." He gave this recital proudly, and added: "I went over to the auction at the Sterne place last month and bought in some plows and harrows and old harness for dog-gone near nothing. But they'll still work. I bought a few mules off some Mexicans that run out of fodder and money and sold mighty cheap. And now I'm all ready to start working that bit of loamy land down in the draw. I figure that they's some good crops in that land."

"It's a hot country, Willie. I've always sent Jennie away through the heat of the summer."

"I could manage it, too."

"Not if she had children."

"Well, that's a little different. But in a year or two, we'd be better fixed."

"Unless you hit a bad season."

"There's chances to be took in everything."

"Maybe."

For the first time, Willie began to fear. This continued opposition might become a stone wall before him. What could he do to climb it? The silence during which he pondered these thoughts lasted for some instants. Then he looked to the older man with a sigh. "If Jennie will take the chance and gamble with me, I thought you wouldn't mind, Mister Martin."

"Did you? Well, Willie, I dunno that I quite agree with you. I've invested quite a little coin in Jennie. I got to think about that. I've fed her and clothed her all these years. I've give her everything she asked for. I've fixed her so's she needn't be afraid to look at anybody in the world. She gets everything I got . . . and what I got, when I die, is worth having. I don't suppose that you thought about that, Willie, when you picked on Jennie and decided to marry her?"

Willie grew crimson. In fact, that she would be the heir to Chris Martin had actually never come into his mind before. He had thought of nothing but Jennie herself, and never had troubled to think of her background. When Chris Martin figured in his thoughts, it was not as a rich father-in-law, but as a possible obstacle to their union, and in no other wise.

Old Hank Ballon, in the meantime, had forgotten the recent injunction of the terrible Chris. His wailing voice now arose again, taking up the burden of the second stanza of "Sally".

> **Her father, he makes cabbage nets,**
> **And through the streets does cry 'em;**
> **Her mother she sells laces long,**
> **To such as please to buy 'em;**
> **But sure such folks could ne'er beget**

So sweet a girl as Sally!
She is the darling of my heart,
And she lives in our alley.

Chris rolled his eyes at the window, but he did not stir from his chair, and his voice, which had now become a sort of a low thunder, was directed at Willie Merchant only.

"Old Hank, he's a type of what comes to men that marry on nothing. Old Hank, his girl was one of the prettiest you ever see. What happened? She worked herself ugly having three babies in three years, scrubbing their clothes, tending the house, doing the sewing, and cooking for Hank. But their shack was so small that there wasn't no room in it for three babies and Hank. There wasn't no peace there for him. He went out and started drinking. He's done it ever since. He's full of moonshine right now. More booze, less work. His blacksmith shop started running downhill. Then along come a bad winter. The kids got colds . . . Hank didn't have money to buy 'em the right sort of food. Dog-gone me if they didn't all die. And that busted their mother's heart and she died right after 'em. And that's all what come from a poor marriage."

From the street the tenor voice of the old man rose again, and now he had sung himself into tune, it might be said, and there was the resonance, or the ghost of it, that had once made him sought for at all youthful parties.

Of all the days that's in the week,
I dearly love but one day,
And that's the day that comes betwixt
A Saturday and Monday;
For then I'm dressed in all my best
To walk abroad with Sally;
She is the darling of my heart,
And she lives in our alley.

Both Chris and young Merchant now remained for a time staring at one another.

"You ain't favoring this here marriage," Willie said stiffly at the last.

"I ain't."

"Then, Mister Martin, with all respect to you, I guess that me and Sally had better go ahead and do the best we can in spite of what you say. We figure that we can't get along without one another."

The voice of Hank Ballon, reinforced by a long swig of colorless moonshine whiskey in between stanzas, now thrilled through the air, young and filled with the music of joyousness.

When Christmas comes about again,
Oh, then I shall have money;
I'll hoard it up and box it all,
I'll give it to my honey;
I would it were ten thousand pound,
I'd give it all to Sally.

Chris Martin was at the window again. His voice was not raised; it was murderously low. "Hank," he called, "go home and wait for me there! I'm coming to see you, *pronto*."

There was a chorus of shrill protest from the little children who had gathered to hear the old toper sing, but Chris slammed down the window and shut out the noise. He had the fuming stub of the cigar between his teeth. It was so short that it burned his lips. But he spoke around it, grinding his teeth into the tobacco, and his clear blue eyes under their wrinkled lids were devilish in their intensity.

"You two'll go on without me, eh? Not by a damned sight, Willie. No, sir, you ain't going on without me. You ain't going at all. You're going back to your work or wherever else you want to go. Understand? You're going to see Jennie, and you're going to tell her that you've changed your mind, after all . . . you ain't ready to marry her yet."

"But I am . . ."

"You lie!" shouted the tyrant. "You young fool, you lie! What'll you marry on? Your scrap of land and your dozen or two cattle? I say, what's that land worth and what's them cattle worth without water? And where d'you get water except from me? D'you think I'll let you have it if you start bucking me? Nope . . . I'll smash you flatter'n the devil, Willie! That's me. I smash men. I got hands made for smashing them. I grind 'em up to dust. You'll marry her whether I want you to or not, will you? Why, I'll turn you and your cattle into skeletons. You'll marry on thin air, that's what you'll do."

It was too true. For water, his cattle went to the great water hole on the Martin lands, that huge spring that never failed to run. Cut off from that supply, he was ruined indeed. His three years' work evaporated. Perhaps a hero would have thrown defiance in the teeth of Chris. Willie was not a hero. He was brave as the next man. No one had seen him show the white feather. But now he was crushed. For, as Chris said, he could not live on thin air — not with a wife to support. He swallowed hard and admitted defeat.

"Mister Martin," he said slowly, "you got me beat. I can't move."

There was a change instantly in the cruel eyes of Martin. He dropped the cigar butt on the floor and ground the tobacco under his heel. "That's sense, Willie. You and me will get along. I knew you had sense. But that fool, Hank Ballon, got me mad with his damned singing. This is what you do. You tell Jennie that you and she got to wait. Don't tell her that you've talked to me. You hear? I ain't going to have any trouble made between me and her. Not a bit. You go tell her that you thought it up out of your own head. Another year and then, maybe . . . we'll see."

But Willie, as he left the room, knew in his heart of hearts that the barrier that Chris had raised to their wedding would never be lowered. Martin had other plans for his niece. And, as Willie had frankly confessed to Chris, he was beaten.

He went obediently to Jennie and told her, not the truth, but what Chris had told him to say. They had to wait for another year.

"When we marry, we want children. They cost money. Another year everything will be hunky-dory. You see, Jennie?"

She looked up to him and nodded, but there was a wrinkle of wistful sadness and surprise in her forehead. "I guess you know what's best, Will," she said.

Willie rode home with dust of ashes in his heart. He unsaddled the roan and had barely the energy to dodge the heels that the vicious brute flung at his head. He went back to his shack. He dropped the saddle in the middle of the kitchen floor, and he went on to the sealed room, dragged open the door, and looked within. Then he dropped upon his knees beside the big rocking chair, and the tears ran fast down his face.

CHAPTER
THREE

Old Chris had conquered, but he was far from contented with his day's work. On the whole, he did not believe in the use of brute force when the other side had any weapon with which they could strike back at him. In this case, the weapon that Willie Merchant had was the love of Jennie for him. Martin was sensible that love is a dangerous adversary at all times, that it is full of tricks and wiles, that it is as remorseless as a poisonous serpent, and that it has a strength that is never spent. And although he did not see exactly how Willie could strike back at him, yet he had been willing to be cautious, and he had planned to be most diplomatic in that last interview. He had planned to put the situation to Willie with advice and insinuation without any overt threat. If he hinted at the use he might make of his control of the water to enforce his decisions, he had intended that it should be no more than a hint. He had wished, in a word, to handle Willie with gloves.

And he had failed in that effort. He had shown his bare, clenched fist, ready to strike. He had roared and bellowed at Willie as if the latter were no more than a tenant of his. He had revealed himself as a brute, and that knowledge made him wretched. In the first place, he did not like enemies. He was too wise to tread deliberately on the toes of others. He preferred diplomacy, always, to the mailed fist, although the single blow was all his instinct.

Such was the mind of Chris Martin. This day he felt that he had made a fool of himself, and he blamed his folly directly upon the voice that had sung the old love tune from the street. In a word, Hank Ballon had been his overthrow. And he determined, before his passion evaporated, to take out his grudge on the old blacksmith.

He went immediately to the shop, and there found Hank lying on the floor in the coolest corner, with his head upon a small sack of shavings, sleeping off the effects of his liquor. A smile of bliss was on his lips. His thin face was flushed by the happy vision that visited his sleep. One old hand lay, palm upward, on the floor of hard-compacted earth. Its palm was calloused like the heel of an athlete. The fingers were shriveled and wasted by age. They were curled almost as far shut as though the familiar handle of the sledge were in their grip. It was a noble and weary old face. Seen apart from his garb, those features would have served a sculptor for the type of a great statesman, wearied with the cares of his nation, and sinking under the burden of public service. The nose was long and finely formed. The forehead was a towering magnificence, with the blue tracery of veins showing distinctly at the temples. The eyes were very large, and sunk deeply, as with long mental labors beneath the overhanging brow. The chin was long, square, and beautifully formed.

Even Chris Martin, who was as devoid from sentiment as stone, was touched with emotion and awe as he looked down upon the sleeper. But awe and emotion could not rule him long. He presently extended his foot and ground the toe of his cowhide boot into the ribs of the old smith. Hank Ballon groaned, clapped his hand to his bruised side, then opened his eyes and saw the face of his visitor. He pushed himself into a sitting posture with his long, thin arms.

"Howdy, Chris," he said pleasantly, and he smiled upon Martin. It was a beautiful smile. In sickness it made him seem whole. In age it made him seem young again.

"Stand up," ordered Chris Martin.

The smith caught hold upon the old anvil that stood near him and heaved himself up. He yawned widely, stretched himself, and was suddenly quite sober and steady. The imminence of the danger that confronted him was sufficient to make him rally all his faculties.

"I come here to wait for you, like you told me to do, Mister Martin," he said ingratiatingly.

Old Chris looked steadily upon him, and a savage satisfaction in his power filled him when he saw the glance of the other waver and fall away. "You been drunk again, Hank."

"Drunk? Me?" began Hank with honest indignation.

"Ain't no good to lie. Not to me."

Poor Hank passed a hand slowly across his forehead, bewildered, as though unable to remember accurately what he had been and what he had done even no earlier than this same day. "Maybe I had a mite too much," he admitted.

"You've been drunk again," said the tyrant. "How much did you borrow from me last month?"

"Ten dollars," said Hank in a dying voice.

"What'd you promise me then?"

"That I'd stop drinking, Mister Martin. I aimed to do it, too, but seemed like this morning . . ."

"Damn what it seemed to you. Looked to me like you'd lied."

At the insult, Hank flushed to the roots of his gray hair. But he looked steadfastly down upon the floor. He was more enchained than any galley slave. He could not strike back.

"How much d'you owe me altogether?"

"A hundred and thirty-five dollars," murmured Hank, almost inaudible now.

"A hundred and thirty-five dollars!" cried Chris, with honest indignation. "A hundred and thirty-five dollars is a lot to be owed . . . by an old gent with one foot in the grave. A damned lot of money."

Hank shifted his weight from his left foot to the right. He sighed, but could not speak, and still he looked steadily down at the floor.

"You been going from bad to worse," said Chris. "You used to have some sense. Damned if you ain't losing even that. You get worse all the time. I'm tired . . . I'm through."

Hank shuddered as the blow struck. He looked up now, indeed, bewildered, incredulous. But the face of old Chris was the face of a demon. He kept his voice low, but the effort made him white.

"I'm through," he continued. "You can move out your things. You can go wherever you please. You can pay me back that money you owe me when you've made any . . . which'll be never, I guess. But I want this shop and the house you been living in. I've charged you low rent on 'em both. I'll put 'em where they'll pay me better, now. Good bye."

He went out, not too hastily, for he wanted to enjoy what was sure to follow. And, just as he reached the doorway, a step came up behind him, and a hand touched his shoulder. He turned halfway around.

"You ain't serious, Mister Martin?"

"Ain't I? You old loggerhead, d'you think I been talking just for lung exercise? Aim to make a fool out of me?"

He was not even answered. Hank clasped his long hands nervously together and looked up and down the street. "I been pretty much tied up to this here town," he commented thoughtfully.

"What good have you ever done for it?" queried the master.

"Outside this town, there ain't nobody I know. I'm considerable too old a man to start out and make a new place for myself in the world."

"It ain't my choosing," announced Martin. "I've give you chances and chances. But you ain't done your part. Now I'm through."

139

He turned away again. He had not the slightest thought that he would be allowed to go. He expected that frightened figure to follow him. His first steps, therefore, were followed by shorter, halting ones. But nothing came behind him. There was nothing save a most eloquent silence; Hank would not beg.

Now it had never been in the mind of Chris, for a moment, to drive the old blacksmith out of his shop and home. He had, to be sure, done things as cruel as this, but on this day he only wished to be repaid for a recent annoyance by enjoying the spectacle of the humiliation of Hank. He wanted to be entreated. He wanted to whip the tears of despair into the eyes of Hank. But he had failed lamentably. The grief of the old man had been terrible and calm rather than ridiculous and weak. And old Chris cursed steadily and softly to himself as he went up the street. However, the matter would have another termination than this beginning. Ballon would not move until he was thrown out, bag and baggage. This, the rich man of the town, cruel and tyrannical though he was, dared not attempt. For he knew that the old smith had wound himself around the hearts of every man and woman and child in the village.

He decided, however, to allow Hank to suffer through the night, but on the morrow he would hunt him out and let him know that judgment was suspended — on a promise of future good behavior. With this resolution, he drove out to the ranch house and ate his supper alone; Jennie was not to be seen, and the cook announced her message to her uncle — that she was troubled with a headache and was lying down.

Heartache, said the veteran to himself. *That's her trouble. Them kind of aches take a time to get over, but they heal up after a while. Besides, Jennie has some sense. In a month she'll be thanking me for keeping her out of the hands of a cowpuncher squatter.*

This consideration so warmed his heart toward her that he could not keep from going to her, after a time. He found her in her darkened room, lying on her bed with her face buried in the pillow. He sat down beside her and removed his after-dinner cigar from his mouth.

"Look here, Jen," he said, "I'm sorry you're all cut up with this here headache. Come out and try the fresh air. It's turning tolerable cooler."

She shook her head.

He pondered upon her for a little while. The tan of her neck was as brown as when, in her childhood, she ran about under the sun with a bared head. The wisps of hair that half curled and half floated at the nape seemed to him strangely childish, too. Indeed, he told himself, she was still only a little girl. The consideration of her weakness of body and of mind and of character brought pity into his mind. He took one of her hands. It was hot and wet; the skin was as soft as a baby's.

"I'll tell you, honey, I'm going to send you out of this darned hot climate where you can draw a cool breath. I'm going to send you up into the mountains. Understand?"

"Dear Uncle Chris," she whispered, and then no more except to shake her head.

141

"You won't go?"

"No."

"What's wrong?"

"We're not to be married . . . not for a whole year, Uncle Chris."

"Why not?"

"Willie wants to make more money. And while he stays here and slaves, I can't be gadding about on vacations, can I?"

It was a side of the picture that Chris Martin had not considered.

"Will it make him happier to have you miserable?"

"But I've got to be a partner, you know. Then, in another year . . ."

"Bah!" cried Martin.

She sprang from the bed and to her feet in an instant, bright-eyed with suspicion. She was not so young and tender after all, he decided. He put on a manner of calm masterfulness. She must do what he told her to do. It would be much better for her peace and her comfort of mind. Stop thinking; he would do that for her. But oil had no effect on the stormy sea of her suspicion. Why had he cried out in scorn at the mention of Will Merchant's name? There was something strange and hidden about this whole affair.

"Because he ain't worthy of you!" cried Chris, losing his temper for the second time that day. "He's yaller. That's what he is. He's plumb yaller, Jen!"

"That's not true."

"Don't tell me, girl. I've seen."

"Seen what?"

"Seen him crumple up like a dog when I threatened him . . ."

"When you . . . Uncle Chris, what does it mean?"

He saw that he had blundered on much too far. He decided to brave it out. "Means that I told the pup that, if he married you, I'd shut his cattle away from the water. He didn't have nothing to say. That's why he come out and talked to you. Puts his cattle above you. A devil of a fine kind of love that is. Love? He loves my money. That's all. That's why he wanted to marry you, Jen. Nothing else. He's a crook, and he's yaller besides."

Thrice she had been about to make a fierce retort, and thrice she had controlled herself. "And that's all true?" she said huskily at last.

"What else made him change his mind?"

"Then," she said, "thank God that I've found him out in time."

She spoke so gravely that Chris Martin was touched with a slight misgiving. He began to feel that he had meddled in something more than an affair of calf love, perhaps.

"I guessed that he was no good," he said. "I wanted to give you time to find it out for yourself."

"I'd like to be alone," said Jennie.

He left her to walk, as he did every evening, up and down under the mulberry tree, smoking his long, black Havana. He made it last a long time, as he did every one of those costly cigars. It endured with him until bedtime. But during the whole space he thought not once of the cigar between his teeth; what was in his mind was that he was in a grave crisis. He was beginning to understand that, if he lost the affection of the girl, he did not care what calamity followed. She was more to him than he had dreamed, far more. She was more, even, than a child of his own could have been. Realizing this, he was more pleased than ever that he had broken that engagement with young Merchant. If only everything turned out well.

CHAPTER
FOUR

He went to bed and dreamed troubled dreams. He wakened with a headache, and no Jennie to sit opposite him and pour his coffee and smile at him while he growled at the world in general. Once, as he looked at her empty chair while the Chinaman awkwardly hovered about and tried to take the place of the young mistress of the house in making the rancher comfortable, a panic came over old Chris.

Martin said to himself that, if love and sorrow had crushed the girl to such an extent — for to miss a meal was not in the comprehension of Chris — perhaps it would be better, after all, to let her marry the youngster. However, he felt that he had taken a step from which he could not recede. He had poisoned the mind of the girl against Willie Merchant, and on that point he was entirely comfortable, for he had only told her what was, to a great degree, the truth. Like all truly masterful liars, indeed, he never based a falsehood upon thin air. His conscience would never trouble him for what he had done, if only Jennie could be made happy again. To help him to that end, he trusted deeply to time, as all wise men do.

Having had a debauch of sternness and cruelty the day before, when he arrived in town the next morning, he opened the three letters that lay upon his desk, read them, answered them with his swift, illegible scrawl, and then finished smoking his cigar. By this time the effect of a night's bad sleep had well worn off; his natural vigor was beginning to assert itself, and he left his office and walked down the street, banging his heavy heels against the boardwalk that was his only needless extravagance in the construction and the maintenance of the village. He reached the house of Hank Ballon and kicked the gate open.

"Oh, Hank!" he called. His voice struck like a blast through the open front door and echoed faintly back to him from the rear wall of the house.

"Hank's got up early, the dog." Old Chris grinned. "Done him good to get a talking to, and he's got up and started in work the same's younger men do. Well, he won't keep it up long. Not him. It ain't in his bones."

He was so convinced of this that he went on down the street toward his office again, but at the door of the hotel he turned sharply about, driven by something that he could not explain. He went hastily around the corner of the street, and there he saw a semicircle of youngsters standing at the entrance to the blacksmith shop, and gaping in the most intent interest.

That was most usual. Wherever Hank appeared, the children were sure to show their faces before long. While pressing jobs awaited his hand, he would sit down on the old barley bin in the corner of his shop and hold forth to all who cared to listen, but particularly to the children. Rocked far back into the shadow, with his long and bony fingers hooked in front of one knee, his head deeply sunk, his eyes either closed or else looking out with startling glimpses of light, he would tell his stories. They were better than fairy stories. They started not with "Once upon a time", or "In a distant land across the seas", but out of the very stuff of which their lives were made, he built his romances. His heavens were no bluer than the skies above their heads, and he, by the mere naming, made the old swimming pools, the twisting white roads across the hills, and the smoky colors of spring upon the desert enchanting.

He was about to turn on his heel again and go to the office, but he decided that he would steal up and listen to the old loafer's voice for a minute or two. So up he crept, all unheeded by the enrapt children. When he arrived, he found that he had apparently come into one of the pauses in the narrative. There was no voice speaking. It was a pause of terror and fear and grief in which the cunning talker allowed their own emotions to work in the minds of his audience. All of those emotions were in the faces of the children who stood so silently around the door of the shop. Old Chris looked around the corner of the shop to take a peek at this eminent faker. But to his amazement, he found that the shop was empty of a single human form. But upon the flooring, near the forge, there had been written with the point of a red-hot iron:

Dear Chris:

Here are all my tools, and I guess that they pretty near pay for the money I got from you. I find it's hard to go, but I'll never come back.

Hank Ballon

This, then, was the meaning of the movement upon the fascinated lips of the children. They were repeating that terrible sentence over and over again: Hank was gone, and he would never come back again.

Then, suddenly, some one of them caught sight of old Chris. There was a white flashing of faces as they turned upon him. Not a word was spoken. Old Chris turned and fled. There was no other word for it. He ran away. As he went, he wondered what under heaven had happened. If the shouting of children was a mere noise and annoyance, why should their silence be worse than a thunderbolt fallen upon him?

When he was at last in the shelter of his office, he did not even light a cigar, but walked up and down for a long time, trying to put his thoughts in order, and failing lamentably in the effort. Hank had left town. Hank had actually taken him at his word and gone. If a dog, that had barked at him a hundred times and then run when he snapped his fingers, had actually run out and put teeth in him, he could not have been more appalled.

He finally decided that he must go down to hear what people were saying of him. He had not far to go. He found half a dozen black brows bent upon him. The very clerk behind his grocery counter would barely bid

148

him good morrow. These were signs, these were portents, indeed.

Then he went out into the street and saw Sam Patrick, and gave him a good morning.

"A darn' poor morning to poor old Hank," blurted out Sam Patrick, and went on past him without another word.

In short, it meant revolution. But Chris Martin thrust out his lower jaw and decided to meet the brunt of the opposition right there on the spot. He called back Sam Patrick with a voice of thunder. Then he told him why he had driven Hank away. The blacksmith was a lazy old drunken ruffian, stated Chris Martin. For years he had not been worth his keep. For years he had been running deeper and deeper into debt. Now the time had come for him to leave. He was incurable.

"He'll he a big loss to the kids," was all that Patrick would say, and so he left Chris.

In the meantime, as they talked, windows had gone softly up, and heads had looked out and even many ears, unseen, had listened carefully to every word from the street. When the tale was ended, each window was closed again all as softly. Not a word was said; not a voice was raised. But old Chris knew well enough all that would follow, and how they would gather together to converse about the thing that had been done. They would have harsh things and hard things to say about him, beyond a doubt. But he resolutely damned them and went on his way. Yet something was stinging him to the heart. What would become of old Hank? Where had the old rascal gone?

149

Then he forgot his pity. It seemed to him that Hank had simply left the town and left that sad and stern message behind him because he wished to raise the hearts of the villagers against Chris. Five minutes before he had been condemning himself for his cruelty to Hank. But from this moment he began to hate the old fellow and wish that even the memory of him might perish from the face of the earth. His anger grew with brooding.

In the meantime, his niece had left her room not five minutes after her uncle left the house. She went to the corral, caught and saddled her own horse, and then flogged at full gallop across the hills and through the delicious fresh coolness of the morning air. Oh, how thin and still and how vast it was. Still it seemed to Jennie that the curve of the great earth's surface was pressing her dizzily up into the sky.

There was no joy in her heart. She went savagely on to the house of Willie Merchant, and she met Willie at the door, just coming out, with his saddle resting against his hip and his head sunk.

She was too blind with anger and rage and disgust to do more than know that it was he. Had she looked any closer, she could not but have been touched by the despair in his eyes. But she saw nothing. There were too many tears in her eyes after she had spoken the first words.

Jennie told him, quick and plain, that she was done with him. She offered him back his ring, and, when he would not lift his powerless arms to take it, she dropped it in the dirt at his feet. She took out a dense packet of

150

letters and tossed them down after the ring. Then she turned and rode away. When she crossed the next wave of ground and looked back, what did she see but poor Willie Merchant standing just as she had left him, with the white batch of letters at his feet, and the saddle resting against his hip, and the quirt dangling in his hand.

"A coward. A coward. A coward," gasped out Jennie as the gallop of her horse rocked her along. And then she cried in the same voice: "I wish I were dead! I wish I were dead! I wish I were dead!"

She rode on blindly until her horse began to stagger. Then she looked about her and found that, instead of heading straight back for the ranch, this wrong-headed beast had turned aside and was veering toward his old home, which was the Jacobson Ranch. So she had to make a detour through rough ground before she could get back through the broken country and come within line of her uncle's ranch again. Thus it was that she encountered old Hank Ballon.

She came over the first rise from which that old ranch house was visible and saw the deserted shack that old Bud Hervis had built there twenty-five years before, in the days of the cattle wars. But it was no longer deserted. Smoke, as gladdening to the heart as the flag of a man's country, waved out of the patched and re-ërected chimney, and snapped away to nothingness in the morning breeze. The door was open, and a broad white piece of new pine showed where it had been recently repaired and held together with nails. Indeed, the old place had come into a sudden and not unpleasant life.

Then, looking down into the hollow, she was amazed by the sight of the bony bay gelding, Timothy, and the goat, Jud, which, as all the world knew, were the property of the good old man, Hank Ballon. She knew all about Hank's faults. But she knew all about his virtues. Like everyone else, except her uncle, she loved him with all her heart.

In her astonishment, she forgot her own grief and rode up to the door and knocked against it with the loaded butt of her quirt.

"Hello," said the familiar voice inside, and then the door opened and the old blacksmith was before her. He came out with a laugh and a wave and took both her hands in his big, bony fingers. "Jen, my darlin'," he said, "how long and how long it is since you've been to see me an' talk to me. Where have you put yourself? Into Willie's pocket, dog-gone him."

Hank knew, then, and that meant that everybody knew. It was going to be much harder than she had at first anticipated.

"There's nothing in that, Uncle Hank."

"I guess not," he said with too much emphasis, and winked brightly at her.

"But what on earth are you doing out here, Uncle Hank?"

"Me? I'll tell you how it is, honey. Dog-gone me if I ain't been pondering and pondering, and I figured it out that there ain't no chance for rest and quiet in a great big place like the town. So I decided that I'd come right out here and take a swing at . . . what you might call suburban livin', eh?"

"But seriously, Hank, you rascal, what's in your mind?"

"Nothing but a wish to get away from the noise, Jen. There ain't nothing more than that. All I want is this little shack and you to talk to half an hour a day, and dog-gone me if I ain't plumb contented."

"But the village, Uncle Hank. Good heavens, what will it do without you? How can it get on?"

"I'm an old man, honey. Folks get along right tolerable well without old folks."

"Uncle Hank!"

"Heavens, girl, I ain't aiming to make you cry."

"Who've you had trouble with?"

"Ain't you going to believe nothing that I tol' you?"

"Not a word."

"This here comes from givin' women votes," pronounced Hank. "Dog-gone me if it don't."

She tried again to make him talk. "I'm just out here restin' and waitin'," was all that he would say.

But when she went on to the ranch, she heard more details. One of the cowpunchers had come on Uncle Hank in the old shack and had helped make him comfortable there.

The message that he sent by the cowpuncher to the world was that he was waiting, indeed — and waiting inside the sight of the ranch house of Chris Martin. Because, he said, when a man had done as much wrong to the world as old Chris had done, it was time that he began to pay for it.

"Someday," he had concluded, "Chris will go smash, and everything that means the most to him'll be lost. I'm just staked out here, waiting to see when it happens."

CHAPTER
FIVE

When Jennie heard this, she refused resolutely to believe that Uncle Hank could ever have said such a thing.

"Why," she said, "I love Uncle Hank, and he loves me, Pete."

"Sure he does," said Pete the cowpuncher. "Sure he does. But nobody can love half as hard as he can hate. And here's where your Uncle Chris comes in for some dog-gone hard hating."

He went away and left Jennie by herself to digest this remark and all that it might imply. She decided at once that, when her uncle came home that night, she would have a long and most serious talk with him.

But a great deal was to happen that day before the night came on and the veteran drove his buckboard home with the dust sluicing off the wheels and the tires bumping over the humps that were hidden beneath the velvet of the dust. For before that time came, a white-faced Willie Merchant came on a foaming horse into the town and entered the office of the terrible Chris Martin.

He stood at the doorway and regarded the landowner as though the latter were a ghost. Chris had vowed not to lose his temper for another month, but he was angered by this interview, and, besides, he despised Willie for the whiteness of his face.

"What in the devil d'you want?" he asked of Willie.

"You lied to me," said Willie in a dead man's voice.

"I lied? You rat-faced brat . . ."

"You lied," Willie repeated.

And Chris saw, with the most utter amazement, that, in spite of all appearances which indicated it, Willie was not afraid. Not in the least. In fact, he was in a fighting fury, and would as soon pull out a gun as a handkerchief. To Chris it was hardly credible — for he prided himself on his ability to judge men. He could not believe that he had gone so far wrong with Willie. Not that he doubted his entire ability to handle Willie in a personal conflict of any kind. As for gun play, although he seldom had a chance to indulge himself in the actual sport itself, he practiced his draw and his shot every day. When he drove home behind the rat-tailed sorrels every night as he bumped along the roads with no one within hearing of him and no one within sight, he used to empty his revolver at least once at stumps and stones. So that old Chris was in perfect practice. Being in perfect practice, he considered himself as dangerous a fighter as anyone in the world, with the exception, perhaps, of a few desperadoes.

He regarded Willie rather with a cold and scientific interest than with a passion of anger. He did not want to kill this boy simply because the boy could not put up a fight good enough to make the war interesting. Old Chris had arrived at that stage of mind.

156

"You're talking big and brave," he told Willie gently.

"I say that you lied when you swore that Jennie shouldn't know about what you and I had talked over. Then you went and told her everything."

"You ain't remembering right, Willie. I said that you must not do any talking to her about this here talk we had. I didn't say whether I'd do no talking or not."

"You can't speak behind that sort of a cover, Mister Martin."

"I never speak any place, Willie. I'm always right out here in the open . . . and everybody in the world knows right where they can find me."

"That's why I've come down here to tell you that you've double-crossed me. She's turned me down, this morning. She come, and give me back my letters and give me back my ring. She said that she was through with me because I was a coward, and because I thought a lot more of my cattle than I thought of her." He shrugged his shoulders. "I guess she heard that from you, Chris Martin?"

"Maybe. Maybe she just made up her mind that she only wanted an excuse to break off with you, and any old thing would do."

"That sort of talk don't bother me none," said Willie with a strange loftiness. "I know what she was yesterday, and I know what she was today. And you're the one that done it." He paused.

Old Chris did not move in his chair. He lighted a cigar and through the smoke peered earnestly into the face of Willie. With each instant he was making astonishing and most delightful discoveries about the

157

rich mines of manliness in this round-faced youth. It always pleased Chris to find a man, under whatsoever guise. But not a gleam of his pleasure, of course, was allowed to appear in his face. The next thunderbolt, however, completely threw him off his guard.

"I been wishing that you was a young man," said Willie. "But you're old, and I can't fight you. You're old, and you're safe from me. But for that, I'd have your gizzard out."

It brought a sort of groan from Chris Martin. "You young fool," he said. "If trouble is what you're after, I can give it to you inches thick. First place, keep your cattle away from my water hole. Tomorrow, I fence it in. That's a beginner. Then I'll follow it right up. I ain't even started to show you what I can do. I'll make this here country so hot for you that you'll howl like the devil for help. Don't forget that."

Willie sighed. "I'm kind of glad that we know where we stand, each of us," he declared. "Let me tell you that, if one of my cows dies because you starve her out of water that you ain't got any need of yourself . . . I'll come and take a fat cow of yours to fill her place."

"You'll steal, eh, kid?"

"I'll take my rights and keep 'em."

"You'll bust the law?"

"When the law busts me."

"That's the sort of talk that makes for murder, Willie."

"I'm rich an' ripe for it, Chris Martin. You can lay to that. I'm all set for it. For heaven's sake don't give me no chances."

Chris Martin laughed. "Get out, kid," he said, and rose from his chair. He waved his arm as toward bothersome flies. "Out of this here room. Never come back. You? I'm going to bust you. If you raise a hand to hit back, I'll have you pinched. If you swipe my cattle, I'll have you lynched. Now get out. I'm tired talkin' to a fool."

Willie Merchant went most obediently. He retreated to the door, backed through it, and then went slowly and steadily down the stairs.

"He thinks that I'll shoot him right in the back if I get a chance," translated the older man slowly. "He don't know me. He don't know the half of me, that fool kid. But he's game."

Four revolver shots crackled through the air of the street. Old Chris hurried to the window, almost rejoicing. A fight was what he wanted most of all. To see one was the next best thing to being in one himself. But all that he saw was Willie sitting in his saddle in the street calmly putting up a smoking gun into his holster. He had fired the four shots himself, a pair close together and then another pair, just like two men exchanging a brace of shots at one another. After which the deathly silence sounded like a double murder.

He gained what he had wanted to gain. In five seconds the entire population of the town was assembled around him. He spoke quietly from his place in the saddle above them, and yet Chris could hear every syllable of his enunciation.

"Boys and friends," he said, looking about him with no signs of stage fright before such an assemblage as

159

this was. "I've just had a little talk with your boss, old Chris Martin. Him and me have agreed to fall out right here. What he aims to do is to shut my cattle away from his water. Well, boys, you know that I've soaked in three years' work on that there little ranch. I've got my own cattle running pretty slick and fat. I've had no help from nobody, and showed that a gent don't need no help in this here country. All I need is water. Martin ain't got cattle enough within marching distance of that water to use it. You all know how it soaks away and goes rambling off into the sand and dies in the desert after it leaves the watering pool. But old Chris says that he's going to shut me away from that there water. And I say that, whenever a cow of mine dies for the want of water, I'm going over and take one of his cows. And I mean it, every word."

Willie paused. The faces beneath him were stunned with wonder and, as old Chris could plainly see, with admiration.

"How this'll all come out," Willie continued, "I dunno. I'll be breaking the law if it gets that far. And then I'll be run off my place, my cattle will die, and I'll probably get grabbed by a sheriff or a deputy while I'm trying to get even with old Chris. But before they start in lying about me, I want to tell you the straight of what's going to happen if Chris bars me from the water, and so help me God."

He actually raised his hand as he swore it, his gun hand — his right hand — and looked up into the white-hot sky. Then old Chris knew that he could never draw back from this solemn engagement. It was a

160

matter of honor — of pride. He had to crush this defiant young fool no matter how much his heart bled for him.

CHAPTER
SIX

After that, old Hank Ballon was not the only one who waited for the downfall of Chris Martin and the dénouement of this strange little war, for the whole range heard the tale and wondered heartily what the outcome of it could be. Of course, on the face of it, there was no hope for Willie Merchant. He had bid defiance to a giant, and therefore he would be crushed. Yet there is an element of suspense even in a lost cause. And the course of that battle was waited for with the keenest expectation. There was hope against hope that justice might somehow be done to the weaker of the two combatants and justice done at the expense of old Chris.

In the meantime, Chris could not help but go ahead. What he prized more than anything else in the world was the fear with which he was looked upon by his neighbors. That which he had spent his life working over was the subjugation of the men of the village so that they dreaded him more than they dreaded death. They were in the palm of his hand, and that sense of power was most delightful to Chris. He could observe the workings of his perfect system now. For no matter what black looks were cast upon him by the villagers, they dared not speak to him of what they thought. They were his men as absolutely as though he were a feudal lord and they his serfs. To maintain himself in that proud position, he must convince them that it was ruin to oppose him. And he could only convince them by promptly crushing young Willie Merchant.

He proceeded at once with the work at hand. He sent his men to erect stout fences that shut away the southwestern lands from his great water hole; now Willie might take care of himself as best he could. The gantlet was down.

After that, the contest was followed with the keenest anxiety in the town. The whole range heard of what was happening, and the whole range wondered how it would come out. Not a man, perhaps, who did not sympathize with Willie Merchant up to a certain point — but suppose that he were actually to cut fences and run off the cattle of the tyrant — what would happen then? What would the law do?

There was no appeal to the law for the time being, however. Willie saw his cattle grow wild of eye. They no longer ate. They waited in front of the fence that barred them from the water hole where they were so accustomed to go. Every day, Willie went out and watched them with an aching heart. Nothing tames the wild so much as thirst. It is more terrible than mere hunger, because it strikes sooner, and the pangs of its torments are sharper in the vitals. The thirsty cattle grew so gentle that they huddled together, but, when Willie dismounted and came among them, not a foot stamped and not a horn swung at him. It seemed to him that they turned their brute eyes upon him with a dumb appeal for help, he who had helped them so often, who brought them through the most terrible winters with a little extra forage, who got them up and scraped the chilling snow from their backs in hard weather, who pulled them from the bogs in spring, who was ever seen through the day, hovering somewhere against the horizon. And so long as that familiar silhouette was near, there was nothing to fear from the wolves. They dared not come near the eyes of the man.

Of course it was sheerest fancy, but it seemed to Willie that all of these things were running in the brains of his cattle as he walked among them.

At times the cowpunchers from the big Martin Ranch came down to the fence and sat calmly in their saddles there and viewed the dying herd. They tried to talk to Willie. But he could not speak a word to them. He knew that if he parted his lips, it would be to curse and rave like a madman. So he would not speak to them. Again he knew that, if he started to talk, his voice would break and he would weep like a woman — for he was very sensitive, very proud. He carried himself with a haughty air, with a chip on his shoulder, simply because he knew that his face was incurably boyish, and he was ashamed of that appearance. He loathed the weakness that made him come close to tears at every crisis. Shame is a terrible power that lives in the human soul, and it was what controlled the life of Willie Merchant.

Sometimes, as he watched his herd and the cowpunchers on the farther side of the fence, he could see them talk to one another and shake their heads. Then a mist of self-pity would make his eyes dim; he would look upon the whole affair as from a pinnacle of a great height. It was a petty matter. He was a sullen fool, and Chris was a stupid old boor, no more. There was nothing here worth dying about.

Sam Hitchcock, the foreman on the ranch of Chris, called to him one day. "Are you getting your guns limbered up, Willie?"

It was half satirical and half sympathetic, the voice that asked this question, and it brought the last phase of the contest into the mind of Willie with a start. He was no expert with guns. He had used a rifle and a revolver ever since he was a youngster, just as everyone did on the range. But he could claim no particular skill with either weapon. His time was put in on the practical part of ranch work — the tending of cattle, and not the shooting of coyotes. He had not wasted three hours in his entire life pumping lead at targets. If he wished to make a showing, and against odds, he must certainly begin to practice at once.

He observed the fellows on the farther side of the fence. There were at least four of them who were infinitely better than he, and all the others were at least as expert as he. Yet, in another moment, he knew that if the time came when he must oppose fighting men, something would happen in him and make him capable of disposing of his work or else enable him to die as a brave man should. For, from this time forth, he began to feel that he was in the hand of a directing destiny that would drive him on to ruin or success as the case might be.

Then came the trip to town and the talk to the banker in an effort to sell his cattle. He had done small business with that banker before. He was astonished now by the price that was offered to him.

"I'm mighty sorry for you, Merchant," said the banker, "but I hear that your cattle are in poor condition, just now."

"They're starved for water, that's all. They need a drink, and then they'll be as good as ever. Two weeks will put them back."

The banker shook his head. That might be, and again it might not. His sympathy was all with Willie, but this was a business proposition. It was not his own money; he was investing for others; the directors would take him to task; therefore he concluded by offering a tithe of what they were worth. It was a joke, thought Willie, and went elsewhere to strive to strike a bargain. But nothing could be done in reason. His honest friends who he knew would not cheat him were all too poor to offer a price. The men who were able to pay wanted the cattle for nothing. Finally one old codger answered his complaints with a bit of dry, remorseless logic.

"Look here, you want a fair price when I know you're cornered and that you got to sell. I ain't a philanthropist. I'm a businessman. I've climbed on the heads of them that have gone down. If I can climb on you, all right. If I can't . . . then sit down and smoke a cigar, but don't try to talk business with me."

Willie went back to the ranch and straight to the herd. The first thing he noted was a cow lying on its side with the upper hind leg stiffly extended. He knew without another look that that poor creature was dead. A sudden panic passed through Willie. What if they were all to die because of the lack of water, simply because he could not get his price for them? Then, with anguish in his soul, he fled to the nearest squatter — a fellow who was playing the same game he had tried to play, and had failed in. It was ten miles of hard riding.

"Come get the cows, Jerry," he told his friend.

"I seen 'em today," said Jerry. "We could never drive 'em this far."

"They'll need watering first."

"Sure."

"Then," said Willie calmly, "they'll have their water."

"How?"

"Leave that to me."

"Willie, you ain't going to play the fool? Because you lose some cows, you ain't going to throw away yourself after 'em, are you?"

"What happens to me," said Willie, smiling, "don't make a bit of difference. I'm just playing the game with Chris. He's won the first move. Maybe I got a chance at the second, though."

At this strange talk, the eyes of Jerry stared. But he rode home with Willie. He helped the latter harness up an old watering wagon that had been abandoned and left there by a wandering hay press. Willie's ingenuity had patched the holes in the iron. Willie's skill and industry had repaired the ruined running gear. Now he hitched six staggering, red-eyed mules to that watering cart, although two could have pulled it in the days of their strength.

"The whole shebang goes to you, Jerry," he told his friend. "These hosses and cows and mules are all done and all in. Now you stay here and wait for me to come back."

Jerry waited, and Willie went straight on toward the ranch of old Chris. Three more cows were dead as he passed the herd. All the others were down, sleeping or resting or dying. He cut a way for himself and the team through the wire fence, and drove on. There was no guard on duty this night. As though Chris were inviting him to break the law.

The cows saw him go through. But not one lurched to its feet to follow him. They were spent in the last stages of exhaustion. So then he hurried as fast as he could go. He reached the great fountain where the spring welled out of the ground, and he tied the mules with fifth chains so that they might not get to the water and kill themselves by drinking great drafts too suddenly. He carried water to them in buckets, poor frantic creatures, until they ceased chafing in their harness and were able to endure the sight of the glimmering waters of the pond in patience. Then he went on to fill the tank of the wagon itself. That was slower work, but, when he backed the heavy wagon under the great pump at the farther side of the pond, he made good progress in filling it. It was a two-man pump, but Willie could have done twice that work with ease on this night. The tank was filled full. The last stroke of the pump sent water swishing cool and black along the sides of the wagon, and then Willie put on the cover, sealed it, watered the mules again, letting them drink more freely this second time, and finally started on toward the gap in the fence.

Jerry was out there to help him, by this time. He had refrained from cutting fence or in any wise breaking the law; he could not help lending a hand to reclaim the cows from death, which were to be his own, and so they passed the water in buckets, and the weakness of those which were down kept them from fighting the buckets out of the hands of their saviors. They could only bellow feebly as the smell of the water reached them. So they were given drink, one by one. Strength returned to them by magic. They rose to their feet. They began to crowd about the wagon, a mass of tossing horns, fighting to get more drink.

By this time they were strong enough to drive, so they started the herd toward the road, and then up the road to Jerry's place.

"You can buy water off Sawyer on the way," suggested Willie, and then left his friend and turned to go back.

"I'm only keeping these here for you," suggested Jerry rather feebly.

"They're yours for always," insisted Willie Merchant. "I'll never take a horn of 'em back again."

"I'll come back and help you tend to the hosses as soon as I get these fair started up the road," said Jerry.

"The hosses are dead," said Willie calmly. "They died today. All except the roan."

169

There was no answer from Jerry, as though he realized that words would not do in a case like this.

Merchant turned back to his ranch alone, while the long train of the cattle that had once been his passed down the road before him, bellowing and fighting, for the water had given them just enough life and energy to make them ugly.

CHAPTER
SEVEN

Back to the ranch went Willie. He had four dead cows, now, to replace. The living ones were no matter. He had saved them by giving them to another man, as poor as himself, one who could never have afforded to buy them, but who would be able to support them. With what he already possessed, this would make the nucleus of a fine herd.

But all this was behind Willie. The live cattle meant nothing. Only the dead belonged to him. He had not forgotten one syllable of the oath he had sworn in the presence of the people of the town. He went straight through the gap he had cut in the fence. He found a group of weather-beaten old cows and four gay heifers. These he drove through the gap and back onto his ranch. After this, he carefully spliced the broken fence, and the sun was just rising when he finished his work.

He went back to the shack. He had been so active this day, that he had not had time to realize all that was happening. But when he put on a pot of coffee and built a rousing fire under it, the first fragrance of the coffee as it passed through the shack made the heart of Willie shrink in him. He threw himself down on the bunk and lay motionless, with his face buried in his arms. The whole agony flooded down on him at once. He had lost the three years of his labors. He had lost Jennie. And the house that had been so much to him was now no more than a coffin to him — it enclosed all of his lost hopes.

Willie slept. And when he wakened, there was a hand on his shoulder. It was the tall form and the stern face of Harry Vance that appeared above him, saying: "You've finished your game, kid. You just hop up and come along with me."

Young Merchant sat up and yawned and stretched the sleep out of his arms until the last of it tingled out of his finger tips.

"Hold out your wrists!" said a voice behind Harry Vance.

It was young Pearson. Willie and Pearson had gone to school together, played together, fought together. They had flirted with the same girls, joined the same gang, followed the same ideals. But here was Pearson, looking at him as though the skin of Willie had turned into the hide of a wolf. There was dread and wonder and hatred in his face as he approached, carrying the handcuffs. Willie, as he obediently extended his wrists, thought the thing over. The conclusion came to him in a flash. He was reported a lawbreaker, a cattle rustler, and, being such, not only were the sympathies of people for him destroyed, but he had actually begun to be an object of hatred and fury.

He did not think of this with a passion of resentment, but calmly, remembering another occasion when he himself had ridden out with a posse to catch a parcel of cattle thieves. He could recall the battle fury that had risen in his breast when he had first sighted the fugitives. He could recall how his fingers had itched to pull out his gun. But the gun had not been drawn, and now the situation was reversed.

He despised and pitied young Pearson, just as he despised and pitied the being which had formerly been Willie Merchant, for far different was he now. It was almost worth the price of the agony he had paid and still was paying, this superior knowledge of the hearts of men that was now his.

"Hold on," said big Harry Vance. "I guess we ain't going to need no irons. Willie's got his brains back again by this time. He ain't going to make things a mess for himself by trying to resist arrest. Besides, he knows me. He ain't . . . a fool." And he frowned ominously upon Willie.

Indeed, Willie knew the deputy well. The whole county knew and feared him, and the greatest of all mysteries was why the good sheriff should use such a creature as a tool.

"We don't need no irons . . . Willie ain't no fool," repeated the deputy. "Leave them handcuffs where you found 'em, Pearson."

Pearson retreated, frowning.

"Cook us up something to eat . . . fix up a snack, will you?" said the deputy.

Willie Merchant went obediently to work. He cooked the best that he had. He had bought some eggs from Mrs. Chundar the day before. He scrambled them now with slices of ham cut criss-cross until they were almost minced. He made strong, black coffee whose fragrance filled the whole house. With an expert hand and with wonderful speed, he mixed fresh batter and fried flapjacks that puffed up as light as a feather pillow shaken by the chambermaid's hand.

The deputy and his assistant ate ravenously. They ate until they leaned heavily back in their chairs and watched the cook industriously puttering about the stove. Neither of them thought to offer to exchange places with him and let him eat while they cooked. They took his service as their due. And he worked most cheerfully, talking as he cooked.

Finally Vance wanted to know why he had been such a fool as to rustle the cattle off the Martin place without running for it after he had done the work. He answered that he had done that rustling not because he expected to escape afterward, but because he had told the townsfolk that he would do that thing, and therefore he must live up to his word.

In the meantime, as he talked, he went back and forth, and finally, still talking, he went out the door of the house to the water wagon. He filled a bucket and brought it in, and turned from the wagon in time to see young Pearson slipping back from the door with a naked revolver in his hand. It made the blood swim across his eyes. Even while he cooked for them and gave them his best, they were prepared to pounce on him.

When he got back, Vance and Pearson were tilted back in their chairs, asking for more coffee. He filled their cups, and then brought forth the ham and scrambled eggs. They had already eaten too much, but, like creatures that cannot turn from good food, they fell to upon the new dish with groans. The deputy shook his head like an aggressive bulldog, and Pearson returned valiantly to the charge. So, placing the last bucket of water that he had brought to heat upon the stove, and picking up another, Willie went out as to get a second supply from the wagon.

He talked as he went. "How about more eggs, Sheriff?" For, by that name, he was complimenting the deputy.

"Why, damn it, Willie. You're a good fellow. But I'm stuffed, damned if I ain't."

Willie had put down the bucket of water and untethered that tall, long-legged, powerful racer of a horse, the gray upon which Vance had ridden out to the ranch house.

"More ham, then, Mister Vance?"

"Not a damn' thing more, but maybe a swaller of coffee, Willie."

"Help yourself," said Willie from the saddle of the deputy's horse.

"What?" called Vance a little anxiously, as though catching a new note in the voice of his host.

"You take my ham, I take your horse," said Willie calmly, and rapped his heels against the ribs of the gray.

At the same time there was a stifled yell from Harry Vance; his knife and fork clattered against his plate; his chair went back with a screech, and then was flung

175

from him and smashed against the wall as Vance dived for the door.

"You rat . . . if you . . ."

Willie heard that much. Then he was gone. He headed the big gray straight along the side of the shack until the front of the house was just behind him, and then he rocketed across the hollows.

Harry Vance came thundering into the open, but by the time he had taken his bearings and rushed around to the front of the house from which he could view the fugitive, there were scores of precious yards between them. Moreover, the sheriff's assistant had no rifle with him. That rifle — a beautiful Winchester with fifteen newly loaded cartridges resting in the magazine — lay in the long holster that extended along the side of the gray and under the right knee of Willie Merchant. And to complete his arming, on either side of the saddle there was another holster, and in each holster there was a fine Colt, finished each like a jewel.

And with only a revolver to work, Harry Vance was quite helpless. His first two shots flew wide. His third was straight enough, but it only kicked up the dust at the flying heels of the gray, and after that the tall horse worked quickly out of range. Harry Vance, for his part, stormed back into the house. He met Pearson on the way, a white-faced Pearson, whose eyes were almost starting from his head.

"What's happened? What's happened?" stammered Pearson.

"You blockhead, what d'you think?"

"If only," groaned Pearson, "you'd let me have my way about them there handcuffs . . ."

"Who stopped you? Who stopped you? You talk like a fool. If you'd had a head about you, you'd've kept an eye on him. That was what I was trusting to you. I couldn't be everywhere. I couldn't do everything. I had to leave something to you."

"On your horse," said Pearson suddenly. "People'll never stop laughing when they hear that he got away on your horse, Harry Vance."

"They'll never forget that. I'll stick on his trail until I've cornered him, and then . . ."

It was absolutely necessary to his physical well-being that he should smash something. So he caught up the heavy stool near the door and hurled it with all his might. It caught the stove, in ring parlance, fairly in the solar plexus. That is to say, it caught the structure fairly amidships and scattered it to bits. It was only a flimsy structure of the thinnest cast iron, hardly able, indeed, to endure the weight of the steaming bucket of heating water that now was fast approaching the boiling point upon its top. At this shock the entire face of the stove caved in. The bucket of hot water dropped to the floor and tipped its steaming contents upon Harry Vance and scalded him to the knees.

At this his fury became madness. He rolled his eyes wildly about him for something alive on which he could wreak his vengeance, but he saw nothing as he danced back and forth outside the shack in an agony of suffering.

Then chance stepped in at this point. For, when the stove collapsed, all the contents of the firebox were scattered across the floor. Some of them fell upon the place where the water had already soaked the floor, and there they harmlessly smoked. But others rolled to the corner where there happened to lie the crumpled wreck of a two weeks' old newspaper. This paper smoked for a moment, and then, as it reached the point of conflagration, burst into a broad tongue of yellow flame that, in an instant, had licked up the whole height of the wall. A loose end of wallpaper caught and passed the flame onto the shade with which poor Willie Merchant had recently covered the window. Then the sashes caught the fire beneath them, for all the wood was baked and rebaked into a state of the most perfect tinder dryness. In thirty seconds more that flame was curling around the eaves of the house.

"What'll we do!" cried Pearson, panic-stricken.

"Stay where you are and drop that water bucket, you fool."

Pearson hastily obeyed, but he wondered what public opinion would be when they learned that Willie's home had been burned over his head.

"Don't you see nothing?" thundered Harry Vance. "He's resisted arrest. You hear? Resisted arrest!" On the tongue of Harry Vance it sounded like the breaking of all the ten commandments at the same instant.

"And resisting arrest," cried Harry Vance, "he turned over the stove himself and set fire to the house!"

"That'll make us seem like fools . . . that we let him get out of our hands."

178

"Not a bit, Pearson. Stick by me and we'll lie our way out of it. You and me turned to and done our best at putting out the fire and paid no more attention to the escape of Willie, because we figure that the saving of the house was worth a pile more than the life of a rascal like him. Pearson, that lets us out. Now let her burn, and be damned."

CHAPTER
EIGHT

It was not the way of Chris Martin to lean unduly upon the law. There was a maxim that he had written in his mind early in his career: "Keep away from the law and the law will keep away from you." But this day he had a particular reason for using it.

Shortly after the morning began, he received word that his fence had been broken, that there were wagon tracks to the pond, and that there were further tracks to show that not only had his water been stolen, but some of his cattle had been driven through the gap. That gap had now been closed, but it was plain that foolish young Merchant had lived up to the letter of his threat spoken before the people of the town. It was now the turn of the rancher to act, and he prepared at once to take back his cows.

First of all, he went to the room of Jennie. But here good fortune had favored him greatly. She was out of the way. She had risen at daybreak, after a sleepless night, saddled her horse, and gone off for a long ride. That put her out of his way and cleared the ground for action.

When he had discovered this, he went out to the cowpunchers and gave them his orders. The whole of them were to ride over to Willie's place, take the stolen cows, and bring them home once more, and, if Willie resisted, they were to act as the occasion justified. This was the order of old Chris, but after it had been spoken, not a man stirred. They merely looked to one another and scowled. Finally the foreman spoke for the others.

"This here," he said, "is a game that I don't like. And none of the rest of the boys like it. Willie Merchant has been plumb badgered into doing a crazy thing. If we go over there, he'll pull a gun on us."

"Are you afraid of him?" roared old Chris.

"Not a bit. There ain't one of us that wouldn't tackle him alone. But there ain't one of us that wants to have his blood laid ag'in' us. He's been a hard-working kid. Now he's cleaned out and plumb busted. Let him go, for all of me. It ain't my job to walk on him now that he's down."

On the tip of the tongue of old Chris there was an order for his men to pack their belongings and ride for town, but he checked himself. If he discharged these old hands, he probably would find it hard to enlist others who would be any more willing to do the work of destroying Willie Merchant. He turned on his heel before that tigerish temper of his should take the mastery. He went back to the house and sat down to confer with himself. He deliberated in the following fashion:

If I ride there myself, I'll meet Willie, and his pride will make him fight. Then I'll have to kill the young fool. If I kill him, what will Jennie think? She's

181

disgusted because she thinks he's showed yaller. If she finds out that he's pulled a gun and started a fight, she'll know that I've lied about Willie. And what'll be in her head then? She'll go on loving his ghost and hating me for a murder. Nope, this is a case for the law.

So he rode to town and swore out the warrant that had sent young Pearson and Harry Vance out on the road to the Merchant place. Then he sat in his office and waited. It was early in the afternoon before the word came in of what had happened, and it was strange tidings indeed. The mild Willie Merchant, with the round face of a boy, had resisted his would-be captors desperately, in a hand-to-hand struggle, it appeared.

"We didn't want to do no murder to arrest him," said big Harry Vance. "I told Pearson that we'd take him with our hands. And he fought like a damned wildcat. Pretty soon he rolled into the stove. A kettle dropped off and the water scalded me. That gave him his chance to work loose. He got away and ran through the door and jumped on my hoss. Pearson wanted to foller him or to shoot him out of the saddle. But in the meantime, the firebox was scattered all over the floor and the fire was catching the wood. I told Pearson that we'd better let the kid go and try to put out the fire in his house. So we started to work and done our best. But it wasn't no good. The fire spread a pile faster than we could put it out. Pretty soon the whole kitchen was flaming, and then we seen that there wasn't no use in working any longer. Nothing could stop the whole house from burning. And up she went in smoke, like a bonfire."

All of these statements were reinforced by the agreement of Pearson. The town promptly voted that it had been an exceedingly generous action on the part of the deputy. They even got a collection together with which they bought him a good horse to take the place of his stolen gray. The kindly old sheriff rode in specially to take charge of the manhunt, which had grown to such surprising proportions, and to compliment Harry Vance for his good conduct.

As for Willie Merchant, public opinion was shocked into another course. There had been nothing but pity and sympathy for him hitherto. There was now a revulsion of feeling. In the first place, they argued, a man had no right to rustle cattle, no matter what happened. To cut fences and rustle cattle was bad, mighty bad. To resist arrest was even worse. And to have crowned all with that unspeakable offense of horse stealing was still worse. In short, men put their heads together and decided that something should be done, and done at once, to bring Willie to his senses and lodge him in jail.

"He'd get off with a pretty light sentence. A couple of years in jail would give him time to think things over," was the final verdict.

Before the evening came, the pick of the town had offered itself to serve with the sheriff and Harry Vance on the trail of the fugitive. They started out, well mounted and armed, from the town of Copper Creek, where the sheriff lived, in the evening of the day. Harry Vance rode at the head of the party.

But there was another shock of common opinion in store. It was produced the following morning. That night, when Copper Creek was dark, a figure slipped into the hotel and, while the clerk snored in his chair, leaned over the register and made out the number of the room that was assigned to young Pearson. Harry Vance would have taken his recent ally with him on the manhunt, but Pearson declared that he was through with the labors of enforcing the law. He had been singed, or nearly singed, in one affair. And now he feared the fire.

Alas, for poor Pearson. He had waited for the blow that now hung over him. The shadowy form now slipped up the stairs, and so softly that not a squeak came from them. It reached the door of Pearson's room. It tried the knob and found that it was locked. Nothing daunted, the midnight prowler went through the hall, up the stairs, into the attic, out the skylight window, and then, like a monkey, climbed down the wall of the building. The window was open. Through the window it passed, and wakened Pearson with the chilly touch of the muzzle of a revolver beneath his chin.

"Wake up," said the voice of Willie Merchant. "I got to have a little chat with you."

Pearson sat up in bed with his arms rigid above his head.

"Now," said Willie Merchant, sitting deliberately upon the bedside and dropping the muzzle of his gun, "I've heard the lie that you and Vance have circulated around the town today. But it ain't going to ride, son.

I'm going to have the truth knowed. I'm going to have it signed with your hand and swore to all, solemn and square. You understand?"

"Wh . . . what?" breathed poor Pearson. "Wh . . . what am I to do?"

"Let folks know that you and the skunk, Vance, burned my house and everything of mine that was in it. Let 'em know that. Give 'em the straight news, and I'm satisfied."

"Vance," groaned the victim. "He'll never stop till he has murdered me, if I do this here thing that you want me to do, Merchant."

"You'd rather have me turn the trick than him, then?" said Willie.

"Would you murder me, Willie? For heaven's sake."

"I'd murder you, son. What's a life to me, more or less? They've ruined me. They've run me out. One man more ain't nothing to me. Will you write out the truth, Pearson?"

Pearson, with a groan, surrendered. "Because it wasn't me that done the burning!" he exclaimed. "It was him. Let him pay for it, then."

"Sure," said Willie soothingly. "Sure. Here's paper. I guess you got a pen. Nope, a pencil won't do. Steady, partner. Take it easy. Wait till your hand stops shaking."

CHAPTER
NINE

The confession that Willie secured, at last, was far more than he had dared to hope for. Under the stimulus of terror, with that long, ominous-appearing Colt beneath his eyes, Pearson wrote more freely that he might otherwise have done. He wrote all that Willie could have hoped, and more. He described every incident of that arrest, of the calm manner in which Willie accepted it, of the meal that was cooked for them and that they ate, of the sudden drumming of the hoofs of horses, and their discovery that Willie had escaped. He told of the fury of the deputy, of how he smashed the stove by throwing the stool at it, of the fall of the firebox and the spreading of the flames, and of the plan that Harry Vance thereupon laid for concealing the truth about that act of vandalism from the eyes of the public. He wrote out this amazing story and signed it with his name, dated it, and dropped the pen. Willie, reading it with dazed eyes, folded it, tucked it into a pocket, and departed through the door, leaving his victim with his head between his hands.

It meant much to young Willie Merchant, the paper that he now held. It fixed the blame for a detestable crime that was, in his eyes, like a murder. The house

186

had been more than a house to him. It had been the work of his hands. It was to him what the picture is to the painter, a thing that cannot be duplicated, once destroyed. And so all the hours of hope and pain and happiness that Willie had put into the building of his shack were gone beyond recall, and those three chairs that had stood in the sealed room — aye, and the room itself, which she could never walk into now. She could never unwrap them. He could never hear her exclamations.

She herself was gone from him and could not be brought back. All that he had been a few days before was scattered to the four winds. A giant had struck his work and his dreams, the concrete and the unreal, and that stroke had demolished him quite. It was old Chris who had done it. When he thought of that grim old man, it seemed to him that the soul of the devil lived in that squat body. Such had been the men who first conquered the mountain desert and made it habitable. Such had been those who blazed the trails that wearier mortals like himself had been able to follow a short way. It was no wonder that Chris had grown rich. Indeed, what Willie Merchant felt for his conqueror was not hatred so much as a sort of reverence. He had not seen how he could be undone, only a short time before, and now he was a fugitive, pursued by the law. He saw before him a dim prospect of a few wild years during which he might live by the gun, riding hard, sleeping in the open, frozen in winter, burned in summer, taking by force, spending in wild debauch, paying for his very food with bullets and eating it in stealth like a wolf.

Such were the thoughts of Willie as he went down the hall of the hotel and then slipped down the stairs. In the lobby beneath, he found the clerk still sprawled in his chair, his mouth open, snoring loudly. The door was wide open, and through it he stepped into the street. There he hesitated, looking up and down. But what difference did it make? All ways and all directions were the same to him; they all led to varying forms of misery.

The question was solved without his own effort. He felt a shadow stir behind him. Then a gun muzzle ground into the tender flesh at the small of his back. An old, stern voice said: "Well, youngster, I guess you and me'll talk."

It was the voice of Champion, the sheriff. What under heaven had brought him there at this time of the night? Or how could he have found the trail so soon? But, after all, perhaps it was better this way.

"Put them hands down, and put 'em down behind you, slow and easy," commanded Champion.

Merchant obeyed. Cold iron touched his wrists, and there was a *snap*. He was hopelessly shackled.

"Now, son, let's have a look at you."

He turned, saying: "Well, Sheriff, it's me. Kind of soft for you, eh?"

"Willie Merchant?" murmured the sheriff. "Well, well, well. Step along." And he waved up the street.

The jail lay in that direction, and Willie needed no explanation. He went calmly to its doors. They were unlocked, and he was taken in. He was brought into a little office. The sheriff sat down at a dusty desk, opened a big book, and asked him many questions. Willie answered them one by one. Only half of his mind was there; the other half was searching out the image of old Chris Martin and wondering what would be the expression of sardonic satisfaction on his face when he heard the news.

The book was pushed back. "I'll have a look through your pockets, Willie," said the sheriff.

He brought out the matches, the cigarette papers, the half ball of twine, the pocket knife. He unbelted the cartridge belt, and swung it off, together with the revolver. Then, from the inside coat pocket, he took out the paper that Pearson had just written.

"Read it, Mister Champion," said Willie.

Champion flicked the paper open and began. "Looks long enough to be a love letter," he said with a grin on his wrinkled face. The grin presently disappeared. He read with an occasional grunt and droop of the eyebrows. When his eyes had run to the bottom of the page, he raised them and began again at the beginning. He now studied out every phrase, as though it were written in a language with which he was only half familiar. When, at last, he was ended, he raised sorrowful eyes to Willie.

"I'd rather have lost a year of life than to've seen this," he said simply. "I'd've swore that Harry Vance was on the square now. But this here letter is straight. Mighty straight. It'd convince any judge and court in the mountains that Pearson was yaller . . . and telling the truth." He shrugged his shoulders and looked at Willie again with new eyes. "Willie," he said, "this kind of changes things. But I'm afraid that it don't help you none. It shows that you're going to have company in jail. But it don't save the fact that you swiped old Chris's cows. Does it?"

"I ain't aiming to save myself," said Willie. "I figure that, after some of the honest men that I've met up with, spending a few years with the crooks in the open will be sort of restful."

"Going to plead guilty?"

"I sure am. Let 'em finish up the case quick. That's all that I ask."

"Willie, what got into you? Mind you, this is after arrest, but what you say *won't* be used against you in court. But open up and tell me what got into you? If I'd been asked to pick out the plumb soberest young gent in the country, dog-gone me if I wouldn't've landed on you right off for a hard-working, money-saving kid. And here you go bust in one grand slam."

"I was needing excitement," said Willie with a smile. "I'd played sober so long that I had to go on one big bat."

"Well," said the sheriff, "I was just curious, but, if you don't want to talk, I reckon that I can't make you."

"Listen to me, Sheriff . . . if you'd never been a friend of mine before, I'd reckon you one now, since you've put the irons on me just when I was getting set to run wild. It's better to go ten years in the pen than to go ten months in the open and wind up like a coyote, with a slug of lead to digest."

"You was aiming to play the game wide open?"

"I was a fool," said Willie, "but my heart was busted, Sheriff."

The sheriff, without another word, rose from his chair and led the way out of his office into the cell room. There, with a rusty key, he turned the wards in the old lock. They screeched as they moved, and he waved Willie into the compartment. There he removed the irons, but still he lingered a little.

"You've lived honest, worked honest, and now you talk honest, Willie. When they send you up to the prison, dog-gone me if it ain't a mark ag'in' old Chris, not ag'in' you. You can lay to this, too, kid, when you get out of the coop . . . come back to me. I'll have a way to give you a hand."

CHAPTER
TEN

If Chris Martin heard the news of the imprisonment of Willie that next morning, he could not relish the word. In his brutal heart of hearts, he had really only one wish about the young fellow, and that was that he would turn outlaw and go the way of that kind. There was other news than that of the capture of young Merchant. Big Harry Vance had been served with a warrant for arson, and he had promptly knocked down the bearer of the warrant, rushed out to a horse, and ridden far away. But Pearson, his accomplice involuntarily, was now in a cell.

The public opinion was put in the greeting of an old acquaintance of Chris who rode in from Cedar Creek that day.

"I hear you've gone out and bagged a couple more, Chris. Having a kind of a nice little game all by yourself, ain't you?" It was spoken with a faint, ironical smile.

Old Chris answered with a grunt. He had received nothing but black looks from the entire village ever since old Hank Ballon vanished.

"Time takes care of hard feelings," he was heard to murmur.

As for his villagers, they would not dare to revolt against him. They were deeply in his power, and they were not free-handed, like Hank. They had wives and children, and they dared not defy him. So secure was he in his hold upon them that he began to relish this new situation. It proved so conclusively who was their master. Every hour of the day he had a new testimony concerning his position. He was, in fact, the undisputed tyrant of the town, and the realization was sweet to Chris Martin. He went home that night whistling half the way, and actually forgot to light a cigar.

The foreman came out and watched him unsaddling his horse, for Martin was at least enough of a democrat not to make any of his cowpunchers do menial work.

"I hear they got Willie," said the foreman.

"When any young fool," said the rancher, "runs into a stone wall, he's going to get knocked down."

That, for him, ended the narrative of Willie Merchant.

"He'll go up, all right," said the foreman.

"Sure he will. He's done."

"How many years?"

"I dunno," said Chris. "It's pretty serious. Cutting wire and then swiping water . . . that's as good as burglary right there, ain't it? And then rustling cows on top of all that . . . the law is pretty hard on cattle rustlers, partner."

"The law'd rather see cows starved to death, I reckon," mused the other.

"Eh?" said Chris.

"Law'd rather see 'em starved," repeated the foreman steadily.

"You aim to be one of them that waste time pitying a blockhead?"

"I do."

"I got no time for soft heads, son."

"I got no time for you, neither," said the foreman. "You can find somebody to take my job. I'm through." And he turned upon his heel and walked away.

Chris was dumbfounded. Here was a new expression of public opinion. Here was a man whose hair was grizzled, whose step was no longer light, who had, for many and many a year, labored like a slave in the service of a hard master. But now he was willing to sacrifice the pension that, in a few years, was sure to come to him, in order to enjoy the exquisite satisfaction of telling the master that he disapproved of his conduct. It was almost bewildering to Chris, but he put it into a maxim and threw the fact behind him.

Some fools blossom early and some blossom late, said Chris to himself, and went to the house.

There was Jennie waiting. She was dressed in riding togs, her best outfit. There were yellow gloves on her hands, and a black, snaky quirt was dangling from her fingers. Her head she held very high. And in her eyes there was something that made him a stranger. It troubled Chris.

She's sulking, said Chris to himself. *When a woman is sulking, the thing to do is to act damn' serious. Like you had a toothache or something. They sure hate a smile when they're on a grouch.*

194

With this in mind, he shied his hat into a corner and slumped into a chair as though the weight of the world had crushed him. But the eye of Jennie remained as frosty cold as ever. It seemed to the old rancher, as he watched her, that she had never been so beautiful. For to him she was beautiful. A man who called her nose too short would have been damned by him as blind to begin with, and a fool to finish. Even her freckles were, to him, each a separate grace. He wondered, as he watched her, how God could have given him the joy to be bound by a blood tie to this marvelous creature.

"Uncle Chris," she said, "I've waited for you to come home before I left."

He refused to admit the meaning of the words. "Left for where, Jen?"

"For Cedar Creek first, I suppose."

"Going to visit the Lorings?"

"No. I'll stay in the hotel for a while."

"Bad place, Jen."

"Perhaps."

"How long d'you aim to be gone?"

"Forever."

He peered at her with a squint, as though he were looking across the blazing sand of the desert at the far, cool image of mountains.

"Forever, Jen?" he murmured.

She rose. "Forever," she answered.

"You ain't joking, honey?"

"Joking?" she said savagely. "No, I haven't your sense of humor. It doesn't make me smile. I . . . I . . ." She

195

shook away tears that were coming, and then stamped a foot to drive away the coming weakness.

"Jen," he told her, "you sort of stagger me. What have I done except love you like you was my own?"

"You've ruined my life," she told him. "You've ruined it. You lied to me about poor Will and sent me there to scorn him and break our engagement . . . and that drove him to all the rest. You called him a coward . . . a coward and . . ." She choked with the immense injustice of it. "And I've learned the whole truth. A coward? He was brave enough to defy the whole law . . . and you . . . and all the rest. A coward."

Public opinion, said a still voice in the heart of Chris. *She's only a part of it. Public opinion.* "Jen," he said aloud, "suppose that you and me was to talk all of this over, slow and easy."

"There's nothing left to talk about. Will's gone from me. The prison will have him. The prison. And you . . . it's all you . . ."

After that, what happened was too stunningly swift for Chris to follow. But it was all stormed out at him. She was going, and never to return. She would stay at Cedar Creek until she had fought the case for Will with her money. For now those old investments that he had made for her had flourished and grown into a small fortune. And she, being of age, would claim them. She would do this, and then, when Will was gone, she would take herself she cared not where, so long as she never had to see her uncle's face again.

Then she was gone, and he watched her throw herself on the back of her horse and gallop away with her head down into the wind. At that he weakened enough to run outdoors after her and cry out, but his throat was cramped and small — not a whisper's volume issued from it. And she did not pause to look back at him, not even when her horse had galloped over the top of the hill to the west. She drove straight on, and presently the horse and rider vanished.

He went back slowly into the house. The screen door stuck, and he plucked at it with numb fingers, rather wondering why he did not curse it. When he went in, the shuffling feet of Wing, the old Chinaman, whispered past him. He saw that the eyes of Wing were wet. At this he wondered, rather dimly. That the very cook should weep because she was gone, and yet from him there came not a vestige of a tear.

Her glove lay in the middle of the floor, where it had fallen, and he plucked it up. He had a foolish pang as he saw it, a desire to go out and call her back. As though she would return for the sake of a riding glove.

So, instead of going out, he sat down, with the glove in his hands, and fell to smoothing it with his stubby fingers. He began to look at it with a new wonder, for it was so small that it seemed to him that Jen must be still a child if her hand could fit into it. She was not a child, however. It was a woman who had raged at him. It was a woman who was about to fight her best for Willie Merchant and save him from the prison if she could.

When he looked up again, the Chinaman was moving softly about the room, laying the table; the thick dusk was everywhere.

"I ain't eating," he told Wing, and went outside again.

He felt at first that it was better outdoors. He could breathe more easily in the freshening wind, and he said to himself: "Time'll take care of all this. I ain't broke. Not yet."

Then, turning the corner of the house, he came on the swing under the mulberry tree. It still hung there in the blackened ropes, although it was ten years since it had been used. It seemed to Chris suddenly that it was ten years since he had been deserted. He turned hastily back, lighting a cigar. But it had no taste. He began to crumble it, bit by bit, in his fingers. He began to think of that old trip to Havana; his interviews with the cigar manufacturers ... That was in the newness of prosperity; that was when Jen had first come to him. Time could never heal him, he knew at last.

"I'm too old," said Chris, and he tossed away the fragments of the Havana.

CHAPTER
ELEVEN

"I want acquaintances," Chris used to say. "I'll get along without friends. I want folks around me that need me . . . not them that I need."

He had lived on that basis so successfully that now he found there was not a friend in the world to whom he could turn, and yet he knew that he needed a friend most desperately. There was no advice that could help him, but although he was aware of that, he felt that he must talk. The mere utterance of words would lift some of that mysterious weight that pressed down upon his heart.

Nothing would do. There was not a living soul to whom he could turn. He spent two days revolving his misery in his mind. Each day he continued his usual routine. He went into the town in the morning and returned in the evening. But now he spent his day not in the office, but wandering around through the village. What he was hunting for, he himself did not know. But finally he made sure that he was looking for one kindly eye, and he found none. There was nothing but the bitterest resentment and suspicion in every face he encountered.

On the third day, his strength melted away, and he surrendered. He would go to Cedar Creek and tell Jen that he must have her back; that he himself would throw all of his giant strength into the battle to save Willie Merchant, but that she must come back to him and stay with him.

So he drove to Cedar Creek that day and actually up to the hotel, before his heart changed. It was not that he minded humbling himself to Jen. It was that some other person might hear how he debased himself and cringed. The walls of that hotel were paper-thin. Even a whisper might be heard in an adjoining room. So he drove on past the hotel, through the town, with his hands cold and his face hot. He drove five miles out on the farther side of the town. By the end of that distance he had made up his mind. He turned the team around and drove them, smoking, back into Cedar Creek.

Martin went to the jail and asked for Sheriff Champion. That veteran upholder of the law was not there. He went to the home of Champion, and the old man came out on the porch to meet him. It seemed a little strange to Chris that he was not asked inside to talk. It seemed a little strange, also, that there was no smile on the face of the sheriff. Yet they were men of the same period. Together they had fought in the cohorts that won the West. Together they had seen the great men of the border rise and fall.

But the sheriff greeted him with a distant eye, as though he were a stranger.

"Sheriff," said Chris, "what'll happen to Merchant?"

The sheriff turned that cold eye upon him, and then looked away again. "About ten years, maybe," he said. "Maybe more."

"Mightn't he wriggle off?"

"Sure. Anything's possible. If you wasn't to appear against him to press the charge . . . if the sun was to stop shining . . . sure, he might get off." And the sheriff smiled, without mirth.

"Well," said Chris tentatively, "he'll learn something in jail, that kid."

"He'll learn to be a bad one," answered the sheriff. "I know the makings of men. Willie had the get-up of a man-killer, Chris. He's high-strung. And he thinks too much. A hard worker will make a hard fighter . . . pretty near every time."

"He'll be still young," said Chris. "He'll be young enough to make another start."

"A gent like you," said the sheriff, "can make a new start any time. But this here setback has made Willie an old man."

Old Chris took his way back to the street and to his team. He had enough to think over. Willie as an old man. Jen would be happy with no other for a husband. What was to be done? After all, the whole problem ceased to be a problem. It became exceedingly simple as he put it to himself in short words.

If he stayed in that country, he could not live unless he were known as Chris Martin, the ruler of men. If he surrendered his case against Willie, he would be broken. The old halo of terror that surrounded him like a mystery would be vanished. He would be a common creature like a hundred other men. And he could not face that end to a long career. But there was another possibility. As the sheriff had said, a man like Chris could never be too old to make a new start. And there were new countries, too; far north among the snows of Alaska there were immigrants conquering a new country. Suppose that he were to surrender here, but go North to make himself as strong and as terrible there as he had been in the southland?

He went back to his own town; he retired to his own office, and there he wrote a letter in his wide, sweeping hand.

Dear Jen: I'm pulling out for the north. Things have got sort of stale and tame here in the south. This is to say good bye.

Merchant will come off clear. I won't be here to press the charge. When he's free, go to my lawyer, Benedict. He'll have something to tell you. Good luck.

Uncle Chris

Martin mailed that letter. Then he wrote another to Benedict, which would make that iron lawyer stare, and then swear with astonishment. But when that was mailed in turn, he felt that he could breathe again for the first time since Jen had left him.

He took for himself $5,000 in cash. He had not had $50 with which to make his first start in the West. Then he went down to the buckboard, gave the team the whip, and whirled out of the town — his town no more — and north and north.

They heard of him no more. Not even Jen could get trace of him. For the northland and a new name had swallowed him. Although they continued to hope for news, none ever came.

As a matter of fact, according to his own maxim, time took care of that. He grew into a legend long before his death, and the children of Willie Merchant and Jen, on the old Martin Ranch, listened to tales of Chris as they listened to tales of fairies, strangely evil, and strangely good.

The Crystal Game

Frederick Faust's saga of the youthful hero Speedy began with "Tramp Magic", a six-part serial in *Western Story Magazine*, which appeared in the issues dated November 21, 1931 through December 26, 1932. As most of Faust's continuing characters, Speedy is a loner, little more than a youngster, able to outwit and outmaneuver even the deadliest of men without the use of a gun. He appeared in a total of nine stories. The serial has been reprinted by Leisure Books under the title *Speedy*. The first short story, "Speedy — Deputy", can be found in *Jokers Extra Wild* (Five Star Westerns, 2002); "Seven-Day Lawman" can be found in *Flaming Fortune* (Five Star Westerns, 2003); and "Speedy's Mare" appears in *Peter Blue* (Five Star Westerns, 2003). "The Crystal Game" was originally published in *Western Story Magazine* in the issue dated April 2, 1932.

CHAPTER
ONE

Council Flat was one of those railway stops in the West where it seems that the planners of the road had grown tired of stretching the steel rails straight across league after league of desert and had marked with a cross the place where a little station house covered with brown paint should be. It was merely to please their fancy, and not out of any necessity or possible use it appeared, they built the place, and there it stood, to make a brief blur before the eyes of transcontinental passengers, shooting past.

No road led down to the station house of Council Flat; there were only three winding trails that, uniting a short distance from the station, led up to it, still winding slightly and without reason over the perfectly level surface. Beyond the point of junction, still meandering as though over rough and smooth ground, the trails separated and wound away into a distant horizon, which was still blurred by the after-effect of a recent sandstorm.

Inside the station, there were three people who had already waited an hour for a train that was two hours late, and therefore they had come to know one another, at least, by name. The middle-aged man was one

Benjamin Thomas, and the girl who accompanied him was Jessica Fenton. The big young man, with the rather stylish clothes and fastidious, supercilious manner, was John Wilson. The three had a common destination in the mountains that were turning from brown to blue in the milder light of the late afternoon.

That destination was Trout Lake, in the middle of those brown-blue mountains. Since they were all bound for the place, the talk turned chiefly on the tales that had come down out of the hills about the gold strikes and of the $300 pans that had been washed at the side of Trout Lake itself, and all around the creeks that wandered down into it through the forest.

They were in the midst of this talk when they heard the thunder of a train. It could not be their own, which was not due to come for another hour, but they went out and stared hopelessly toward the small spot that was swelling out of the horizon, seeming to grow larger without actually drawing nearer. It was a way of killing a few brief minutes, at least, to watch that train come and go, and it would be a melancholy pleasure to see it dwindling down the tracks where they should have been speeding an hour ago. All the time that they had waited, they had a sense of time rushing past them at a frightful rate, time hurtling toward glorious possibilities in the future, and they, in the meantime, were caught and held in wretched stagnation.

So with irritation, with amusement, with sympathy, they saw the train approach. It grew so slowly before the eye that it was apparent almost at once that it was merely a freight train that was coming. This, however, was very much better than nothing at all. They would try the sharpness of their eyes in reading the signs along the sides of the boxcars. They would try to recognize the initials and names that might represent lines as far away as Florida and Maine, and they would guess at the contents.

The passing of the train, in fact, was accomplished at not more than twenty or thirty miles an hour, because of a grade, scarcely noticeable, but a factor to be reckoned with in hauling forty loaded cars. Swaying and snorting, casting out fire at its feet and a mist of blowing steam from its head, the engine went roaring by finally, and their eyes still followed the caboose as it hitched along at the end of the train. It grew smaller. Its flag dwindled out of sight; the whole train was enveloped and lost within the thin cloud of dust that whirled up behind it. Then it appeared again, as a small black spot. Finally it was gone.

The three had watched the passing of the train with their eyes squinted, their ears assailed by the roar of the monster. Now they began to look at one another and shake their heads, so that it was hard to say whether they wished they were on that train, pursuing their way, or thanking heaven that they remained behind where peace and quiet reigned.

It was about this time that the girl, whose eye was quicker than the others, saw an odd fellow come out of the bush on the farther side of the track. He vaulted lightly over the two fences that railed in the track. He was enough to set people staring in any community, because he was dressed in a long robe of silk, striped with red and yellow, and he had on his head a red and yellow turban-shaped cap of the same material, and there were red and yellow slippers on his feet. This attire gave him the appearance of an Oriental. His face, too, and his eyes were dark. One immediately placed him among more ancient races. Furthermore, his face was so delicately cut it looked less like flesh and blood than a statue chiseled out of marble. Yet, with all this, it was a face not lacking in decision.

This fellow, as he came up to the station platform, saluted the others by crossing both hands on his breast and bowing low, so that the tassel of his silken cap fell forward. The manner of the others in answering the greeting was characteristic. Young John Wilson started to part his lips, started to raise his hand, but, instead of doing either, simply nodded curtly without uttering a sound. The other man, Benjamin Thomas, was so surprised at the bow that he actually put his hand up to the brim of his hat to lift it, but recovered himself in time to turn the gesture into a salute. The girl looked at the dark-faced stranger with a smile and gave him a pleasant good afternoon.

He straightened from his bow and went on through the door of the station house. He had the look of one who does not wish or dare to look on the faces of strangers; although he went with his head erect, his eyes were so lowered that it seemed impossible that he could see beyond the tasseled toes of his slippers. The lids were so far down that the black lashes made a semicircle of shadows under each eye, like a painted line.

210

After he had gone into the station house, the other three looked at one another. Mr. Thomas shrugged his shoulders and winked one eye expressively, as though this were a question that he knew all about, although he was holding his tongue. John Wilson had a faint glimmer in his eyes, but immediately afterward relapsed into his high-headed, supercilious attitude. But the girl said: "That's a wonderful face. Let's go look at him, if we can manage it without being too rude."

She was first through the door of the station house, followed by the others. They found that the stranger was seated, cross-legged, on a bench on the opposite side of the room, his feet being drawn up under him like a Turk. The light came in over each of his shoulders and showed him engaged in an occupation that was even stranger than his appearance. He had a small crystal, about two inches across, spinning on the upright tip of the forefinger of his left hand, and while it spun, the finger never wavered to one side or the other, yet the crystal kept its balance as though it were fastened by a rod through the center of the finger bone.

The length of time that the ball continued to spin was one of the most remarkable points of the matter. If it were resting upon flesh, no matter how smooth, the friction would presently cause it to slow down and stop, but it whirled and whirled until one felt that the very breathing of the stranger must be the cause of its rotation. Perhaps it was balanced, with really marvelous exactness, upon the very tip of the fingernail. At any rate, it continued to spin almost as though it were revolving in a vacuum.

While it whirled and flashed, the stranger kept his downward look upon it with the look of a Hindu devotee — that is to say, with an expression of stony but breathless absorption. One might have said that this odd ceremony was some sort of religious pantomime.

Ben Thomas crinkled his eyes, critically, as though he were looking straight through the performance. Then he shrugged his thick, athletic shoulders, and leaned back in his place.

John Wilson stared, lost his supercilious look, resumed it again, and also leaned back.

But the girl crossed the room and stood before the stranger. "We're terribly curious about that spinning crystal," she said. "I wonder if you don't expect us to be?"

CHAPTER
TWO

The beauty of a cat lies half in its movements. Your dog is full of effort, tug, and strain when it is jumping about. But a cat will get up out of a sound sleep, slope from the branch of a tree to the ground, and nail a squirrel as it comes out of its hole all in a half second. The cat always seems to be folded up in utter repose, but it unfolds with wonderful ease. It is always loaded for trouble; it sleeps no more than a gun does. There is always a trigger finger ready to exert pressure.

As a cat slides from sleep into waking, so the man in red and yellow rose from the bench and the crystal ball disappeared in a flash from the tip of his finger. He was gravely attentive to the girl before him. "That is my business," he said. "I am a crystal-gazer, and I make my living by looking into glass."

"Oh, you're a fortune-teller?" she said.

"Fortune-teller?" he said in a voice whose silken gentleness matched the beauty of his face. "Well, I am rather a reader of the past than of the future, but I see something of the future, also. But shadows of light are harder to decipher than shadows of darkness."

"I don't understand that," said Ben Thomas. "That kind of beats me, Jessica," he added, drawing nearer.

John Wilson also drifted toward them, maintaining his aloof air, as though his feet were bearing him forward without the intervention of his will.

"Why," said the girl, "I suppose he means that he looks at the future as that part which has the light, and the past is the part which throws the shadow."

"Eh? Maybe, maybe," said Ben Thomas. "What's your country, stranger?"

"I come from the country of Kush," said the other, "from above the Fifth Cataract and the Oasis of El Badir."

"Kush? Cataract? El Badir? That's the dog-gonedest address I ever heard," said Benjamin Thomas.

"Cataract . . . that refers to the Nile, I suppose?" said the girl.

"It does," said the solemn crystal-gazer.

He had been standing with lowered eyes all this time, eyes so extremely downcast that his face had the blind look that one sees in the head of a Grecian statue. Now he suddenly looked straight at the girl. She straightened a little, astonished at the sight of those remarkable eyes.

"Then you're an Egyptian. Is that it?" asked Ben Thomas.

"I am an Ethiopian," said the other.

"Negro?" exclaimed Thomas.

"The Ethiopians of the pure blood are not Negroes," said the stranger.

"Well, this crystal-gazing," said Ben Thomas, who was a practical man. "How d'you go about it?"

"I look for you into the crystal as it turns," said the youth.

214

"And what's the price?" asked the practical man.

His companion glanced at him with a sudden shadow of distaste in her eyes.

"Whatever you wish to give me, so long as it is silver," said the man from Ethiopia.

"Well, a dime's silver," said hard-minded Ben Thomas.

"That, also, is enough," said the stranger.

"All right, start in crystal-gazing, then," said Ben Thomas. "And here's the dime." He chuckled as he drew a fistful of silver from his pocket and produced a dime between thumb and forefinger.

The youth shook his head. "Afterward," he said. "There will be time to pay, after I have finished looking in the crystal. Sometimes I see nothing but whirling lights and whirling shadows without form. And sometimes I am able to see a little truth. It is not I, but the crystal that speaks . . . sometimes I am too dull to understand it. In the end, if you have found some truth in what I say, you may pay me as you will, or not." He finished, and waited.

"That's a good dodge, too," said Ben Thomas. "Nobody'll refuse a coin to a fellow with a game like that. Go on, then, and start the ball spinning, if that's the way you go about it. Then you can tell me what you see. I'm gonna learn," he continued, looking toward the girl and John Wilson, "that I'm a man with two legs and two hands, a heart and a pair of lungs. I'll find out that there's been a woman in my past and there's gonna be a woman in my future. Oh, I know the kind of tripe that the fortune-tellers give out. But we gotta have some way to waste the time."

"It may not be a waste in spite of that," said the girl, but her voice was so soft a murmur that no ear caught the words except the man of Ethiopia. And he heard because the furry ear of a cat was not more acute than his.

"Are you prepared?" he asked. He was looking at Ben Thomas.

"Prepared? Sure I'm prepared," said Thomas, shrugging his thick, powerful shoulders. "You go right ahead, sonny." And he laughed.

Suddenly in the hand of the man from Ethiopia there again appeared the crystal ball, and he raised it until it stood on the tip of his delicately tapering forefinger at such a height that it was between his eyes and those of Ben Thomas.

"You are ready," he said. "And therefore . . ." He flicked the ball with his right hand, and it began to whirl rapidly about with a flicker of reflected sunshine trembling in its depths. The face of the Ethiopian turned to stone; all life died out of his eyes as they stared.

He spoke, and his voice was a dead, wooden thing. "In the past there is a red shadow, and in the future there is a red light."

"What kind of red? Paint? Or whiskey?" asked Ben Thomas. The heavy lines of his face wreathed in a smile once more and his mustache bristled with pleasure.

"Blood," said the boy.

216

"Hello, there!" exclaimed Thomas. "Blood? I've been a butcher, eh?"

"Of men," said the boy.

"What say?" exclaimed Thomas. "What's the idea in this here? Trying to get more coin out of me by . . . by pretending that you . . . Look here, young fellow." He reached out to grasp the arm of the Ethiopian, the arm that was supporting the whirling crystal ball.

The arm disappeared smoothly, but not abruptly. The crystal ball was gone at the same instant, and the Ethiopian stood before Ben Thomas with his eyes on the floor, his hands thrust into opposite sleeves, very like a Chinaman.

"What sort of bunk is this, young fellow?" asked Thomas.

"Uncle Ben," protested the girl, "you asked him to play his game. You mustn't be angry with him for the way he plays it."

"I'm gonna find out something!" cried Thomas. His voice rose to an angry roar. "Look me in the eye!"

The Ethiopian looked up, but the dark blankness of his stare was utterly impenetrable to the other.

"Now tell me where you get that stuff about blood in my past?"

"From the crystal, sir," said the mild-voiced youth.

"Hey? Oh, rot!" exclaimed Ben Thomas. He was an angry man, indeed; in the swelling of his rage, it seemed as though he were about to lay violent hands upon the smaller man. But the Ethiopian, slender, erect, immobile, kept a blank but fearless stare fixed upon the face of the rancher.

"Suppose that the crystal should have told him something about the days when . . . ?" began the girl.

"Bosh," said Ben Thomas. "You know me, do you?"

"The crystal knows you, perhaps," said the youth. "I never have seen you before today."

"I don't believe it," said Ben Thomas. "You know me, and you've heard yarns about the vigilante days. That's it."

"No, sir," said the crystal-gazer. "I heard nothing about you. I give you my word that I never have seen you before today."

"I don't believe it," muttered Ben Thomas. "But . . ."

"He talked about the past, but he talked about the future, too," remembered John Wilson, aloud.

Ben Thomas jerked his head toward the big young man. "Yeah, and that's true, too," he said. "Whacha mean about the future?" he added, whirling back on the Ethiopian.

"Sir," said the youth, "the crystal sees not only the deed but the mind. It sees the red of blood in your mind."

"Well, now, I'll be . . . " began the rancher. He checked himself. "I've half a mind," he declared, losing control of himself, "to teach you to . . ." The hand of the girl on his arm quieted him. He shrugged his shoulders and turned away. "Never heard such bosh in all my life," he declared.

"There is the silver, then," said the Ethiopian. "You pay, but only if you are satisfied."

218

"I've got ten cents' worth of heat out of your lying," said Thomas. "Take it." He threw the dime on the floor.

The Ethiopian leaned with an unhurried movement that was swifter and surer than the dropping of a bird's head to pick up a seed. The coin that had rolled in a flash across the floor disappeared under the shadow of his hand. He straightened again, unperturbed.

John Wilson said: "I'd like you to try with me, if you please?" He flushed a little as he said it, and strode up before the smaller man.

"Thank you," said the crystal-gazer. "I hope that there will be something to reward your faith, sir. Are you ready?"

"Yes, quite ready," said John Wilson. He turned a deprecating smile and shrug toward the girl, as though to assure her that he took no stock, of course, in this sort of thing, but was merely trying to make up for the atrociously bad manners of the other man. He was met by a glow of approval in her eyes that made him glance hastily away again, flushing.

The blank, sightless eyes of the gazer were now again considering the winking lights inside the ball of crystal. "There is a coldness, sir," said the dull voice of the Ethiopian. "There is a coldness that fills my mind from the crystal."

"What coldness?" asked John Wilson.

"It is fear," said the gazer.

"Fear?" said Wilson. "Fear of what?"

"That I cannot see. But there has been much fear about you, and fear in you . . . fear for its own sake, I should say."

The color rushed out of the face of the big young man. He said nothing, but stared, and the girl looked up at him with an expression of much pain.

"In the past there is more strength than was needed," said the youth who watched the crystal. "In the future there will be enough strength, at least."

A shudder ran uncontrollably through the body of John Wilson. "In the future, there will be strength?" he said haltingly.

The girl drew back a little, as though she were troubled by being within earshot of this speech, as though she felt that she were playing the part of an eavesdropper.

"There will be strength. There will be sufficient strength and sufficient trouble, also."

"Danger?" asked the big young man.

"Danger that you can avoid."

The breast of John Wilson rose. "And suppose that I do not avoid it?"

The crystal-gazer remained silent for such a long moment that the turning of the crystal grew perceptibly slower and slower. "If you do not avoid it, you still have strength enough," said the crystal-gazer.

An exclamation burst from the lips of John Wilson, beyond his power to control. "Thanks for that," he gasped.

CHAPTER
THREE

The voice of John Wilson was not loud, but there was a fervor in it that changed the whole atmosphere, and gave it significance. He stepped hastily back, and, turning to the girl in a way that showed that she had been constantly on his mind, he murmured: "I've made a fool of myself. I'm sorry. I've been an ass."

She shook her head, regarding him, however, with a little constraint as she answered: "I know how it is. It gets on the nerves . . . it's like hypnotism, I dare say. One goes to pieces. I've been at a séance and had the thing happen to me." She smiled reassuringly at him, out of the largeness of her heart, but he knew that inwardly she was despising his lack of control.

He was deeply flushed when he pulled a dollar from his pocket and dropped it into the hand of the crystal-gazer.

The latter murmured his thanks, his face as expressionless as ever, and he seemed about to sit down when the girl said: "It's my turn. Let the crystal talk for me, too, if you please."

She stood before the Ethiopian, smiling a little, very steady of eye and assured of manner. He, without a word, made the crystal spin again. There was only one important distinction this time — being shorter by several vital inches than the crystal-gazer, she could look more fully into his eyes, and it seemed to her that she could see lights forming and dissolving in the large, dark pupil. It was like the light of energy, rather than the light of thought. The smile vanished from her face.

"In the past there are only small shadows," said the crystal-gazer in that silken voice that fell like an enchantment upon her. "Except one near shadow out of which you have hardly stepped. A shadow of grief, a shadow of sorrow."

She caught her breath.

John Wilson, lingering, shame-faced, nearby, watched her hungrily. As he saw the words strike in, his own expression of protective concern spoke quiet volumes.

"You are still in the shadow, but it is not so deep. You are searching, and you are full of hope. You are searching now. You are walking forward into a bright light of questing. And there I see . . ." He paused. The blankness left his eyes. A troubled frown appeared on that delicately modeled forehead.

The crystal turned no more. It disappeared into his flowing sleeves as he folded his arms once more.

"You still have something to say," said the girl. "You've been wonderfully right. There has been a great grief. And now I'm searching and hoping to put an end to it. All that is quite true."

"Don't be such a gull, Jessica," snapped her guardian.

She raised her hand to stop him, and waited hungrily for the next words of the crystal-gazer.

Still the latter delayed. "I cannot tell," he said.

"You can," urged the girl. "If there's something ugly that you see, please let me know. I'm terribly interested. I find myself believing."

"Believing a cheap fakir like that?" cried Ben Thomas. He came slowly forward, with short steps, scowling at the Ethiopian, his dislike only too evident.

"There is one darkness of which I cannot speak," said the stranger.

The girl lost color. Then, nodding, she said: "You mean death?"

He looked straight at her, but his eyes were kept utterly blank. He said nothing.

"Death?" she repeated. "Is that what you mean?"

It was plain that face of stone would not give her a reply. There was no sullen refusal in it, merely utter blankness. The words would never be spoken.

Ben Thomas brushed in between now. "I never heard such rot in my life!" he exclaimed. "There's been a lot of nonsense about death and strength to our friend, Wilson, here. And blood . . . for me. Yeah, blood in the past and in the future. That sort of thing. Why, Jessica, I think that you half believe what the liar tells you."

"Don't talk that way, Uncle Ben," said the girl. "I don't like it. It makes me unhappy."

"Let me talk to this beggar," said Benjamin Thomas.

"Don't," said the girl. "You know your temper, Uncle Ben. Please don't." She had brought out a dollar and slipped it into the hand of the Ethiopian.

"Wait a minute," said Ben Thomas. "I've got myself in hand. I just want to show up the silly fool. He's got a

223

rigmarole, that's all. Look here, you. You say there's red blood in my future, eh?"

"So the crystal shows me," said the other.

"What kind of blood did you say it was?"

"The blood of murder," said the crystal-gazer with perfect calm.

An exclamation, as though from the force of a blow, escaped through the open lips of Ben Thomas. "You dirty little hound!" he shouted, and struck hard, with the flat of his hand.

It missed the mark. The crystal-gazer had slipped back a trifle, shifting his ground with the speed of a stepping cat, and his blank eyes were blank no longer, but filled with a curious light of pleasant contemplation as he looked at Ben Thomas.

"Uncle Ben!" cried the girl.

"Mister Thomas . . . " began John Wilson, hurrying forward.

But the rage of Thomas had mastered him, at length, and now he lunged straight at the throat of the stripling. "I'm gonna show him!" he roared. "I'm gonna break . . ." He jumped back suddenly, crying out: "He's broken my wrist!" He was holding his right wrist with his other hand, and holding it hard, as he glared at the Ethiopian.

The girl had seen — but barely, because the movement had been almost too fast for the eye to follow. It was an upward stroke of the hand of the crystal-gazer, so that the edge of the palm had struck straight under the wrist of her companion.

"I'm sorry," said the crystal-gazer. "But I had to do something. I couldn't let him keep his gun hand intact until after I've left. But the wrist isn't broken. The tendons and the nerves are a bit numb. That's all."

Ben Thomas, panting with helpless rage, turned suddenly and rushed out into the open air to let his passion dissolve. The distant rumble of an approaching train was growing louder.

The crystal-gazer calmly slid out of his silken robe, his turban-like headgear, his striped slippers, and appeared before the others in ordinary clothes, with a deep-visored cap on his head. He folded the clothes he had taken off. Being the sheerest silk, it was easy to make them disappear under his coat. But what seemed the chief miracle to the girl was the change in his appearance. In the conventional clothes he now wore, his skin seemed three shades lighter.

"You are no more an Ethiopian than I am," she said suddenly.

"Oh, certainly not," he said, "when I'm not in those clothes."

She sighed, and the smile came back to her face. "If it was all a sham, it was a very good sham," she said. "I was believing, for a moment, that there was some occult power ... oh, I was having a pretty bad moment."

"And I was having a fairly good one," said John Wilson, shaking his head and sighing in turn.

"Why, you see," said the stranger, "everything that the Ethiopian told you had been told to him by the crystal, and, of course, it was perfectly true. I wouldn't discredit fortune-telling, if I were either of you." He shook his head, and, at the same time, he was smiling cheerfully at them. "Here's my train, now," he said.

"It's a freight," said John Wilson as he and the girl followed him onto the platform.

"That's it," said the stranger. "I often use them. Lots more room on 'em than the passenger outfits. Good bye, and thank you both."

"Hold on," said Wilson. "I wish you'd tell me your name."

"My Ethiopian name?"

"No, your American name."

With that flashing smile that had newly appeared to take the place of his former Oriental solemnity, the boy answered: "Why, people don't bother a great deal about my name. Nicknames are what they generally use for me. A great many call me Speedy."

"Speedy?" murmured the girl.

"Well," murmured Speedy, "the fact is that sometimes I've been accused of taking people for a ride, and that the riding generally is quite expensive. But don't believe a word of it. You'll find out that it isn't true."

As he spoke, the second freight was thundering past the station, and into the dust cloud, into the uproar, he walked, turned, raced with the speed of a panther beside the hurtling train, swerved, and, panther-like, jumped with feet and hands extended. The next ladder down the side of a boxcar streaked under him; he grasped it, and, as he swung back, holding by one hand, he took off his cap and waved to them.

The dust cloud swallowed him and the train, and the girl walked back into the station with John Wilson. Something led them toward the spot where the crystal-gazer had stood, and she, with a cry, ran forward and picked from the bench a shining silver dollar. "Look," she said, turning.

"He wouldn't take the fee from one of us," exclaimed Wilson. "He wouldn't . . ." He was stopped by his own thoughts as he stood staring at her.

She, doubling her hand about the coin with a tight grip, managed a wan smile and nodded her head. "He said that I was to die," she murmured. "And that's why he left my money behind him."

CHAPTER
FOUR

Thomas was quite over his temper and full of apologies, before the train arrived. He apologized to the girl; he went to John Wilson, and, as though shame and pain were fighting in him, he confessed the bad part that he had played, and laid it to the credit of an evil temper.

"I'll tell you what, Wilson," he said, "a wicked temper's a curse. I'm sorry that my poor father didn't beat it out of me when I was a youngster, but I was only a child, and I was spoiled. The result is that I'll be kicked in the face many and many a time again before I come to the end of the trail. There was that youngster, a bright lad, too, and I've sent him away thinking that I'm a skunk."

John Wilson was full of sympathy. "It was too bad," he said. "But when a man's temper goes wrong, what's to be done? Praying is about the only thing that could do any good, after that. Oh, I know all about that. My father was a fellow with a temper, and he took the heart out of us children while we were still little." His voice trailed away, and his eye hunted the distance. He shook his head, finally concluding: "It's too bad, that's all.

228

And particularly because that fellow Speedy must be a man in a million."

"I think he is," said Ben Thomas. "He's a clever rogue, at least, and he's got magic in those hands of his, real magic, I can tell you." He made a wry face at this, and rubbed his sore wrist.

This seemed to restore good nature to everyone except the girl, who was still dreaming into the future with a pale face, the silver coin clasped in her hand.

"Did you see what he did?" asked Ben Thomas.

"No."

"Hit me under the tendons of the wrist with the edge of his hand, damn him. That's what he did. Jujitsu, that's what he's a master of."

"The Japanese wrestling?"

"Yeah, you can call it wrestling, if you want to. But I'd sooner call it murder. You take one of those Jap experts, and they turn their bare hand into knives and cleavers and clubs, like they wasn't made of flesh and blood, but of iron."

"I've heard something about their tricks," said John Wilson. "They work on the nerve centers. Isn't that the idea? They paralyze the other fellow by hitting at just the right places."

"Yeah, that's it," said Thomas, sighing. "And that fellow Speedy, he hit at the nerve center, all right, when he hit me. My hand still tingles. Only, he made me mad, Wilson. Talking about blood and murder!"

"Why, I can guess how it was," said Wilson, "if you don't mind."

"I'd like to hear!" exclaimed the older man eagerly. "Why d'you think that he talked like that?"

"Because you were just a little rough with him, at the beginning," said Wilson. "Just a little rough, and I suppose he got angry and decided . . ."

He paused, and Ben Thomas muttered: "Decided that if I wanted trouble, he'd give me plenty of it. Was that it? Well, maybe you're right. I was thinking . . ."

His own voice trailed away, and there was still much distant thought in his eye when their train arrived at last. It was loaded with men and excitement, all bound for Trout Lake. In the coach they entered — the least filled of all the line — they were only able to get separate places. But that hardly mattered, for the girl was soon in conversation with a cheerful young cowpuncher who had a sack full of tools between his feet and nothing in his mind except hope to make a quick million in the new diggings.

Ben Thomas, on the other hand, had beside him a leathery old veteran, quite without teeth, so that the point of his brown chin came very close to the point of his red nose. He, like the younger men in the car, was full of good cheer and high expectations. That was a perfect opening for the conversation that Ben Thomas wished to introduce. In five minutes, he had turned the conversation on the subject that was now nearest to his heart.

He said: "Somewhere or other out here, I've been hearin' about a fellow by name of Speedy, a queer fellow and a queer name. Ever heard it?"

"Speedy?" repeated the other. Suddenly he snapped his fingers. "Hey, wait a minute," he said. "What kind of a looking gent do you mean?"

"Well," said Ben Thomas, "I'll tell you. The gent that I seen was not so big, not more'n middle height. Not more'n a hundred and fifty or sixty pounds. Dark hair and eyes, and pretty well tanned up. Might've been a Mexican, or something, by the look of him, except that the eyes were different. Handsome, too, almost like a woman, he was so damned good-looking."

"Yeah, that's Speedy, and he ain't no woman, neither," said the veteran. He paused to chuckle a moment.

"You know him?" asked Thomas.

"Me? I dunno that I can say that I know him. Nobody knows Speedy. I know some things about him, that's all. What was he doing?"

"Oh, spinnin' a little crystal ball on the end of his finger, and telling lies about what he seen in it."

"That's him," said the other. "Juggling things around is what he's always doing. I seen him, once, keep seven knives in the air, and sink 'em all in the same crack in the wall, when he finished."

"*Humph!*" said Ben Thomas. "If he's a knife thrower, he's likely a greaser, then, the same as he looks?"

"He ain't any more greaser than you nor me," said the other. "But juggling is his game. He don't throw knives into flesh, neither, unless he gets real pressed. And only a damn' fool would press Speedy. No, sir, he don't need no weapons, and he don't carry none . . .

He's got his bare hands, and that's enough for him, no matter where he is."

"I could think of places where a gun would be a pretty big comfort for anybody to have along with him," said Ben Thomas.

"A lot of other folks've thought that," declared his companion. "But when they put the pressure on, they find that they don't make no impression on Speedy. His hands is enough for him."

Ben Thomas was silent, remembering a certain moment with increasing vividness. "What sort of a gent is he?" asked Thomas. "Kind of a loafer?"

"You said something that time," said the older man. "He never was knowed to do a lick of work."

"Oh, just a thievin' tramp, eh?" asked Ben Thomas, rather relieved.

"Him? He tramps around, but he don't steal nothing, except from them that steals from others," declared the prospector.

"Now, whacha mean by that?"

"I mean what I say. If you was around Speedy, your money would be safe in your pocket, and so would mine. And if I was busted, I'd get a new stake from him, maybe, whether he knew me or not. He gives away, like water, to gents that he knows."

"*Humph*," muttered Ben Thomas. "Where would he be getting his coin, then?"

"Suppose," said the prospector, leaning forward and marking off his points with a gnarled forefinger against a callused palm, "suppose that you was a crook at cards, say, and stacked the deck, or worked the brakes on a roulette wheel, or something like that, and that you trimmed a lot of poor suckers for a thousand or so every day of your life."

"Go on," said Ben Thomas, greatly interested.

"Well," said the prospector, "if you was that kind, you wouldn't like to see Speedy come to play your game, because he'd be sure to beat you and the roulette wheel, too. He'd find ways if you stacked the pack, he'd stack it better. If you tried tricks, he's got about a thousand tricks up his sleeve, and he's always ready to use 'em, too."

"*Humph*," muttered Ben Thomas again, and he frowned, as though this were a matter of the most serious importance to him.

"I'll tell you what I heard a gent say about Speedy," declared the prospector.

"Go on and say it, then."

"The gent says that Speedy is a frigate bird."

"Whacha mean by that?" asked Ben Thomas.

"I mean," said his companion, "that I didn't know, neither, till I got it explained, and this is the way of it . . . Out there at sea there is fish hawks, eh?"

"Yes, I guess there are fish hawks at sea, too." Ben Thomas nodded.

"Well, after the fish hawk catches a good fat fish," said the prospector, "and has got him placed right, with the head pointin' forward, he starts risin' out of the water, and he steers for the land where his nest is. As he rises, and works along to a good height, out of the sky on top of him comes a bird with long wings, big talons, and a big beak. There ain't much to it except speed and teeth, you might say, but it makes a flying swoop at the hawk and scares it. The hawk, if it don't want the talons sunk into it's side, changes its mind and drops its fish, and the frigate bird, it turns over in the air and drops faster than a stone, catches up with the fish, and carries it off for dinner."

"Yeah?" muttered Ben Thomas thoughtfully.

"The same way with Speedy," said the prospector. "Them that don't make trouble for other folks don't have no trouble with Speedy, but them that live on their guns and their wits, they're the meat for him. They're what he lives off of. The fish hawks, they do their work, and Speedy, he takes their fish away from 'em." The idea pleased the prospector so greatly that he began to stir from side to side and laugh heartily.

But Ben Thomas was not so pleased, and he remained for a long time lost in thought, with a puckered brow and a darkened eye. He plucked at his mustache in the extremity of his absorption, but no pleasant solution seemed to come to him for the problem that was occupying his mind.

In the meantime, the train was leaving the flat and entering the foothills of the mountains that held Trout Lake.

CHAPTER
FIVE

They reached the station nearest to Trout Lake well into the night, then they took the stage. In the dawn of the next day, they wound down into Trout Lake, a weary lot, but fighting weariness with the hopes they carried with them.

When the stage topped the last crest in the rose of the morning, they could see white-headed mountains shining in a bright sky, and mighty forests of pine trees robing the slopes darkly to the bottom of the valley. In the midst of the valley lay Trout Lake, sparkling with blue light. It was a jewel of such a size that the entire world could come to it and chip away wealth, and still there would be enough for all.

The girl, who had slept a great part of the way, with her head sunk against the shoulder of John Wilson, wakened now and looked up first at the mountains and the sky, and then at the face of Wilson, raised above her. She did not know, for a moment, where she was, and merely wondered, vaguely, with the detachment of a child, at the rigid strength of the chin, thrusting forward, and at the pallor of the handsome face. Then she remembered suddenly and sat up, blinking.

"Rested?" asked John Wilson rather huskily, for he had the chill of the long night in his throat.

"Yes, thanks to you," she said. "You ought to have waked me up. I've been leaning against you I don't know how long."

"That's all right," he said. "I didn't mind." He flushed a little, and, at this, the girl frowned slightly and might have smiled a little, also, except that she suppressed it. She understood.

She looked at Ben Thomas, sitting opposite her, big, burly, immovable as a rock, in spite of any discomforts of body or soul, and he gave her a brief salute. Weariness did not show in his face. The lines of life had already been run too deeply there to show the fatigue of a single night, or the effect of a single act, she thought.

John Wilson was saying: "You're thinking of something."

"Yes," she said. Suddenly she turned and looked straight at him. After all, she felt that he was kindred spirit and that there was in him a certain depth of kindliness. "I was thinking of what Speedy said," she answered.

"About you?" he said. "Oh, that was only a joke."

"It wasn't a joke," she answered. "And I wasn't thinking about that, either. I was remembering what he had said about you." She was sorry, that moment, that she had spoken as she did, for she was remembering the exact words of Speedy as he told Wilson that there had been fear in his life and that his strength was greater than he thought. She was sorry because the proud face of Wilson was drawn with pain instantly.

236

But he answered at once: "You're right, and he was right. Fear. That's it. Fear. I . . ." He paused, and locked his jaws together.

A great pity awoke in her, reached her lips, and stopped there. A moment later it came again, seeing him sitting with a face of stone, and she touched his arm.

"More strength than you think. He said that, too," said the girl quietly.

He did not look down at her. He did not need to, for she felt the tremor that ran through his body. The rock that was in him had been stirred, at least.

Then there were things to occupy them other than the contents of their minds, for the stage driver began to make his grand entrance into Trout Lake, which consisted in whipping up his six horses to a full gallop and taking the stage through twenty sharp curves and corners on the lower part of the road into the mining town. The trees rushed beside them in a solid blur. The cold air of the morning leaped at their faces in a strong gale, numbing them to the bone. They clung to the sides of the coach and smiled faintly, with frozen lips, as though they were striving to enjoy this dangerous adventure.

She looked askance at big John Wilson and saw that his eyes were still abstracted, looking into the future. If there was fear in him, it was not the sort of fear that was fed by the danger of six maddened horses rushing around the bends of a half-made mountain road. Again she changed her mind about him, suddenly and completely. There was finer mettle in him than she had

237

thought. What was the mystery about him? Into what danger was he passing? Into what danger was she, also, moving? Or had the prediction of Speedy been mere foolish words of the professional fortune-teller? She did not think so. She had heard from Ben Thomas, by this time, the gist of his conversation with the prospector, and Speedy became a figure of even more consequence in her mind's eye.

At last, they rushed with the thunder of hoofs into the rosy gold of the sunrise and down the main street of Trout Lake. It was like a hundred other mining towns. It was built of logs, boards and, above all, of canvas. It was a huddling mass of lean-tos, looking as though a single strong blast of storm would blow down each house of cards.

Men were already moving about the streets. A sixteen-mule team was laboring through the deep dust, and two wagons, behind the animals, rocked among the ruts as the stage itself was rocking. Everything was rough, but everything was purified with hope and the sweetness of the mountain air that went to the bottom of the lungs with every breath.

They dismounted. They were taken into the warmth of the single hotel and seated at a long board, where they ate venison steaks, and corn pone, and drank powerful black coffee, all at a prodigious price.

Her father's friend, "Uncle" Ben Thomas, seemed pleased by all of this, but the face of John Wilson had not altered, except to grow more and more like pale stone, with a supercilious, meaningless smile engraved upon it. He certainly felt that he was closer to some hour of trial. What could the trial be?

After breakfast, Ben Thomas hired a pair of saddle mules.

He and the girl mounted and were off, up the valley, with the clangor of work beginning and the sound of men's voices singing here and there, among the trees, near at hand and far off.

"It seems," she said suddenly to Ben Thomas, "as though nothing but good could be in the air, doesn't it, Uncle Ben? And yet . . ."

He filled in the pause. "You're thinking about that fellow Speedy, eh? Aw, forget about that. He was only playing a game."

"Do you think so?" she asked, but not as one who can be easily convinced.

"Well, look-a-here," said Thomas heartily, "you don't believe in the dog-gone crystal ball, do you?"

"Well, I suppose not," she said.

"Answer one way or the other. D'you or don't you believe?"

At this, she finally shook her head. "No," she admitted. "I don't really believe any of that."

"What's left then?" asked Ben Thomas.

"I don't know," said the girl. "Unless he were a sort of mind-reader."

"What mind did he read to find you dead, Jessie?" asked the other roughly.

"Yes, that's true," she answered. Then she shrugged her shoulders. "I don't know," she said.

"Just a lot of rot, and that kid, that Speedy, he knew how to do his tricks, and make it seem something real. That was all," said Ben Thomas, dismissing the whole idea. "Now, you take this . . . Hello, there's the place . . ."

"The two black rocks and the pine between 'em!" cried the girl. "That's it! That's it!" She hurried her mule into the lead down the trail, and at the same time a tall man in ragged clothes came out from behind one of the rocks, and sent his cry of welcome ringing down the valley toward them.

CHAPTER
SIX

The tall man was Oliver Fenton, big and gaunt, as gray as one of the huge mountains about them, and he carried in his face a look that was partly savage and partly sad. For three years he had been a hunted man because the death of Henry Dodson had been laid to his account. Pursuit by manhunters for three years is enough to whiten a man's hair and line his face. But he was illumined with happiness as he held the girl close to him, with one great, brown hand smoothing her hair.

He turned from her to grip Ben Thomas by both arms, making him shake and tremble in the force of that grasp.

"There was nobody in the world that I could turn to, Ben," he said, "but I knew that I could trust you. And I was right. She's here, and you're with her, and it's the first happy minute I've had in these three years. But get into the trees as fast as you can. Nobody has found the diggings yet. Hurry, man, hurry! There's a horse coming up the trail, now. Hurry, will you? I heard a horse neigh right down the trail."

They pushed on past the two black rocks, and then turned sharply aside among the trees. Instantly they were climbing over the most difficult sort of path. For

241

the pine trees were set almost at random, here and there, in earth, upheld by the great boulders. They had to dismount, then sweat and toil up the ragged surface, leading their mules.

For half an hour, at least, they struggled on up the mountainside, keeping their breath for the climbing, rather than for talk, although Oliver Fenton was ever turning back, as he led the way, to watch his daughter overcoming the obstacles right gallantly and making a wonderful effort to keep up with the men. He nodded, and smiled, and gloried in her.

Then, at the end of the climb, they came out into the flattened shoulder of the mountain, to a small natural clearing. There the trees stood back from a little trickle of water that widened into a pool two steps across. The heads of the pine trees and the blue of heaven, crossed by a shining white cloud, were reflected in that tiny pool.

"This is the place," said Oliver Fenton. "This is the place, Ben. I've been watching over it like a miser all these weeks since I wrote to you. I knew when I tried the stuff that it was a fortune. I knew when I washed the first pan that it was like another Klondike. Look. Here's a pan. Washed out some of that black stuff here . . . right here . . . yes, or anywhere along the creek, if you're to call that runlet a creek."

Ben Thomas, frowning to disguise his eagerness, caught up the pan. Digging in the soft black clayey soil required no great effort. With the pan, Thomas scooped out some of the earth and washed it rapidly in the runlet. There remained in the pan, when Ben Thomas had finished, a little heap of golden grains and dust. Thomas sifted it into his hand; it made a respectable little pyramid. "That's about eight or ten ounces," said Thomas, considering. He was like a man in a dream, looking before him, seeing wonders.

"Nearer to ten ounces, I take it," said Oliver Fenton. He was smiling and nodding, not looking toward Thomas, but at his daughter, and she kept her own gaze fixed on Fenton as though all this matter of the gold were a small thing to her. She studied him, pitied him, grieved over the leanness and the savagery that had come into his face.

"Take one long day of work," muttered Ben Thomas, "and a man, he could wash out the price of my whole ranch, and the cows that're on it . . . I mean, with the mortgage considered and all."

"A man could do that, Ben," agreed the fugitive.

"Look," said Thomas huskily. "I've been and worked all my life, since I was a kid. I've worked hard, and I've worked honest, ain't I?"

"You've always been a hard, honest worker," agreed Fenton.

"And look at what I've got," said the rancher. "Nothin' but a bit of no-good land and a couple mangy cows."

"You've got a good place, man," argued Fenton. "You've made a living out of it for a long time."

"I could've made a living breaking rocks, too," said Thomas. "I could've made a living out of a blacksmith shop, too. It's been the sweat of my brow that's made the money, not the land. And here . . . here you take and wash the price of that dog-gone ranch out of the mud in one day." He dragged down a great breath.

"Why, Ben," said Fenton generously, clapping his hand upon the powerful shoulder of the other, "you can give up ranching now, if you're tired of it. You can give it up, man, and you can live in a town, if you want to. You don't need to think that I'll forget that, in the pinch, I could turn to you? No, no, Ben. I'm going to make your fortune for you, along with ours. I'm going to make you rich, Ben. We'll split the thing three ways. One for Jessica, one for you, and one for me."

Ben Thomas did not seem to hear. He lifted his rugged face, and a splotching of sunlight and thin shadow fell over it, so that the eyes seemed to blaze like polished metal. "What kind of Providence is there that they say watches over things?" he asked. "What kind of Providence is there, I mean to say. I go and work hard and honest, half a life, and here you come and wash out a fortune in a day. That's the kind of Providence there is. That's what they mean by Providence."

"Uncle Ben," said the girl, protesting. "Didn't you hear? You're to have a full third share in it. Look. It means millions, I suppose."

"No, it won't mean that, hardly," said her father. "I've washed up and down this creek. It's a mighty rich patch, but the gold is all pooled in this shoulder, do you see? It's a rich pool, but there's nothing higher up and there's nothing lower down than this little plateau. Not millions. Maybe half a million. Well, maybe a whole million, too. But at any rate there's enough for all three of us." He turned to the girl, and his eyes drank her in slowly, luxuriously. "You've had a bad time, Jessica," he said. "Your mother's had a bad time, too."

"It hasn't been so bad," she answered.

"Not bad?" he exclaimed. "You working out, washing, sewing, teaching music, anything to keep soul and body together? And you say that you haven't had a bad time? Your mother, too, making a slave out of herself and your name disgraced by me? You say that isn't a bad time? Oh, but I've groaned for you."

"We've never doubted you," replied the girl. "And the rest was nothing."

"I'll clear myself one day," answered Fenton. "One day I'll show that my hands are clean, after all. But now I can do something for you, in a way. Here it is, in the ground, and you go down to Trout Lake and file on this ground. File the claim. Ben, take her down with you, will you? You know the way, now. Stake it, and go down to Trout Lake. I can show you the best places here. Stake for her, and stake for yourself. Naturally you can't stake for me. Ah, I've had nightmares, waiting here and watching. Every day I heard voices somewhere near. They've prospected the whole side of the mountain, I reckon. They'd've come here, except that the run of water doesn't go on down the slope. It ducks into the rocks, out of sight. But every day I've been seeing the nightmare of some other man coming here, trying this ground, washing a handful of it and seeing . . . why, I've thought that I would be guilty of murder, if that happened." He turned to Thomas. "You've found the place, Ben. We'll stake it, and then you start, will you? Start fast. We haven't any time to waste. Listen."

245

He held up his hand. Far away they could hear the stir of voices coming faintly through the thin, pure mountain air.

Ben Thomas aroused himself from a trance and turned to the others. "I'm ready," he muttered. And he added to himself, under his breath: "Half a life of slavin' . . . and then this . . . just blundered onto."

"And no one has seen you here?" the girl was asking her father anxiously.

"Nobody. I've lived here like a wildcat in the shadow," he answered her. Then he urged them on. "Quick! Quick!" he exclaimed. "I'll be staying here in a sweat until you come back again. Stake it out, Ben. Here, I'll help. I've got everything ready. Here's the description written out, locating it. I know enough surveying for that. This is a description that will fit to a T. Hurry along. I'll take you down as far as the trail."

He escorted them away, a hand on the arm of the girl, a hand on the arm of his friend.

As they disappeared, among the shadows along the bough of a great pine that bordered the clearing, another shadow stirred, moved, sat erect — a man. He was on the lowest bough and had been stretched there, face downward. Now he climbed down, a considerable distance, with nothing to aid him but shallow finger and toe holds in the roughness of the bark and in knotty projections, here and there. But he came down with such surety, it seemed that he was possessed with claws, like a cat. At the bottom, he sat down on one of the great roots that projected like the coil of a brown python from the ground and pulled on the shoes that had been slung about his neck. Then he stood up, dusted his hands, took out a small pocket knife, and with the edge of the blade carefully removed a small shot of brown resin that adhered to his trousers leg. After that, he stepped out of the shadow into the patch of sunlight that broke through the foliage above him. Carefully he moved, never stepping upon the soft soil, but only from projecting rock to rock, until he came to the edge of the runlet. There he stooped, scooped out a palmful of the earth, washed it with a rapid and gentle trundling motion, and looked down curiously at the glittering yellow grains of gold that remained in the wrinkles of his cupped hand.

"Gold," murmured Speedy. "Yes, and murder, too. I guessed it before, and I know it now. Murder . . . red murder . . . the air's full of it."

His voice, as he spoke, was not at all in keeping with the solemnity of his words, for there seemed to be a bubbling cheerfulness about him, and he had a half smile about his lips, as though from amusement or from sheer happiness and content with this world as he found it.

With quick glances he noted down the spot and the guiding headlands that appeared, looming through or above the trees. When he had finished that quick survey, he could have found his way to this place even through the thickest darkness, so long as there were a faint foreshadowing of any of the neighboring mountains through the heavy gloom.

He was still lingering at the spot, when he heard other voices approaching from the side, and at this he

247

drew back as silently as a shadow that moves beneath a cloud across the surface of the earth. The trees received him; the big trunks swarmed and thickened between him and the clearing, and so he moved back and back until he was at a sufficient distance to give over his caution and to stride boldly and freely away among the forest aisles. He did not walk, however. Walking was not for him at such a time as this, for there were vital miles between him and Trout Lake, where he had much to do.

He broke into a run, an easy and light striding as the run of a Navajo Indian, those matchless desert runners that can put 100 miles behind them between sunrise and sunset, and in a week outmarch the toughest mustang. So, weaving among the trees, he sloped away across the mountainside, and still, as he ran, he was smiling.

CHAPTER
SEVEN

When Ben Thomas reached Trout Lake, his mind was entirely made up. He had been turning various possibilities over in his thoughts during the journey back, and his decision, he believed, was entirely practical. The moment he got to the town, therefore, he started to act on it with the fine, quick decision of a man of affairs.

He dropped the girl at the hotel, merely saying: "We have to hurry, Jessica. You have the mules put up . . . here's money to pay for 'em. I'll hurry over and arrange things at the bureau, so that there'll be nothing for you to do except to sign your name when it comes to filing the claim. I'll be back here in a few minutes . . . maybe a half hour. Will you be ready?"

"Ready?" said the girl. "I'll be waiting on pins and needles. Do you know what it means to me?"

"It means a fortune in hard cash, or soft yellow gold, any way you look at it," suggested Ben Thomas with a grin.

She shook her head. "It means that there'll be enough money to hire one good lawyer, and I know that one good lawyer will be able to clear Father before the world."

He nodded, waved, and was off, smiling reassurance at her over his shoulder. As a matter of fact, her last remark had made him feel that what he was about to do was not a crime at all, but almost a virtue.

Who is it that does not know that lawyers are a quicksand that will swallow up a fortune as a shark swallows a small fish? Therefore, if the girl intended to spend her fortune on the law, it was far better that she should have no fortune to spend. That money would round out the sum that he needed.

He never had seen himself satisfactorily as a small rancher. The picture of Ben Thomas that he retained in his inmost mind's eye was of a great power, a man of nationally felt force, one whose name would be familiar to the captains of finance.

He was sure that he had in him the brains and the mental resource to employ great good fortune, if ever it came his way. But the cattle business had not brought him luck. On the contrary, he seemed apt to buy high and sell low. Then there was the matter of the infernal mortgages. He had thought himself a lucky man when he was able to raise the money at the banks. He had assured himself that in two years, at the most, he would be able to pay off the debt. As a matter of fact, he had increased his indebtedness, and never lowered it a penny. That he constantly attributed to bad fortune, not to lack of energy or ability on his part.

In the back of his mind, there was established a sneering contempt for most other men who he met. He was always seeing political posters along the roads, nailed or pasted up, and reading in place of the actual names: **Ben Thomas, for state senator; Ben Thomas for sheriff; Benjamin Thomas, the people's true friend, for governor; The Honorable Benjamin Royce Thomas, for the United States Senate!**

In those terms he saw himself, and they were the reality. This actual self that moved through the world, unappreciated, slapped upon the shoulder as hearty, hail-fellow-well-met, Ben Thomas, the rancher, was merely the sham that bad luck forced him to maintain against his will, against his higher nature.

Now, as he walked rapidly down the street, he saw the future with amazing clearness. There might be half a million, perhaps a million in that black clay on the shoulder of the mountain. Half of that sum he could put in investments, and he knew just where to place the money — in small loans to ranches that would soon go under and whose owners could be squeezed out into the road while he, Ben Thomas, properly organized the places. The other half he would use to pay his debts, build a good house, enlarge and restock completely the old place, and suddenly step forward as a public-spirited citizen, ready to assume the burdens of legislation and law enforcement.

Well, he felt that he had the presence, for one thing, and for another he was confident that he had the brains. It might be that he had failed so far to make a great position for himself, but that was simply because he never had been able to fill his hands with opportunities large enough to fit his grasp.

This was the humor he was in, when he came to his first and most important destination, a little shack on the street, with a shingle sticking out over the door and painted with the inscription: **Office of the Sheriff: Samuel Hollis.** He turned in under the sign and found himself in a little room, one half of which was clouded with the blue-brown of cigarette smoke.

Through that cloud he saw a man whose hair was so straw-colored, and whose eyes were so pale a gray that he looked like an albino. There was something startling about his nondescript features. He was standing by a table and revealing himself in boots and long, spoon-handled spurs. His chaps were of worn, scarred leather, hanging over the back of a neighboring chair. He was not very big, and he was not very impressive. Ben Thomas wished that he had found a more startling and formidable-looking man.

Another man had preceded Ben Thomas. This visitor was dressed up in the semi-official costume of a gambler, from the long coat to the wide-brimmed hat of gray felt. He was a big, important-looking fellow, but now he was sagging, as though under a weight. And the gentle, soothing voice of the sheriff was heard saying, in a mere murmur: "The only thing is, that I wouldn't do it again. Mind you, I ain't got a thing ag'in' you. I don't want to have a thing ag'in' you. I'm only telling you . . . I hope that I won't hear a yarn like that ag'in, with you in it."

"You won't hear a thing like that again," said the other. "On my word of honor."

"Don't go to promising. Go to doing," said the sheriff. "So long, and good luck to you, brother."

The gambler walked to the door, blinked at the sun, and then slid away to one side with a furtive, dodging movement, as though he were afraid that a gun might be leveled against him from behind.

The opinion of Ben Thomas about the sheriff rose a great deal. He stepped forward and said: "Are you Sam Hollis?"

"That's my name," said the other gently.

"I'm Ben Thomas. I've brought you news."

"News that comes to a sheriff ain't often good news," said Sam Hollis. "But what is it?"

"You've heard of Oliver Fenton?"

"Ain't he the man that killed Henry Dodson?"

"That's the one. And he's the one that Missus Dodson will pay ten thousand dollars for, once he's brought to trial."

"Ten thousand is a lot of money," said the sheriff.

"I can tell you where to pick it up."

"You mean, where to pick up Fenton? Ain't that the idea that you're drivin' at?"

"That's the idea."

The sheriff nodded. "That'd be right friendly," he declared. A mild, childish interest began to flicker in his pale eyes.

"Here's the place," said the other. Quickly he dictated the description of the way to the shoulder of the mountain where Oliver Fenton had struck the pay dirt.

253

"That sounds good to me," said the sheriff. "Maybe I could pick up that fellow. You don't know him?"

"I know him pretty well."

"Know whether he's much of a fighting man?"

"Every Fenton's a fightin' man," declared the rancher, "and Ollie Fenton is a scoundrel, that's all. He's a demon on wheels. He ain't a youngster, but he's fast, and he's strong."

"I wasn't exactly talking about fist fighting," the sheriff drawled naïvely.

"He can use guns, too," said Ben Thomas. "He's a mighty good shot."

"He might be a good shot, but is he a cool head?" asked the sheriff.

"He's the coldest that you ever seen, when it comes to a pinch. He's the kind of fire that don't sputter, but it burns through steel plate like shingle wood."

"I've seen that kind of man, I reckon," said the sheriff as mildly as before. "I'd kind of like to have a look at this Fenton, too. The ones that fight cold are always interesting. Show me a gent that has to warm himself up by swearing a little before he pulls a gun, and I'll mostly show you a gent that shoots crooked, too . . . unless he's Irish." He smiled a little, as he added the last words, and shrugged his lean shoulders.

Thomas was satisfied. He was convinced that he was in touch with a man who knew his work. "You'd better take some others along with you," suggested Thomas.

"When I go out to bring in one man, I go alone," said the sheriff. "Now, about a split in the reward, if any reward turns up. Whacha think should be your split?"

"My split? Well, what do you say?" asked Thomas, always pleased to bargain.

"One third," said the sheriff.

"A half, sounds more like it to me," said Thomas.

"He's a fightin' man," said the sheriff. "I notice that you didn't bring him in yourself."

"Him? I couldn't bring him in myself, and I can't be mentioned. I know him, d'ye see?"

The eyes of the sheriff narrowed for a shooting instant. "Might be that you're a friend of his?" he suggested.

"I ranched near him," Thomas responded uncomfortably.

The sheriff nodded. "I see," he said. As he considered Thomas, the latter found that his face was rapidly growing very warm. "We'll make it a half, if you say so," said the sheriff, half turning away.

"Aw, a third would do, too," said Thomas, red but amiable. "Let it go at that. And where's the bureau? I'm gonna file on a little claim ..." He reached, as he spoke, for the full description of the claim that Oliver Fenton had written out and given to him. To his amazement, the papers were no longer in his coat pocket.

CHAPTER
EIGHT

There was a reason for the disappearance of the prize from the pocket of big Ben Thomas. When he had reached the hotel with the girl, across the street, in the smoky mouth of a blacksmith shop, Speedy had been standing, breathing rather hard from his long run across the uplands and through the woods. But he had been content because he had arrived in town before Thomas and his protégée. It was not for nothing that he had lain out on the limb of the pine tree and studied the upturned evil in the face of the big man, back there in the clearing.

Now, eager and keen as a hunting hawk, he watched the girl take the two mules, while Thomas turned down the street.

Speedy was after him at once, and his movements were like the flight of a snipe downwind. For he did not go straight forward. Pursuing an irregular course, pausing here, halting there, and then cutting at a diagonal across the street, he came up behind his quarry just as Ben Thomas paused to allow an eight-mule team to turn in the street, the tossing heads of the leaders swinging across the sidewalk.

"Good work!" called Ben Thomas cheerfully to the teamster at that moment and waved his hand. As he waved and the wagon straightened out down the street, the coat of Ben Thomas belled out and under the flap of the pocket Speedy could see the glint of white, the top edges of the papers.

His hand dipped in like the beak of a bird and came out again, bearing the prize, which disappeared into his own coat with such speed that even if any passer-by had been looking, he would have seen hardly more than a flash of light as Speedy turned on his heel, shook his head, and frowned like a man who must retrace his steps because of something forgotten. He hurried back up the street to the hotel.

Only once he paused and risked a glance behind him, and that glance showed him Ben Thomas turning in under the sheriff's sign. It was enough to indicate that he needed speed, but he had to be nonchalant, also.

He went to the hotel clerk and asked for Miss Fenton. She would be called. The clerk himself went to do it, and a rusty-headed boy slid in behind the desk to take up the duties of handing out and receiving keys.

Through the register, the fingers of Speedy sifted, found that day's arrivals, and glanced at the handwriting of the girl. A second and longer glance printed the characters in his mind, and the next moment he was writing a by no means clumsy imitation of her hand:

Dear Uncle Ben: I've just seen an old friend, and he asked me to go down the street to see his father. I'll be back in a half hour or so. Wait for me here.

Jessica

He folded the paper and pushed it across the table to the red-headed boy. "Give this to Mister Ben Thomas when he comes in, will you?" he asked.

"Sure," said the boy, and stuffed the paper into its key box.

When Speedy turned, the clerk was coming toward him, and Jessica Fenton along with him. There was first a shock of surprise in her face, followed at once by the most brilliant of smiles. Genuine pleasure made her hold out her hand and grip Speedy's.

"I might have known that you'd be traveling toward the most excitement," she said. "How are you, Speedy? Or do you really want people to call you that?"

"I can't help myself," he said. "I'm one of those poor chaps who can't keep a name of his own. I've tried all sorts of names, but they won't stick. They roll off me like water off a duck's back. I've brought you a message from Mister Thomas."

"Oh, you've seen him?" asked the girl.

Trouble was in her eyes, the old trouble, as she watched her companion.

"We're not enemies," said Speedy, "because of that little trouble at Council Flat. Mister Thomas was in a crush of business, something that he had to do at once.

258

He begged me to do something for you and, of course, I said that I would."

He drew the papers from his pocket, and her eyes widened as she recognized the handwriting of her father.

"Here's the description of a claim that he wants you to hurry down to the bureau and file."

"But he has to go along and file with me," said the girl. "That's the agreement."

"Is it?" Speedy said. He went on smoothly: "Thomas doesn't want any part of the claim, according to what he says. His idea is that, if anything happens to him, well, people wouldn't know that he owed it all to you, and that it's really your property. He was only going to file to help you hold the property."

He had ended rather lamely on this note, but the girl had not the slightest suspicion in her mind.

"That's great-hearted!" she exclaimed.

"Well, he's a big man, and he has to have a heart that will match his size," said Speedy calmly. "We'd better start. He said that there was the greatest sort of a hurry."

"He was in a hurry," admitted the girl. "We'll go along. Do you know the way?"

"Yes." He had, in fact, spotted the place on his first visit to the town. He was not one who could settle blindly into any nest, for the world was filled with enemies for Speedy, and he dared not close both eyes at once, either by night or day, in new surroundings or old ones.

He waved her on, and paused again for a moment to say to the clerk: "What's the sheriff look like?"

"You mean Sam Hollis?"

"Yes, of course."

"Why, you can't mistake Sam. Smallish, and ain't got no color in his hair and eyes, but Sam's a real man that'll . . ." He broke off with a grunt, for Speedy was already gliding away to the door, where he joined the girl and turned down the street.

There was much, there was very much for him to do, and, because of it and the danger that lay before him, he smiled and hummed as he walked along.

"This is a happy day for you," said the girl.

"It's the mountain air," he answered her. "It goes to the bottom of the lungs, to the bottom of the heart, too. It gives a fellow life."

She drew out a broad silver dollar and held it out. "I owe you this," she said.

The happiness went out of his face and left it grim. Then he shook his head: "I can't take it. Not yet," he said.

It seemed to her that half the brightness went out of the morning by that change in his expression and by something coldly ominous that lay behind the words. Death had been his word to her the day before, and death, she felt, was in his expression again at this moment. Yet happiness returned to her. For it seemed that both she and her father were on the upward path. How could trouble come when the very soil of the earth was yielding up treasures to their hands?

They turned into a long, low shed, filled with smoke, from which there issued an uproar of angry voices as half a dozen men disputed before another man on the other side of a desk, which was made of a flat board laid over two hurdles. The man had a tired face.

"You see him?" asked Speedy.

"Yes."

"He'll record the claim. It won't take long, once you get to him. But I'll tell you something more, you want to get in there as fast as you can. Shove in, Miss Fenton. You'll get ahead faster by yourself than you will if I wait here. Shove straight ahead and try to close up the deal. I have to leave you. These fellows will give way to you when they know that you only have a half hour."

"A half hour?" she asked him with suddenly increased interest.

"Just about a half hour," he said.

"What do you mean? Is there something that you're keeping back from me?"

"Nothing that would do any good, if it were told," Speedy replied cheerfully, making his expression brighter for her sake.

"But how can you know that there's exactly a half hour?"

"It's something that I got out of this good clean mountain air as I was coming down the street. It's just that I have a pretty keen sense of time, d'you see?"

She eyed him, shaking her head. What there was behind his words she could not, of course, guess, but her mind groped blindly, striving for some clue. But he was waving goodbye, and now he stood at the door. She

261

saw his head turn to the right, and then to the left. There was something infinitely cautious about him. Just in this fashion she had seen a cat pause at the open door of a house before stepping out into the mystery of the open night. Somehow, very strongly, she felt that Speedy was heading into danger. However, that would never be solved by her, and she stepped forward into the waiting line.

Speedy, in the meantime, got into the street in time to see a man dismount from a lump-headed yellow mustang, a $50 antique, with a $10 wreck of a saddle cinched on its back.

"How much for that outfit?" he asked.

"To you, brother, only two hundred bucks," said the other, grinning a little in the eyes, but not with the lips.

$200 in currency was suddenly counted into his amazed hands.

"Hold on!" he exclaimed.

"See you later," Speedy announced, and sprang into the saddle.

The Westerner watched him go down the street, bounding high with every stride of the mustang.

"Another damned fool of a tenderfoot," he said to himself, and began to count his money over again.

CHAPTER
NINE

A mile up the ravine, Speedy, already well pounded and hammered by the clumsy gait of the mustang, passed another single horseman on the way, pushing his horse ahead at a steady, easy dog-trot. As Speedy went by, he noted the pale hair, the paler eyes, the keenness of his glance, and something quietly efficient and self-reliant about the way the man sat his saddle. That was Sam Hollis, he could lay his bet, and, if it were Hollis, then there was still plenty of time to do the work that he had in mind. He was glad to reduce the pace of the yellow mustang, therefore, and still he was reasonably sure that he had gained a good half mile on the man of the law by the time he came to the two black rocks with the evergreen tree between them.

He dismounted, led the horse, trailing and stumbling behind him for a short distance into the woods, tethered it there, and then went at full speed up the hillside.

A mountain lion would hardly have climbed faster than he did, leaping over rocks, almost always in fast motion, no matter what the grade he was managing. As he worked, his eyes were still shining, and his face was bright.

He had gone on for some distance before he began to call — "Oliver Fenton!" — cupping his hands so as to direct the sound straighter and farther before him. Again, after he had run ahead, he paused and shouted once more: "Oliver Fenton!"

He got no answer out of the wilderness, but he hardly expected one; he simply wanted to send a warning of his coming, so that the hunted father of the girl would not slink away at the noise of footsteps.

At last, breaking into the clearing, he swept it with a glance, and shouted for the final time, with all his might: "Oliver Fenton!"

He was silent, then, straining his ear to distinguish an answer, perhaps far away. Once he thought that he heard a sound, but he could not be sure whether it was a human voice coming toward him, or some noise among the trees, for a wind had risen and was bending them slowly from side to side.

It was a crossing of his plans and his hopes that he had not counted on, and he snapped his slender fingers with annoyance. Everything depended upon his ability, he felt, to get to the spot in time to speak with the fugitive, warn him of the coming of the sheriff, warn him, above all, of the treachery of Ben Thomas. And now, having arrived at the proper place, he found that his quarry was gone. He groaned impotently.

There was nothing for it, however. He drew back among the trees, found a patch of thick brush, and behind that he crouched, waiting.

A full half hour went slowly and wretchedly by. He heard not a single sound of approach, but suddenly a smallish form was standing in the clearing where, a moment before, there had been nothing. It was Sam Hollis, beyond a doubt. It amused the watcher as much as it caused him anxiety to watch the prowling movements of the sheriff. He admired the way Sam Hollis handled himself. As he moved, so would Speedy have done under similar circumstances, with the same cat-like silence, the same deftness of foot, the same uncanny wariness of ear and eye, for always Hollis was probing the silence and the shadows of the trees about him while he stepped here and there, never stepping where the print of his foot would remain upon the ground or even upon the cushion of pine needles, but always from rock to rock where he could be reasonably sure that only a microscope would betray the fact that he had come and gone.

Now he was stooping beside the runlet of water; now he had broken out a bit of earth from the bank; now he was washing it in the hollow of his hand. When he arose, it was with a sudden stiffening of his body, and Speedy saw that the face of the man had become hard and cold.

That was what the sight of the gold would always do. Murder was in the air of that quiet little clearing, into which the rays of the sun sifted down so pleasantly, and left little pools and patches and charming embroideries of light upon the ground.

The sheriff drew back and disappeared. There was nothing to see, nothing to hear — only the burbling of the water as it ran with a sound like a secret whisper and the occasional murmur of the wind in the tops of the trees. Then a squirrel came out and squatted in a patch of sunshine, sitting up, examining something that it held in its little black claws. It remained for only a moment, turning its head with bird-like movements from side to side. Then, suddenly, it scooted away, made a gray streak up the side of a pine tree, and was presently chattering harshly far up among the branches.

Then big Oliver Fenton came slowly out into the clearing and looked about him with a frown. "Funny damn' thing," he said aloud. "I kind of thought that somebody was hollering my name around about in here. Some man who . . ." His voice trailed away to join his silent thoughts.

Speedy, tiger-keen with eagerness and anxiety, continued a movement that he had begun as soon as the fugitive from justice appeared. He had hoped, if Fenton came down to the clearing, he might pass close to the spot where he was lying and receive the timely warning. But, in fact, he had come in on the farther side of the clearing and was closer to the place where the sheriff had disappeared.

So Speedy slid out from the patch of brush, where he was securely hidden, and approached the clearing little by little, gliding swiftly from the protection of one tree to another, as though every open glimpse of the little brook were a flight of arrows driven at him. He was almost at the edge of the clearing when the sheriff stepped out from a tree behind Fenton, with a leveled revolver in his hand. Speedy noted that the gun was held low, hardly more than hip high, and thrusting out half the length of the curving arm. That was the way an expert always handled his weapons in this part of the world.

For the thousandth time in his wild young life, Speedy wished that there were a gun under his coat. But that wish was one that he would never gratify. He knew his own nature too well, and the temptations that come from carrying human lives within the crook of a forefinger.

The sheriff had not spoken a word, had made no move that was audible, when Fenton, as it seemed, became conscious of an unseen danger. With a stifled exclamation, he whirled about, saw the man and the gun, and reached for his own weapon.

"Stop!" shouted Speedy.

That unexpected, ringing call out of the woods caused both the sheriff and Fenton to glance to the side. They saw nothing. Speedy had flattened himself out close to the ground, behind a small, spreading shrub that sheltered him fairly well from view while it enabled him to peer out at the pair in the clearing.

"I've got you covered, Hollis," said Speedy. "And I'll put a rifle bullet through the middle of you, if you try to pot him. Fenton, don't be a fool. Keep your hand off your gun. Don't you see that he has the drop on you?"

Oliver Fenton, there was no doubt, would never have submitted to the silent pressure of that leveled gun. He had risked his life too many times in the past three years to surrender himself to the law without a fight, no matter against what desperate odds.

But now that voice that called from the near distance, and seemed to come from a friend, stopped him, because it gave him another hope.

"Whoever you be that's layin' up back in there, you're interferin' with the law," said the sheriff. "D'you know that? Or do you think that I'm a hold-up artist, maybe?"

"You're Sheriff Sam Hollis and a good man with your hands," said Speedy. "But the point is that you've come for the wrong man."

"I've come for Oliver Fenton, and this is him," said the sheriff.

"Steady, Fenton," cautioned Speedy as the big man seemed about to go for a gun again. "Steady, there, partner, and we'll work this out without any gun plays."

CHAPTER
TEN

The sheriff had come, without question, to a full halt, and stood in an utter quandary while Speedy commanded briefly: "All right, Fenton. Back up into the woods, will you, and keep going for a while. I'll take care of the sheriff."

Fenton nodded, and, stepping back, his face still toward the man of the law, he found sanctuary within the forest.

"Now, partner," said the sheriff, "what's the end of your play? You've got the drop on me, and I ain't fool enough to play ducks and drakes with a rifle that I can't even see."

"Wait a minute," urged Speedy. "I've got to think it over for a moment."

Even as he spoke, he was drifting away to the left, and, once behind the trunk of one of the great pines, he worked rapidly and silently away through the forest gloom, making a swift semicircle that had a radius of a furlong, at least.

Behind him, he heard the sheriff speak again, but, now that he was away from the place, the sheriff, for an instant, was out of his picture and he wanted to see Sam Hollis no more. What was of a keener interest to him was the shadowy form that presently he spotted before him, moving quietly forward among the trees. That was big Oliver Fenton, and, coming close up behind, Speedy spoke.

Fenton whirled, with gun ready, hip-high; Speedy raised his hands obediently in the air.

"It's all right, Fenton," he said. "You don't need a gun for me."

A change came in the savage face of Fenton. "You're the fellow that covered the sheriff," he muttered. "And a good thing for me that you were there, but what brought you? Where's your rifle?"

"My rifle was a bit of bluff. It was dirty work that brought me, Fenton."

"Whose work?"

"That of Ben Thomas."

Fenton scowled. "You've done me a good turn, lad," he said. "Don't be undoing it by running down the whitest man on earth. He's as true as steel."

His eyes burned as he brought out his confession of faith, but the boy shook his head.

"Listen to facts, Fenton. I was lying up in a pine tree, yonder, when you and your girl and Thomas were talking together."

"You were what?" exclaimed Fenton.

"You try to believe me. I met the two of 'em at Council Flat, and I didn't like the look of Ben Thomas. It was intuition, if you want to call it that. I talked to him, and my ears liked him even less than my intuition."

270

"I don't understand what you're driving at," said Fenton, "but, man, Ben Thomas has been the best friend and the truest man that ever . . ."

"That ever cut a friend's throat, eh?" finished off Speedy. "When I heard that they were heading for Trout Lake, I came here ahead of 'em . . . I was waiting for 'em, and I trailed 'em out of the town. I worked up the valley behind them, and, when I got their line from the black rocks, I cut ahead and spotted you in the clearing. It was no trick to slide up the back side of a pine tree and lie out on a branch over your head."

"No trick for a wildcat . . . I never saw the man that could do it, though," answered Fenton. "But go ahead."

"Why, I saw the evil in the face of Thomas, when he got the gold out of the pan. He looked up, and I looked down, and there was murder in him, plain to see. But you and your girl were too much taken up with one another to watch him. I followed them back to town. I stole the claim papers out of the pocket of Thomas and watched him go down the street and turn in at the office of Sheriff Sam Hollis."

"Ha?" cried Fenton. His face turned gray as he listened, and his eyes stared.

"That's what I saw him do," said the boy, "and any child could have guessed, from that point, why he wanted the sheriff. He had left the girl in the hotel. He'd send the sheriff for you and he'd file the claims in his own name. Consequences could go hang. Is that a clear story?"

271

"If there's no truth and loyalty in Ben Thomas," said the other, "there's no loyalty or truth in the whole world."

"There's not much of it, I suppose," said Speedy. "When a fellow's down, everybody takes a kick at his face."

"Ben Thomas," muttered Fenton. "I've bunked with him, ridden herd with him, nursed his children, lent him money, fought his enemies, loved his friends, and now you try to tell me that he's a crooked hound. I won't believe you."

"Then, why else am I here?" Speedy asked.

"I don't know. You're a demon, for all I can make out."

"It was a gun play, back there in the clearing," pointed out Speedy. "You were going for your gun while Hollis had the drop on you, and he's not the man to miss that sort of a shot."

"I'd be on my back, dead," agreed the other. "Yes, and I know it. But what was it that dragged you into this?"

"That doesn't matter," said Speedy. "It's a game that I like. That's all that I can say. But here's another point. When I saw Thomas go into the sheriff's office, I went to the hotel again, persuaded your daughter that Thomas had sent me back there after her because he had to be busy elsewhere, and got her to the bureau to file the claim in her own name alone." He shrugged his shoulders as he added: "I left her waiting in line while I came sloping up the valley and found you here."

"You did all this for your own pleasure?" demanded the other grimly.

"Never mind why I'm doing it. I've told the yarn for you up to date. How'll you play it from this point on?"

"I'll get to Ben Thomas if I have to walk through fire every step of the way. When I see him, I'll get the truth out of him, or . . ."

"Or kill him, eh?" asked the boy, pressing the point.

"If he's done what you say, he's a Judas."

"You'd kill him, eh?" Speedy repeated his question.

"What else is he fit for but killing?"

"That puts two ropes around your neck," said Speedy. "Listen to me, will you?"

"Of course, I'll listen," said Fenton.

"You're to keep your hands from Ben Thomas. If you meet him, as you're likely to before long, you're to smile in his face. Will you do as I ask?"

"I'd rather tear out his heart."

"And hang for it," the youngster reminded him.

"I'm to hang for one man already. What's the difference if I hang for two?"

"Because you didn't kill Dodson," said the boy.

"Ah, didn't I?" muttered the other. "And who was it did kill him, then?"

"Slade Bennett."

"Slade Bennett!" cried Fenton, throwing up one hand before his face as though a light had blinded him with the words. "Slade Bennett? That scoundrel? Was it him?"

"It was Bennett, I think," said the boy. "I remember the story of that killing, now. Dodson was a neighbor of yours. There was bad blood between you. He was going downhill, losing money, mortgaged up to the eyes. He'd been drinking and threatening you in a saloon in town. When you heard of that, you saddled your horse and rode away from your place, with your wife and your girl begging you to stay at home. That's the story that was told, at least. You came back late that night. The next morning, you were arrested. Dodson had been found dead inside his house, from a knife wound in the throat. The sign of your horse was traced straight up to Dodson's door. Besides, Slade Bennett swore that he'd ridden by, heard voices shouting in the cabin, then a quick silence and the noise of a horse galloping away. That was what made the case against you."

"That was the case." The rancher nodded. "And what makes you think that I didn't kill Dodson, when killing was just what he needed?"

"Nobody needs killing," Speedy said with a shrug of his shoulders.

"What makes you sure that I didn't kill Dodson?" insisted the rancher.

"The look of you tells me that," said the boy. "You're ready and handy enough with a gun, but you wouldn't use a knife on another man."

"And what makes you think that Slade Bennett did the job?"

"Because Slade would use a knife. He'd used one before. And because he was the man who swears that he heard Dodson name you as the killer. Did Bennett have anything against you before that?"

"Not that I know of."

"He was waiting to see Dodson about something or other," said the boy. "He listened while you and Dodson had your talk and your quarrel. When you rode away, he stepped in, finished his man, and gave you the credit. That's the story, as I see it."

Fenton, breathing hard, stared for a long moment at the smaller man before he answered, with a nodding of his head: "Seems to me like I see it all lined out. And you're right. You're dead right. Slade Bennett did the trick."

"You can be freed from any crime that you didn't commit," said the boy. "But if you kill Ben Thomas, it's murder, no matter what the provocation. You have something besides yourself to think about. You have Jessica, eh?"

"What's she to you?" asked Fenton with a start.

"A fine girl, a straight shooter, and a thoroughbred," said Speedy calmly, "and nothing else in the world."

"Nothing else?" asked Fenton, narrowing his eyes.

"Nothing else," Speedy answered deliberately. "Now, I want to know what you'll do. Will you go to Trout Lake and make a fool of yourself on the trail of Ben Thomas, or will you stay somewhere up here in the woods?"

"I'll stay here," said the fugitive. "That is, I'll stay here if I can. But Hollis will have out a hundred men to comb the woods for me."

"A thousand couldn't find you, if you take to the trees, or to the ground. Stay where I can find you."

Fenton rubbed his knuckles across his forehead. "Man," he said, "you seem to have me in your pocket. I'd like to know your name."

"I have a lot of names," said the boy. "More names than suits of clothes. But a good many people call me Speedy."

"Speedy?" exclaimed the other. And then he threw back his head and laughed softly. "I might have guessed, by the wildcat ways of you," he said. "I've heard of you, Speedy. Mostly I've thought that the yarns they tell about you are just fireside lies. But now I guess they're true. Only, you must be his younger brother, not Speedy himself. The Speedy I've heard about must be forty years old. You haven't lived enough years to do all the things that Speedy has done."

"Why, man," said Speedy, "I haven't done a great deal. But when a fellow gets gossiped about, the gossip multiplies everything by ten. It's fixed, then, Fenton? You stay put, up here."

"I stay put," agreed Fenton. "If you'd told me your name at first, I wouldn't have argued so much. Speedy, eh?" He stared with increasing wonder at the youth.

Speedy brushed this complimentary wonder away, remarking: "If you see Ben Thomas, be friendly with him?"

"I'll do that, if it breaks my heart."

"It won't break your heart. Trust Ben Thomas like a snake in the grass, watch him every second he may be with you, but don't lift a hand."

276

Fenton nodded. "You're gospel for me, Speedy," he said. "But what of Jessica? She's in the hands of that hound?"

"She's not in his hands," answered Speedy.

"Why, she's in Trout Lake, with him acting uncle to her."

"She's with him, but I think that she's in my hands," said Speedy. "Stay here. Don't worry. But keep your eyes open, and we'll find the best way out of this trouble."

CHAPTER
ELEVEN

Speedy hurried rapidly down the hillside. When he came to the spot where he had left his horse, he walked more slowly, cast a half circle about the place like a beast of prey that studies the wind on three sides of a victim before venturing on to the attack. Then he stepped up to the tree where the mustang was tethered.

He had unknotted the reins, when something caused him to stop short. This something was the mark of a heel print, dimly seen on the ground where it had not been trampled over by the restless yellow mustang. He looked up with a jerk of his head and stared into the black muzzle and along the steel-blue barrel of a gun held by Sam Hollis.

"It's you, Speedy, is it?" said the sheriff.

Speedy simply murmured: "Yes, it's I. What's the matter? And who are you?"

"I'm not one of the thousand thugs who'd like to have you where I have you now, Speedy," said the sheriff. "But you know mighty well who I am."

"I never stood in front of you before in my life," said Speedy.

The sheriff remembered an odd bit that he had heard of this famous man. For it was said that he would not lie, no matter how closely pressed, but fell back upon some slippery prevarication, rather than direct falsehoods. He determined to test him, and said now: "Speedy, answer me, yes or no. Were you lying up there in the woods, near the clearing where I found Oliver Fenton?"

"You can see for yourself that I've come down from the woods," said Speedy. "What clearing do you mean?"

"Fenton's clearing."

"What Fenton?"

"Oliver Fenton, the man you've just finished talking to back there somewhere. Answer me, yes or no."

"Every man has his own way of getting information out of a witness," said Speedy. "Your way is like a good many others that I've listened to. But what do you want with me and who are you?"

The sheriff grinned suddenly. "You're Speedy, all right," he said, nodding. Then he added: "I kind of thought that there was something about your face that I'd oughta know, when you went by me on the trail. But when you went on, you sat that mustang so bad, that I couldn't believe it was really Speedy."

"I'm a mighty bad rider," said Speedy.

"You are, if you don't mind me saying so," said the sheriff. "You're a mighty, thumping bad rider. Now tell me what you've got to do with this here business. What's Fenton to you?"

"What's Fenton to me?" Speedy repeated. "What Fenton?"

The sheriff laughed, but softly. Still, he did not move his gun out of line with the youth. "It's a lot of information that I'm giving you, I suppose," he said, "if I tell you that I'm Sam Hollis, the sheriff of this damned wolf-eaten country. I guess it surprises you a lot to hear that?"

"I'm always glad to meet another sheriff," said Speedy.

"Are you?" answered the other. "Speedy, I've got to run you into the lock-up."

"I'm mighty sorry for that," said Speedy.

"You've put your hand in between me and my job," said the sheriff. "And I can't have that."

"I don't know what you mean," said Speedy.

"Sure you don't," agreed the other. "You wouldn't be such a fool as to know what I mean. Will you give me your word to ride in, calm and peaceful, to Trout Lake, or do I have to lash you onto the back of that mustang?"

Only for an instant did Speedy hesitate, but in that instant his dark eyes became as coldly shining as black diamonds. "I'll go into Trout Lake quietly with you, Hollis," he said. "But I'd like to know . . ."

"The crime you're charged with, eh?"

"Yes."

"Interfering with the law," said the sheriff. "Maybe the charge won't hold in front of a judge, but it'll hold long enough to keep you in jail for a few days while I'm cleaning up this case. I'm sorry, Speedy. You're not the kind of a man that the law works ag'in', but duty's duty."

280

"I know it," said Speedy. "I'll go along with you. I've given you my promise."

It was the sheriff's turn to hesitate a little. Tradition said that the word of Speedy was an inviolable bond, that his naked promise was better than the sworn oaths of any other man. Finally Sam Hollis decided that it was worthwhile to treat the tradition experimentally. First, he would examine another legend — that Speedy always went unarmed. That was quickly done. He merely had to order those slender hands, those famous workers of trouble, into the air. Then he patted the clothes of the other dexterously, and located a small pocket knife only.

"It's true," muttered the sheriff. "Well, then, follow me." He led the way down to the trail, where he mounted his horse. Speedy ranged along beside him.

A peculiar warmth of pleasure filled the honest heart of Sam Hollis. He began to look with strong and sudden favor upon his prisoner. He recalled, out of the past, a hundred legends of the great deeds of this man and the work of those incredibly cunning hands. A thousand knavish performances, no doubt, could be traced to them, but in the long run they had always worked for the welfare of the honest man and the downfall of the thug. Yet now he was obviously interfering with the clear duty of a sworn officer of the law and he would have to be put aside.

Speedy was saying, calmly: "How are things in Trout Lake?"

"How are things in any mining camp," asked the sheriff, "in this part of the world? I can't stop the killings. I just manage to keep down the daily average, that's all. They're a pretty hardy lot just now. The judge doesn't have to work overtime, but the gravediggers do."

"I know," said Speedy. "The fellows all want their fling. I sort of sympathize with 'em, at that. Speaking of gunmen, I thought I saw Slade Bennett in town . . . just had a glimpse through a window as I was going down the street."

"Yes, he's in town," said the sheriff.

Speedy started a little, the merest trifle, but it was enough to have meaning to the quick eye of the sheriff.

"That was a cast in the dark. You didn't have no idea that Slade Bennett was in town, eh?"

"I know now, though," said Speedy. "I'd expect him at this sort of a show."

"You call him a gunman, eh? I know he has that reputation, but always self-defense."

"Yes, that's his game. It's an old one, too."

The sheriff nodded. "I've got nothing on Slade Bennett," he said. "Speaking about Fenton . . ."

"Bennett," — Speedy interrupted, not loudly, but softly, as though pursuing his own thoughts and unaware that the other had spoken in the interim — "is one of those fellows who practices two hours a day with his guns and his knife."

"Knife?" said the sheriff. "Why d'you say it like that?"

"I hope to tell you, one of these days," said Speedy. "Depending on how long you keep me locked up in the jail."

The sheriff smiled a wry and twisting smile, but his eyes were dancing. "I know your dodges, Speedy," he said. "Locks and walls ain't made to hold you. You ferret your way out through 'em, somehow or other. But I'll try what a double guard can do with you in an open room, and the lights on twenty-four hours a day."

Speedy nodded. "That's a hard combination to beat," he agreed. "After you have me put away, I'd keep my eye on Slade Bennett, if I were you. He's an actor that'll probably be found in the middle of a play, and holding down the center of the stage."

"Thanks," said the sheriff. "I'll take your advice. I'd like to ask you something."

"About Fenton?" said the boy.

They were coming close to the first shacks of Trout Lake as they talked.

"About yourself," said the sheriff.

"Every man loves to talk about himself," said Speedy.

The sheriff shrugged his shoulders, and then shook his head. "It's hard to corner you and make you talk, Speedy," he said. "You've made a fool out of me today, but, damn me, I don't seem able to feel no malice on account of it, and that's a fact."

"You've got an oversize heart and that's the reason," commented Speedy. And his eyes met those of the sheriff gravely, steadily.

The sheriff flushed a little. "I'll tell you what I'll do," said the sheriff. "If you'll keep out of the way between me and Fenton, and answer one question about yourself, I won't bother you with the lock-up. I'd like to have you free. You're likely to do Trout Lake more good in a day than I could do in a month."

"Thanks a lot," said Speedy, "but what's the question?"

"It's this . . . What do you get out of it? I mean . . . out of this wandering about, fighting the fights of other men, never cashing in for yourself?"

Speedy squinted at a distant cloud. "Why do people stretch a tight wire from one tower to another, and then walk across it in a wind?" he asked softly.

The sheriff started. "I understand," he muttered. "I believe you, too. So long, Speedy. I ought to lock you up. But I've got more instinct than brains in me, and instinct tells me to set you loose. Get on your way."

CHAPTER
TWELVE

Speedy went straight to the hotel. In the dusty, smoky, crowded little room that served as lobby, he ran straight into Ben Thomas and the girl. The man glared at him in a rage. Jessica Fenton was pale with anger and silent, while Thomas exploded: "You've come back, have you? After you finished your monkeyshines! You sneak thief! You stole out of my pocket . . ."

He was in a frenzy of anger. But Speedy lifted one finger and smiled past it in such a singular way that Ben Thomas stopped short, at the risk of choking over his own unspoken words.

"I've seen Fenton," said Speedy. "He knows a snake in the grass from an honest man, by this time. Thomas, remember one thing . . . night and day, I'm watching you." He turned on his heel and went out into the street.

He was sorry, in many ways, that he had had to show so much of his hand, face up, on the table, but he was troubled about the girl. By revealing part of what he knew and what he had done, he hoped he might so paralyze Ben Thomas that he would perhaps fade out of Trout Lake. Besides, there might be enough in what he had said to give the girl warning. However, he could not give himself up, for the time being, to this part of the problem. Other things swarmed before him and must be attended to. The time was short, how short he could not tell.

He paused at the next saloon, pushed through the doors, bought a glass of beer for a dollar, and sipped half of it. "I've got a message for big Slade Bennett," he said. "Anybody seen him around here?"

A little smooth-faced, pink man came up, touched his arm, and looked at him out of confiding eyes. "Across the street, brother," he said softly, and winked.

Speedy did not stay to finish his drink. He turned on his heel and crossed the street into Haggerty's Saloon. It was like most of the others, but perhaps a little more pretentious. The prices charged in Haggerty's were higher, because of the long mirror that ran the length of the room behind the bar. It had been brought up from the railroad line in several boxes, and it was screwed in place in sections, which might not be as splendid a mirror as one in a long piece, but which had the great advantage of breaking only one by one, if bullets flew that way. Even now, one panel was splintered diagonally.

It was well into the afternoon by this time and, since the sun was hot outside and the wet sawdust on the floor of Haggerty's promised coolness within, a score of men were already drinking, shaking dice for the drinks, leaning their elbows on the bar, or seated at the small, round-topped tables that fringed the wall.

Two men stood out from others instantly, not because they were bigger or better than some of the rest, but because the electric tension of danger had come between them. One was John Wilson, standing down the bar with his head high, his face colorless, the lips compressed in a straight line; the nearer man, his face turned only in profile to Speedy, was Slade Bennett. The triangular scar that disfigured his cheek was enough to identify him.

What had happened, Speedy could only guess. But whatever it was — word or gesture or something else — it had happened just before he entered the saloon. The men along the bar were beginning to straighten and turn around to watch the pair. Those at the tables were turning, also, and two of them had jumped to their feet, tense and nervous.

It was apparent that some vital offense had been given. It was also patent, from the leaning head and the forward thrust of the whole body of Slade Bennett, that he had spoken; John Wilson, crystallized to white ice by the stroke of the thing, raised his head still higher.

"You can't talk like that to me," he said.

"Oh, can't I?" purred Bennett. He raised his head deliberately; he tilted it back, and he laughed, so that all could see the derision and the confident scorn in his face.

"What'll keep me from saying it twice over, you yellow hound of a tenderfoot!"

It was time for a gun play, of course, or for a man-size punch, at the least.

But John Wilson was still as a stone; lips began to curl as the men watched. The tension went out of the air. It seemed perfectly patent that Wilson was going to

287

take water. His eyes wavered from the leer of Bennett, and Speedy caught that eye and jerked his head shortly to the side, to indicate the side exit.

John Wilson, as though hypnotized, turned and made a long stumbling stride toward freedom.

"Wait a minute!" thundered the voice of Bennett, cruel exultation in his eyes.

Speedy made a step forward to the elbow of the gunman. "Don't make a fool of yourself, Slade," he said.

"Who says fool to me?" said Bennett, snarling and turning like a tiger. He looked down from his height into the eyes of Speedy. A big and splendid man was Bennett, and the fury of the bully was in him now, the fury that had taken the place of his desperate hunger for a fight fairly throttling him. With a side glance, he saw that his intended victim had reached the door and gone out through it, and there was no guffaw of laughter for the exit of the coward. Interest had been too suddenly arrested and concentrated upon this new arrival, and his singularly bold speech to so famous a warrior as Slade Bennett.

"You ... Speedy ... eh?" muttered Bennett in surprised tones. His eyes worked an instant as his thought and desire struggled within him. It was only a split part of a second that separated him from the drawing of his gun, but Speedy's mysterious hands were still closer than that. Too many legends had been told about their works of wonder; one of those works, Slade Bennett had seen.

Still, too much had been contained in that sentence of Speedy; there had to be an accounting or the taking of water would be suddenly shifted to Slade Bennett. Therefore he demanded in a harsh voice: "What d'you mean by calling me a fool, Speedy?"

"Calling you a fool? I didn't call you a fool, Slade," said Speedy gently. "I wouldn't do that. I said don't be a fool. There's a good deal of difference, isn't there?"

His smile was so calm, and his eyes, withal, so very steady, that the other men in the room began to shift their position a little. No two of them recognized the name that Bennett had given to the stranger, but everyone was able to see that this was a man of mark; otherwise, Bennett would have crushed him to the floor and gone after his first victim.

"I don't see much difference," said Bennett, "but I don't mind hearing you try to explain."

"Certainly I like to explain," said Speedy cheerfully. "It's like this, Slade. Are you listening?"

"Yeah . . . what else would I be doing?" growled Bennett, taking as much ground as this formidable opponent allowed to him.

"Why," said Speedy, "you didn't know that fellow was John Wilson, did you?"

"He might be John Smith, for all I know," said Bennett. "He's a yellow dog, is all that I know about him."

Speedy shook his handsome head. "Oh, you're wrong, Slade," he said. "You're dead wrong. I'd rather sit in the electric chair than face a John Wilson when that cold, white look comes over 'em. That's when they kill, and I've never known a man fast enough and straight enough with a gun to hold 'em off. His father was the same way."

"You're joking, Speedy. This is one of your tricks," said Slade Bennett. "Didn't I see the dirty cur sneak out of the place?"

"You saw him go to get a gun," Speedy advised, smiling steadily. "That's all you saw him do."

"If he's a man, he'd wear a gun," declared the other.

"Why, he wore a gun too often," said Speedy. "I hear that he's had to swear to his father that he won't wear a gun. He uses it too well, I understand."

"The mischief he does," said Bennett. "If ever I saw a scared kid, he's the one, just now."

"That's the Wilson look. I don't know how many men before you have gone wrong about it. A lot of 'em, Bennett," said Speedy. "A lot of people have taken the white look of a Wilson for a look of fear. And a lot of people have died, I understand, Bennett. That's why I called out to you when I saw the look on his face. I didn't want you to go wrong. That wouldn't exactly do . . . seeing that you're an old acquaintance of mine."

"I'm trying to believe you, Speedy," said the other, plainly troubled.

"I know him. I'm a friend of his," Speedy said confidently. "And I'll try to go and steer him in a new direction, away from you. Otherwise, he'll be back here in a few minutes and the saints help your unlucky soul, Bennett."

"Is that so?" said Bennett, rearing his head again, although his color was not so bright as it had been the moment before. "If he's a friend of yours, Speedy, you tell him that right here is where he can find me, and that I stand by what I said."

Speedy sighed. "Well, Slade, I've warned you," he said.

"Cut out the warnings," said Slade Bennett. "Everybody up to the bar."

"Not for me, thanks," answered Speedy. "I'm going to get hold of him and see what I can do. It'll be a hard job, but I'll try my best for you, Slade." And he departed, hastily through the side door of the saloon.

"Who's that?" asked someone of Bennett, who stared at the still swinging door.

"That?" answered Bennett, rousing himself from a trance. "Oh, that's a streak of poison and greased lightning, that's all it is." And he turned for his drink.

CHAPTER
THIRTEEN

Speedy went for the hotel with all the speed that he could make. He felt that his hands were more than filled, because he had a double task before him — the problem of Oliver Fenton was enough, but the problem of John Wilson was equally big and difficult.

When he reached the hotel, he found that Wilson, as he expected, had already gone to his room. He got the number and was instantly at the door, rapping.

After a moment a heavy voice asked who was there.

"Speedy," answered the youth. "I've got to see you."

"I can't see anyone," Wilson said drearily.

"I've got to talk to you," insisted Speedy.

"I'm seeing no one," answered Wilson.

"Wilson, let me in for half a moment, will you?"

There was no answer. Speedy, balked by this unexpected opposition for a moment, paced cat-like up and down the hall. Then he drew a short length of fine steel spring from a pocket and leaned over the lock of the door. Only for a minute or so did he work with this odd tool, and then there was a faint grinding sound as the rusted bolt turned in the lock and the door fell open before him.

John Wilson had not heard the sound. He lay face down on his bed, his head in his arms and his hands, bent backward, clutching at his hair. Beside him was his revolver, and Speedy, as he closed the door softly behind him, shuddered a little at the sight of the gun. He knew well what it meant.

Now, shadow-like, he crossed the room, picked up the weapon, and fondled it for a moment with his too-familiar hands. It disappeared presently inside his coat; at the same time, he touched the shoulder of the boy, saying: "Well, Wilson, we can talk it over. Will you do that?"

John Wilson came wildly to his feet and glared savagely down at the smaller man. Then he glanced at the closed door. "How did you get in?" he asked. "That doesn't matter. You can do miracles, everyone says. You can read minds. You can tell fortunes. But you don't have to be a prophet to see that I've ruined my life today. I've shown yellow. I've taken water. I'm a cur that every man can kick out of the street." His own agony bent his head far back and silenced him.

"You left the saloon to get a gun," said Speedy. "You come out of a dangerous fighting family. I'm your friend. I knew that you didn't have a gun with you, because you can't trust yourself with one. The fighting spirit comes out in you with too much of a rush, and you can't control it. So I hurried over to the hotel to try to stop you from going back to the saloon and killing Slade Bennett."

The young man stared. "What are you saying, Speedy?" he demanded.

"I'm telling you the truth."

"And they don't see clearly that I'm a worthless cur?"

"No, they don't see that, because it wouldn't be true."

"I could feel my face was frozen. They saw the white of it. They must have seen that."

"They saw the Wilson look, which I told them about afterward. The Wilsons all turn white when they're ready to kill. Just the same some Irishmen cry when they're ready to murder you."

"You mean to say that they believed you?" murmured Wilson. "They don't think that I'm a dog?"

"Listen to me. Did anybody in the place laugh or taunt you when you left the saloon?"

"No. That's true. I've been wondering about that. I thought they were all too sick with the feeling of my shame."

"No, they were sure that trouble was in the air, and that you'd left the saloon meaning to come back."

"But I can't go back," Wilson insisted.

The face of Speedy puckered a little. "Not now, perhaps," he said. "But you're going back later on."

"I can't go," said Wilson. "Look!" He held out both hands, and Speedy saw that they were trembling. Every nerve seemed to be twitching, making those big, powerful hands as helpless as a child's. "I'm like that all through," declared Wilson. "I'm shaking all through. I'm hollow inside. I'm not a man. I never was a man. I'm only a rotten shell that looks like the real article." He changed his gesture, and suddenly pointed at

Speedy. "You saw straight through me the first time," he said.

"I saw that you carried your head so high because you weren't sure of yourself. That was all," said Speedy. "And I saw that you had a lot of strength that you wouldn't trust."

Wilson sank down on the edge of the bed and held his head in his hands. "You're wrong," he said. "I'm no good. That's the truth about it."

"They're waiting for you in the saloon," said Speedy. "Now, you start in and try to pull yourself together, will you?"

"Let them wait," groaned Wilson. "I'm going to sneak out of town while they're still waiting."

"Very well," said Speedy, "I'll write a note saying that I've managed to stop you for the time being and advising Slade Bennett to get out of town. You understand? I'll send that note over to Haggerty's Saloon. Then I'll come back up here and talk to you again."

The young man made no answer, and Speedy, with a sigh and a shake of the head, hurried from the room and down the stairs. In the lobby he scribbled:

Dear Slade: This fiend, Wilson, is still in a white fury. He wants the carving of your heart, and I'm afraid that he'll have it, if you don't give him room. You can slide out of this, and nobody will have it against you. I've persuaded him not to go over at once. That's all I can do. Before long, he's likely to break

295

away from me. There's no handling him when his temper gets the best of him. And if he gets at you, Slade, he's a dead shot and sure poison.

> **Yours,**
> **Speedy**

He folded that paper and shoved it into an envelope. Then he gave it to the rusty-headed boy to carry to the saloon, with a quarter for the errand. "Take that to Haggerty's and give it to Slade Bennett," he said. "There's no answer to wait for. Just put it in his hand, and then slide out."

Speedy then went back up the stairs to the room of John Wilson, to find that the man had not altered his position. He closed and locked the door. "Wilson," he said, "you've talked and thought yourself into a panic. You started running, and you ran backwards, instead of ahead. That's all that's wrong with you. You came out West to prove yourself a man, or die trying. And you've still got your chance to fight . . . to win or go down."

Wilson jerked up his head. A twisted, tormented grin was on his face. His voice was changed as he said: "I came out here to try to make myself a man. There's nothing inside me that is worth the making, though. Not a thing. I'm hollow. I always was hollow. I am just a big bluff. I've always been a bluff, too."

"I don't believe it," said Speedy. "A man can't live as long as you have without being called, sooner or later."

"You don't understand," said John Wilson. "When I was a youngster, I was years in one school. Right after

296

I got there, a boy tried me out, challenged me to fight. I had to do it. I stood like a stone, sick. He rushed in at me. I threw out my hand at his head. We clinched, and he lost his footing. We fell, with me on top, and, as we dropped, my elbow struck his head. He lay stunned. It was an hour before he came to. And all the boys standing around thought that it was my one blow that had knocked him out. He was so dazed, that, when he came to, he accepted what they all were saying. From that moment, everybody was afraid of me. I was supposed to have a terrible power in my arms. None of the boys would fight me, and, as long as I was in the school, I was considered a lion. I never dared to play football, for fear they'd find out that I was yellow. I never dared to box, because that would give me away. But I knew all the while that I was a cur.

"Then I went to college. But college boys don't come to fisticuffs very often. A lot of the students from my own school were there before me, and they'd spread the reputation of my terrible strength and my dangerous punch. I wouldn't turn out for any of the athletic teams . . . only crew. There was no physical competition, no physical contact in that. I did pretty well. I pretended that I wasn't interested in anything else, although I was perishing to get into football togs.

"That's my history down to today. Finally I've been called. And you see what happened. I thought that if I came out here into the wild West, to a rough mining camp, I'd be thrown into a corner, and then I'd have to fight my way out, but, when the pinch came, I simply lay down like a yellow dog."

"How did the trouble start between you and Slade Bennett?" asked Speedy.

"I don't know. My mind's a haze. All I could see was the gloating in his eyes as I broke down before him. I couldn't even face his eyes, to say nothing of his gun. I came back here to kill myself . . . and I didn't have the courage for that."

"You have the nerve to row through a four-mile race," said Speedy. "That's a form of courage."

"But I can't face an angry man," said the other. "I never could. I'm . . . a dirty coward, Speedy."

"You've thought about yourself for years," said Speedy. "You've worked up an idea about yourself and the idea's stronger than the fact. I'll tell you one thing."

"What is it?"

"You listen to me, and you've got to believe me."

"I'll listen to you, Speedy," Wilson said grimly. "No man in the world but you could listen to me like this without turning sick. What is it?"

"This is what you're going to do. You're going to wait here till I get word about Bennett. It may be that my bluff has worked, and that he's clearing out. If not, you're going back to the saloon and face him. Here's a knock at the door, now. Maybe that's our answer."

CHAPTER
FOURTEEN

At the door, when he opened it, Speedy found the rusty-haired boy of the hotel. He had a letter that he shoved into Speedy's hand.

"I dunno what you wrote to Slade Bennett," said the boy, "but it certainly heated him up a lot."

Speedy waved the messenger off, and, turning back into the room, he saw the drawn, tense face of John Wilson, staring at him in mingled fear and hope.

It turned the heart of Speedy cold, that fixed, pleading stare. Opening the letter, he found that Slade Bennett had scrawled on the back of the paper that Speedy had sent: **I'm waiting, right here, for another half hour. And then I'm coming over to get the low hound**. There was no signature. The big firm handwriting spoke for itself. Evidently Slade Bennett saw through Speedy's bluff.

"It's no good," said Speedy. "There's the letter. You've got to go back and face him."

John Wilson seized the slip of paper and read it over and over. It seemed to be a thousand words, from the length of time that he took over it.

Speedy, looking through the window, saw the golden and purple dust of twilight filling up the landscape and dimming the great mountains. Only their crests glistened with re-doubled and polished brightness.

Then the hard voice of John Wilson said: "Speedy, I've got to write some letters home, in case anything happens. I'll meet you downstairs. I'd rather be alone for a few minutes. Just leave my gun behind, so's I can look it over before I go down, will you?"

It was a pitifully poor attempt at deception. Suicide was what poor John Wilson meant, and Speedy knew it perfectly well. As he stood there, facing the sunset and setting his teeth hard, he strove to grope his way through this difficulty and find the solution of it. But no solution presented itself to his mind. He needed time to think the thing over, time to ponder on it. Besides, it was highly possible that Wilson really did wish to be alone to write farewell messages.

"I'll leave you alone for a few minutes, Wilson," he said at last. "But then I'll come back and see you. And I'm not leaving the gun behind." He left the room as he spoke, regardless of a feeble protest from the young man.

In the outer hall, as he stepped from the room, it seemed to him that he saw a shadow draw back through an open doorway into a room not far from him, the shadow of a tall man. He hurried to the place. "Who's there?" he asked of the empty darkness beyond the open door. As there was no answer, he asked again, a little more loudly: "Who's there?"

A subdued murmur answered him: "Is that you, Speedy?"

He knew that voice. It was not so very long since he had been hearing it. "Fenton," he said, and glided instantly into the room.

By the glimmering light of the dusk, he saw the big man in a corner; the sheen of a naked gun was in his hand.

"Fenton," said Speedy, "you promised to stay there in the woods. Why did you go and break your word?"

"I didn't give a real promise," muttered the deep, husky voice of the fugitive. "The more I thought about Ben Thomas, the more I knew that I had to see him face to face and have a little talk."

"With guns, eh?" said Speedy.

"With guns," Fenton affirmed grimly.

"Nothing's proved against him, so far," said Speedy. "Nothing except my word. Are you going to kill on the word of the first man you hear talk against an old friend?"

"I'm going to find Thomas," said the other. "His room's right down this hallway." He moved to the door.

"Stop where you are," Speedy commanded.

"You can't stop me," said Fenton. "He's in the hotel, and I'm going to get him. If I die for it afterward . . . well, dying's a small thing to me. There's not much good left in the life that I have in front of me."

Speedy was utterly helpless. "Fenton," he murmured, stepping closer, "you're a fool. Will you listen while I try to . . . ?"

"I won't listen," said Fenton. "I've made up my mind."

"Listen to me, and stick up your hands, Fenton!" snapped the voice of Sheriff Sam Hollis, just behind him, in the dimness of the hallway.

Fenton, with a groan and a curse, whirled, instead of throwing up his hands. At least, he had not come this far to surrender without a fight. But there was no chance for him against the preparedness of such a fighter as Sheriff Sam Hollis. The gun of the latter barked, and, as Speedy sprang forward, the tall body of Fenton toppled back into his arms. He lowered the weight to the floor.

The sheriff was saying, panting as he spoke: "Had to do it. Speedy, it's you, isn't it? I'm sorry, but I had to."

"The foul fiends take you and what you had to do," Speedy answered bitterly. "You've murdered a better man than you'll ever be."

"If a killer can be a good man, he may be one," said the sheriff.

"He's not dead," announced Speedy, who had been touching the bleeding body with his hands. "He's knocked out, he may be dying, but he's not dead."

Footfalls were beginning to hurry down the hall in the direction from which they had heard the heavy, booming sound of the gunshot, but the sheriff slammed the door in the face of the curious as Speedy lighted the lamp that stood on the table in the center of the room.

As the light flooded his face, Fenton opened his eyes. He was perfectly controlled and aware of everything about him. "I guess that's about all," he said. "I was a fool, Speedy. Just as you said. Get Jessica, will you? I'd like to have her near while I pass in my checks."

Speedy was back on his knees beside the wounded man, tearing away the coat and shirt, now splotched with red, to lay bare the wound. It was almost exactly above the heart and yet the heart was still beating. He turned Fenton over carefully. In the very center of the back the bullet had come out, and around the side was a purple streak, rapidly growing darker.

Speedy gasped with relief. "You're knocked out, Fenton," he said, "but you're not going to die. The bullet glanced around the ribs. You'll be walking in a week . . . the sort of a fellow you are." He raised his head, as he ended, and looked at Sheriff Sam Hollis. "You have your streaks of luck, too," he said slowly, and the sheriff, although he understood perfectly what was meant, returned no answer. It was not particularly easy, at that moment, to meet the concentrated light and bitterness in the eyes of Speedy.

They laid Oliver Fenton on the bed. Speedy went to find a doctor, located one in the lobby of the hotel, and waved aside the questions showered upon him by the people in the hallway. Then he went to the room of Jessica Fenton and tapped at the door.

She opened it at once and, at sight of him, cried out: "Speedy, I've heard you talking to poor John Wilson! If you drive him back into a shambles at that saloon, if you tempt him to risk his life, God will never forgive you, and I'll despise you forever!"

"You can despise me to your heart's content," he answered shortly. "But now come with me and take care of your father. Sam Hollis has shot him down. He's not dead . . . he's only hurt. But he wants you."

She swayed to the side and put a hand against the wall. He made no effort to support her. Oliver Fenton and John Wilson were the only people in his mind at this moment; as for this girl, she was simply a trapping of the situation, nothing essential to his mind. Then, as she hurried from the room, he led the way to Fenton, and watched her drop on her knees beside the wounded man.

"Speedy was dead right, Jessica," said her father. "I should have kept away. But I wanted to find that hound of a Ben Thomas."

Speedy was already in the hallway, speaking to the sheriff. The curious crowd had dispersed when it found that no information about the gunfight was leaking out.

"What'll you do with him, Hollis?" he asked.

"He goes to jail as soon as he's fit to be carried there," said Hollis. "That's all the news you need from me, and that's about all you get."

"Good," said Speedy. "That's the way for a sheriff to talk. Wash the blood off your hands, and get ready for a new job, Sheriff. You may be needed again before the evening's over."

He went slowly back to the room of John Wilson, slowly, because the sense of failure was a bitter weight upon his heart. He had failed with Fenton. The man would be tenderly nursed back to life by the men of the law, and then securely hanged by the same careful hands that had tended him in sickness. That was the end of him. Jessica Fenton would go on through life with the stigma of her father's shameful death on her name. The other problem, John Wilson — well, Wilson would probably never be urged on to toe the mark.

When Speedy opened the door of the room again, he saw that not even the uproar in the hall had drawn Wilson away from his writing. He was addressing the letter, when Speedy came in, and he winced at the sight of the small man.

Speedy went to the window and sat on the sill of it, and he wondered bitterly and callously how many men, passing in the street, would put a charge of buckshot or a rifle bullet in his back, if only they could have known who was sitting there, a helpless target.

"Ready now?" he asked.

The stone-pale lips of the other made no answer.

"Jessica Fenton can't be wrong," said Speedy. "She and I both can't be wrong about you."

"What does she say of me?" groaned Wilson.

"It isn't what she says about you," Speedy responded. "It's the way she looks about you that counts."

CHAPTER
FIFTEEN

It was no matter to Speedy how far he carried deception, so long as he could make his point, so long as he could force John Wilson to play the man even for a moment, even though he were to die under the bullets of Slade Bennett the next minute. Jessica Fenton? She was not to be considered, if only her name and influence could make the blood of Wilson respond.

In fact, Wilson had risen from the table, as one drawn upward by a hand. "What about Jessica Fenton?" he asked.

"What about her?" echoed the other. "Why, you're not a fool as well as a coward, I hope. You can see what's in a girl's face, when she shows it as openly as Jessica Fenton has showed it to you."

The white face of the young man flushed crimson. "Maybe I'm both a fool and a coward," he admitted. "Only, Speedy, has Jessica said anything to you?"

"She didn't tell me that she'd go on her knees across the Rocky Mountains for the sake of one kind look from you," said Speedy. "She didn't tell me that. She didn't write it on paper, either, and sign it before a notary. That's the only kind of information that you'd be interested in, though, I suppose."

Big John Wilson, breathing hard, glared out the window, then he looked back toward Speedy. "I've worshipped her from the day I first laid eyes on her," he said hoarsely. "But I thought . . ."

"It's all right," said Speedy. "She'll soon be over caring anything about you, when she hears that you've taken water. She'll find that out soon enough, when Slade Bennett comes over to kick you out of town."

The young man closed his eyes and groaned.

The heart of Speedy sank like a stone in thinnest water. It struck bottom. Then a cold demon got him by the throat and made him say: "Go over there and face him, you rat."

"I can't, I can't," breathed Wilson.

"You can, and you will," said Speedy. "There's your gun. Take it, you dog, and go over and face him. Throw open the saloon door. Thunder out his name. Ask . . . 'Where's Slade Bennett?' And then start shooting. You can shoot straight and fast. Every coward learns how to use a gun like an expert."

"It's no good, all my practice," said John Wilson. "There's nothing in me. I can't do a thing. I've got to get out of town . . . I've got to go." He started for the door.

Speedy stepped in front of him. "You're not leaving town. You're going with me to Haggerty's Saloon."

"No!" cried Wilson.

"Then, I'll take you."

"Curse you," rasped Wilson. "Get out of my way!"

In his frenzy, he struck for the dark head of Speedy, but that lightning-quick eye of Speedy saw clearly

307

enough the coming of the blow. A dozen ways he could have avoided it, but a new thought had come to him and stopped him. There he stood, patient as a log, and let the stroke crash home against his head. It knocked him flat with a force that skidded him on the floor. A cloud of darkness, mingled with red sparks, flew up across his eyes. Through that cloud, he saw Wilson leaning above him, and heard the astonished voice gasping: "And that's Speedy!"

Speedy lay still.

"If I can do that to him," muttered the voice of the other, "what's a bully like Slade Bennett to me." Suddenly he had snatched the gun from the table on which Speedy had laid it and rushed for the door.

Speedy gathered himself from the floor and followed. His brain was still buzzing and his jaw felt as though it were broken, but there was triumph in his heart. There was a hidden manliness in big John Wilson, and he, Speedy, had finally opened the door upon the secret treasure. He was hurrying on now to face Bennett, this young man who had newly discovered himself. In another thirty seconds, he might be dead. But from the viewpoint of Speedy, that mattered nothing, or little more than nothing. To die like a man, from his conception, was far better than to live like a coward, haunted forever by fear. If only the impulse would last and carry John Wilson across the street, and through the door of Haggerty's Saloon.

Speedy, running fast, saw the big fellow lurch out of the door of the hotel and crash across the verandah, then race on across the street. In Wilson, too, there was probably a dread lest the heat of the impulse should cool before it had been given form in action. Speedy was on the heels of the runner, when the latter reached the swinging doors of Haggerty's Saloon and, casting them wide, strode in, shouting: "Where's Slade Bennett?"

As a ripple of water curls around a stone, so Speedy slipped around big John Wilson, and stood some distance along the wall of the saloon.

It was brief. Slade Bennett was standing near the head of the bar and, as Wilson's stentorian shout reached his ears, he wheeled suddenly about with a deep, muffled cry, a revolver flashing in his hand like the gleam of a knife.

There was even time for Speedy to see Wilson, also, as he stood just inside the swinging doors of the saloon, with his head thrown up and back, his face deadly pale. Such was the strife of emotion within his spirit, but there was an overriding gleam in his eyes that, it seemed to Speedy, had been born back there in the hotel room when he leaned above him as he was stretched on the floor.

He had a mere half second to see these things. Then, as big Slade Bennett turned and fired, John Wilson, calmly, deliberately, as it seemed, drew his own gun and shot Slade Bennett down.

Twice had Slade fired, so much greater was his speed of hand than Wilson's, but twice he had missed, and the first fire of Wilson brought down his man.

Speedy went across the floor in an instant and was on his knees beside the fallen man. He tore open coat and shirt, and found the purple spot out of which the blood was oozing gradually, a mere drop at a time, and, with that glance, and by a look at the purple-white band that was forming around the mouth of Bennett, he knew that the end had come for the gunman. Slade Bennett did not open his eyes, but in his breathing he groaned and there was a bubbling in his throat.

Other men came up. A hard, ringing voice, just over the head of Speedy, said: "I'm sorry for this. And I'd like to help. What can I do for him?"

Speedy looked up and saw John Wilson, a man transformed. The color was back in his face; his eyes flamed; a sort of swelling and transcendent power was quivering in his voice and in his eyes, like an overcharge of light or electricity.

Speedy said coldly: "The thing for you to do, and all the rest, is to take off your hats. Slade Bennett's dying. Where's a doctor?"

There was always at least one doctor present in such a crowd in those days, and now the man of science came forward to do what he could.

But Speedy did not leave the fallen man. He said: "Slade, Slade. They've found out about everything. They've found out that you murdered Dodson. What are we going to do about it?"

The eyes of Slade Bennett flashed open and closed again; his mouth sneered. "Dodson had to get it," he said. "You know why I killed him, Jerry. After I stabbed him, I made it look as though that fool, that Oliver Fenton, had turned the trick. Honest people are all jackasses. The sheriffs have been hunting Fenton, and

I've walked about the streets. Jerry, open the window, open the door, I'm choking." He raised himself on his hands with his eyes wide, but frightfully unseeing. On his hands and his heels, his body stiffened an instant, then he collapsed.

Speedy, reaching past the doctor, closed the eyelids as faithfully as that Jerry for whom his voice had been mistaken. And he murmured, not without emotion: "'And all the king's horses, and all the king's men, can never put Humpty Dumpty together again.'"

Slade Bennett lay dead on the floor, and the men who had gathered close for an instant to look down into the dead face were now scattering to find their drinks in another saloon.

Speedy heard a voice that said: "Wilson, that was the coolest trick and the best gun play that I ever seen. I wish that you'd come and have a drink with me. My name's Thompson."

Speedy listened to the voices depart; for his own part, he remained fixed and still beside the dead man, looking steadily down into his face, watching the dawning of the death smile and feeling once again, as he had so often felt in the past, that something out of his own bright spirit had fallen and lay like a dissolving shadow there, before his own eyes.

CHAPTER
SIXTEEN

Then, in the saloon across the street, he found John Wilson celebrating in the midst of a circle of new-found friends who, only the moment before, were so ready to howl like wolfish ghouls over his downfall before that hero, Slade Bennett.

He touched the arm of the young man and, looking up, he saw Wilson turn and look down at him with eyes of liquid fire. The icy barrier of half a lifetime of restraint and discontent had fallen, and John Wilson was just beginning to enjoy himself as the thing he had never dreamed of being. But when he saw Speedy, he stepped through the crowd at the bar and laid his hand on the shoulder of the smaller man.

"I know part of what you've done for me, Speedy," he said. "I can guess at the rest. You let me hit you back there in the hotel room. Nobody can manhandle you, if you don't want 'em to, but you let me slug you. Speedy, is that right?"

Speedy made a brief gesture to disclaim the suggestion. Then he muttered: "Wilson, you've done part of the great job. Now go over and collect on it."

"Collect on what?" asked Wilson.

"On the killing of Slade Bennett."

"I've got an idea," said Wilson, suddenly frowning, "that I never could have done anything with him, except that the bluff that you'd put up for me unnerved him a little when he heard me rush into the saloon and bawl out the words that you wanted me to shout. There's nothing for me to collect out of the killing of Slade Bennett, except a chance to pay his funeral expenses, and I'm glad to do that."

Speedy nodded rather grimly as he surveyed the other. "You're a good fellow, and a white man, Wilson," he said. "And I'm mighty glad of that. But I'll tell you what you're to collect. That's the girl . . . Jessica Fenton. Come down with me to the jail this moment . . . No, they won't have moved Fenton, yet. He'll still be in the hotel. And we'll go and take Fenton away from the sheriff."

Wilson frowned. "I don't know what you mean, Speedy," he said. "If the law . . ."

"The law has nothing to do with Oliver Fenton," said Speedy. "Slade Bennett has barely finished confessing that he killed Dodson. That's enough to suit the law. Oliver Fenton is free, and you can stand in on the party as the hero of the hour."

"You're laughing at me," Wilson said gloomily.

"I'm not laughing," answered Speedy. "I mean what I say. Now, you come along with me." He took the big hand of Wilson and drew him out of the saloon.

As they came under the open stars, in the fresh air of the night, Wilson halted suddenly.

"Speedy," he said, "I seem to be seeing the face of the world for the first time. And I've you to thank for that and I do thank you. Will you believe me?"

"Of course, I'll believe you," said Speedy.

"I've never come so close to happiness before . . . I've never felt happiness before," said the other. "And I'm only beginning to know what to thank you for. But I can see more and more clearly, Speedy, that you played on me. You led me on . . . you made yourself the victim, and let me knock my first spark of fire out of you. Isn't that true? You let me manhandle you, just to raise my spirits, and get me started?"

"Nonsense," Speedy dismissed carelessly. "I don't let people manhandle me, if I can help it, as a rule. Come on, man, come on. You strike while the iron's hot. Jessica Fenton's up there. She's the one that would like to hear from you."

"Did you know," said John Wilson, still immovable in the street, "that I confessed everything to her about . . . about what I've been in the past?"

"No," said Speedy.

"I did, though," answered Wilson. "And she told me that she had faith in me. You know what she based her faith on?"

"What?" murmured Speedy.

"On what you'd said to me back there in the station house at Council Flat . . . that there was the fear of danger in me, but that I was stronger than I thought."

"Go see her now," said Speedy, "and see if she's glad to know that you found yourself for her sake."

"But it wasn't exactly for her sake," admitted Wilson. "I was just a shaking cur, thinking only about myself and wanting to die, if I could find the courage to meet death. Then you put the spark in me. You set me on fire and I still seem to burn, Speedy. The cold demon is gone out of me. Perhaps it'll come back into me, later on."

"You've talked enough," Speedy said not unpleasantly. "Now go up there in the hotel. Step along. See Jessica Fenton and talk to her. You've started in the right direction tonight, man, but you'll need a woman like that to keep you there."

John Wilson, with a start, straightened and then hurried across the street. Speedy followed more slowly, and came into the lobby of the hotel a sufficient distance behind the new-made hero to appreciate the silence that came over the buzzing room as Wilson entered.

All eyes were turned toward the stairs up which Wilson had disappeared at a run, and Speedy followed, smiling faintly. It seemed that his work was drawing rapidly to a close, that there was little more for him to do, in this case, except to look on at the fruition of his work.

He got to the upper hall in time to see Wilson knock at the door of the room in which the wounded man was lying. The door opened, and he heard the outcry of a happy girl's voice and saw the sheen of her hands in the lamplight as she put her hands on the hands of Wilson and drew him into the room.

Well, the news had come before him to the hotel, and the Fentons knew that Oliver Fenton was free.

Speedy nodded and sighed. He stepped closer. Voices boiled up within the room like water in a tea-kettle. The door opened again, and the sheriff came out with a wide grin on his face.

Speedy was near enough to hear, as the door closed, the voice of big John Wilson saying: "It's nothing, Jessica. I didn't come here to be thanked. I only came here to say that, for your sake, I wish that I could have faced down a dozen like Slade Bennett. And . . ."

The closing of the door shut off the voice of the man, and the girl's voice cut in with words that could not be distinguished. Yet there was no need for words. The music of the miracle of happiness was rising like a bright fountain from the throat of the girl.

The sheriff laid his hand on the arm of Speedy. "There it goes, Speedy," said Sam Hollis. "You've spoke some hard words to me, lately, but I'm ready to forget 'em. Now that Fenton has turned out innocent, and Slade Bennett was the guilty man, why, it looks as though I was pretty mean to Fenton. But I had nothing against him . . . it was only the law, not me, that wanted him."

"Where's Ben Thomas?" asked Speedy.

"Ben Thomas won't be seen around these parts for quite a spell," said the sheriff soberly. "He showed up to ask his share of the blood money when he heard that Fenton was caught, and I told him that he could have all the blood money, when it was paid, and, in the meantime, he could have my opinion of him. When I

316

got through talking . . . and I talked in front of the whole crowd . . . he sneaked out. There was some talk of tar and feathers, but I guess all that the boys did was to give him a mighty fast ride out of town."

"It would be a lot better for him if he had had a bullet through the brain," said Speedy. "When I first saw him with the girl, I smelled blood as surely as any hungry cat, Sheriff, but he's still breathing, yet he'll never be able to look a decent man in the face from now on. And the blood I smelled was Slade Bennett's."

"Yes," said Sam Hollis, "heaven help him and every other man that lives by knife and gun, like me, Speedy, or like you, though the only tools you use are your bare hands. Come and have a drink with me, will you?"

"Yes, a drink is what I need," Speedy concurred. "But wait a minute." He paused, raising his hand in the dimness of the hall and canting his head to listen.

"Aye," said the sheriff, "they're all contented enough now. There was a rope around the neck of Fenton ten minutes or so ago . . . and the girl was breaking her heart for him . . . and John Wilson was thought as yellow-livered as a Chinaman. And now listen to the three of 'em laughing together."

"They're laughing," Speedy agreed as he moved down the hall again, hooking his arm through the sheriff's. "I only hope that they're not laughing too soon."

"Now, whacha mean by that?" asked Sam Hollis.

"Nothing, nothing," said Speedy hurriedly. "Let's get to that drink."

About the Author

Max Brand® is the best-known pen name of Frederick Faust, creator of Dr. Kildare, Destry, and many other fictional characters popular with readers and viewers worldwide. Faust wrote for a variety of audiences in many genres. His enormous output, totaling approximately 30,000,000 words or the equivalent of 530 ordinary books, covered nearly every field: crime, fantasy, historical romance, espionage, Westerns, science fiction, adventure, animal stories, love, war, and fashionable society, big business and big medicine. Eighty motion pictures have been based on his work along with many radio and television programs. For good measure he also published four volumes of poetry. Perhaps no other author has reached more people in more different ways.

Born in Seattle in 1892, orphaned early, Faust grew up in the rural San Joaquin Valley of California. At Berkeley he became a student rebel and one-man literary movement, contributing prodigiously to all campus publications. Denied a degree because of unconventional conduct, he embarked on a series of adventures culminating in New York City where, after a period of near starvation, he received simultaneous recognition as a serious poet and successful author of fiction. Later, he traveled widely, making his home in New York, then in Florence, and finally in Los Angeles.

Once the United States entered the Second World

War, Faust abandoned his lucrative writing career and his work as a screenwriter to serve as a war correspondent with the infantry in Italy, despite his fifty-one years and a bad heart. He was killed during a night attack on a hilltop village held by the German army. New books based on magazine serials or unpublished manuscripts or restored versions continue to appear so that, alive or dead, he has averaged a new book every four months for seventy-five years. Beyond this, some work by him is newly reprinted every week of every year in one or another format somewhere in the world. A great deal more about this author and his work can be found in *The Max Brand Companion* (Greenwood Press, 1997) edited by Jon Tuska and Vicki Piekarski. the Captain.